BLAST ANYTHING THAT MOVES!

Fernandez saw a hand appear at the top of the stairs holding a grenade. Before it could be thrown, Fernandez drilled the arm with three rounds, and the small bomb dropped out of the Kenyan's hand and three seconds later exploded.

Fernandez looked back at Lincoln and nodded. He sent covering fire up the stairs until he felt Lincoln slide into place beside him.

"No response up above," Lincoln said. . . .

Fernandez used the mike again. "L-T, we could use about four good men in here. The stairs is ours."

Moments later Adams, Lampedusa, Bos'n's mate Ted Yates, and Quinley ran into the room and found cover.

"Quinley," Lincoln said. "You and me up the stairs. Side by side. You've got the left. Blast at anything that moves. . . ."

SEAL TEAM SEVEN
Battleground

By Keith Douglass

THE CARRIER SERIES:

CARRIER
VIPER STRIKE
ARMAGEDDON MODE
FLAME-OUT
MAELSTROM
COUNTDOWN
AFTERBURN
ALPHA STRIKE
ARCTIC FIRE
ARSENAL

THE SEAL TEAM SEVEN SERIES:

SEAL TEAM SEVEN
SPECTER
NUCFLASH
DIRECT ACTION
FIRESTORM
BATTLEGROUND

SEAL TEAM SEVEN
BATTLEGROUND

KEITH DOUGLASS

BERKLEY BOOKS, NEW YORK

SEAL TEAM SEVEN: BATTLEGROUND

A Berkley Book / published by arrangement with
the author

PRINTING HISTORY
Berkley edition / June 1998

All rights reserved.
Copyright © 1998 by The Berkley Publishing Group.
SEAL TEAM SEVEN logo illustration by Michael Racz.
This book may not be reproduced in whole or in part,
by mimeograph or any other means, without permission.
For information address: The Berkley Publishing Group,
a member of Penguin Putnam Inc.,
200 Madison Avenue, New York, New York 10016.

The Penguin Putnam Inc. World Wide Web site address is
http://www.penguinputnam.com

ISBN: 0-425-16375-X

BERKLEY®
Berkley Books are published by
The Berkley Publishing Group, a member of Penguin Putnam Inc.,
200 Madison Avenue, New York, New York 10016.
BERKLEY and the "B" design
are trademarks belonging to Berkley Publishing Corporation.

PRINTED IN THE UNITED STATES OF AMERICA

10 9 8 7 6 5 4 3 2 1

To my good friend, writing
critic, and advisor in all things Navy,
Cyndy Mobley.
To the ever-vigilant man on
the firing line, my agent, Jake Elwell.
And to my research assistant, language
guru, and constant critic, Chet Cunningham.
To one and all I say thank you.
I couldn't have written this
book without your help.

SEAL TEAM SEVEN

THIRD PLATOON*
CORONADO, CALIFORNIA

PLATOON LEADER:

Lieutenant Blake Murdock.
WEAPON: H&K MP-5SD submachine gun.

FIRST SQUAD

David "Jaybird" Sterling. Platoon Chief. Machinist Mate Second Class.
WEAPON: H&K MP-5SD submachine gun.

Ron Holt. Radioman First Class. Platoon radio operator.
WEAPON: H&K MP-5SD submachine gun.

Martin "Magic" Brown. Quartermaster's Mate First Class. Squad sniper.
WEAPON: H&K PSG1 7.62 NATO sniper rifle or McMillan M-88 .50-caliber sniper rifle.

Eric "Red" Nicholson. Torpedoman's Mate Second Class. Scout for the platoon.
WEAPON: Colt M-4A1 with grenade launcher.

Kenneth Ching. Quartermaster's Mate First Class. Platoon translator/Chinese, Japanese, Russian, Spanish.
WEAPON: Colt M-4A1 with grenade launcher.

Harry "Horse" Ronson. Electrician's Mate Second Class.
WEAPON: H&K-21A1 7.62 NATO round machine gun.

James "Doc" Ellsworth. Hospital Corpsman Second Class. Platoon corpsman.
WEAPON: H&K MP-5SD or no-stock 5-round Mossburg pump shotgun.

*(Third Platoon assigned exclusively to the Central Intelligence Agency to perform any needed tasks on a covert basis anywhere in the world. A top secret classified assignment.)

Lieutenant (j.g.) Ed DeWitt. Leader Second Squad. Second in Command of the platoon.
WEAPON: H&K MP-5SD submachine gun.

Al Adams. Gunner's Mate Third Class.
WEAPON: Colt M-4A1 with rocket launcher.

Miguel Fernandez. Gunner's Mate First Class. Speaks Spanish, Portuguese. Squad sniper.
WEAPON: H&K PSG1 7.62 NATO sniper rifle.

Ross Lincoln. Aviation Technician Second Class.
WEAPON: H&K MP-5SD submachine gun.

Les Quinley. Torpedoman's Mate Third Class.
WEAPON: Colt M-4A1 and grenade launcher or no-stock, 5-round Mossburg pump shotgun.

Willy Bishop. Electrician's Mate Second Class. Explosives expert.
WEAPON: Colt M-4A1 with grenade launcher

Ted Yates. Bos'n's Mate Second Class. Squad machine gunner.
WEAPON: H&K-21A1 7.62 NATO round machine gun. Second radio operator.

Joe "Ricochet" Lampedusa. Operations Specialist Third Class.
WEAPON: M-4A1 with grenade launcher.

1

Sunday, July 18

0120 hours
Dockside at Pier 12
Mombasa, Kenya

Colonel Umar Maleceia waved his silent platoon forward. The combat-outfitted Kenyan rangers blended into the deep shadows along Pier 12 and waited. Colonel Maleceia moved into the glow from the lights on the USS *Roy Turner,* FFG 68, and marched up the steel gangplank now almost level with the pier.

The sailor on duty on the quarterdeck watched as the Kenyan military officer strode up to the rail. The sailor hurried onto the weather deck and to the rail next to the brow. The six-foot-five-inch 300-pound officer wearing Kenyan Army combat greens stopped three feet from the American and saluted the American flag, then the sailor. The petty officer first class returned the salute.

"Identify yourself, sir, and state your business," the sentry said.

Colonel Maleceia lowered his right-hand salute and at the same instant brought his left hand up from his hip. The silenced Heckler & Koch USP combat .40-caliber automatic whispered twice, and two rounds jolted into the sailor's heart. He died before he could cry out.

At once ten of the dark-green-clad troopers from the dock's shadows raced to the brow and hurried silently up it.

Half went forward, the rest aft on the 453-foot U.S. Navy ship. Each man had a special assignment. A moment later Colonel Maleceia motioned, and twenty more Kenyan Army rangers rushed onto the ship.

Aft, Gunnery Chiefs Winslow and Harper had just checked the Sikorsky SH-60B Seahawk helicopter that sat on the pad on the fantail outside the chopper hangar. Both men had returned from a night in the Mombasa saloons and were not entirely sober.

"Told you this baby has the new R-standard ASW sensors," Chief Winslow said. "Told you so. You can see the antenna right there."

"You're drunk Winslow. You wouldn't know a sensor from your mother's army boots." They both laughed and nearly fell down. "Pay up, Winslow."

Just as Winslow reached for a roll of bills in his pocket, two Kenyan rangers surged out of the chopper hangar with the 20-mm six-barreled M 15 Vulcan Phalanx perched on top of it. The Kenyans fired their AK-47's as soon as they saw the U.S. Navy men. A dozen rounds slammed into both chiefs and threw them against the side of the Seahawk, where they died instantly.

Seaman Roberts, on his regular security patrol rounds, heard the shots aft, and then heavier booming blasts from up forward. He ran that way up the weather deck on the starboard side past the alleyway that traversed the middle of the ship. He drew his issue .45 1911 automatic and charged a round into it. Damned big trouble somewhere. The firing sounded like shotguns. Somebody shooting shotguns on the *Turner*?

Below the wing of the bridge, two figures rose out of the darkness. Twin flashes from the pair made Roberts dive to the left. He was too late. One of the AK-47 slugs hit him in the chest and drove him backwards into a giant pool of blackness.

The first shots stirred activity on the quarterdeck. Lieutenant Marvin Foster, the Officer of the Deck, came away from the podium and looked at Seaman Johnson.

"You hear shots?"

The seaman on roving security patrol nodded, drew his .45, and headed for the port side. He never made it. A dark figure with a shotgun edged into the passageway and fired one shot of double-aught buck. It almost cut the sailor in half. The second round slammed Lieutenant Foster against the bulkhead, where he slid down, drawing grotesque patterns of blood on the fresh paint.

Chief Bos'n's Mate Randolph stepped cautiously into the starboard door of the passage to the quarterdeck. He had a five-round shotgun, and fired one round of double-aught buck into the gunman who had just killed the OOD. He bent at the side of the dead officer and pulled out a ring of keys. Quickly, before any more attackers came onto the quarterdeck, he found the right key, turned it in the slot, and hit the General Quarters alarm. The rhythmic metallic gong sounded again and again through the *Roy Turner*. Now Randolph figured maybe some of the men would have a chance.

Belowdecks, the Security Alert Team leader heard the General Quarters gong and unlocked the armory door. Inside, the light was always on. He quickly took the lock off the long weapons, shotguns, and M-14 rifles, and pulled out a pair of Mossburg shotguns. A dozen men surged toward him reaching for .45 automatics and 9mm pistols and their magazines. Some took shotguns and pockets of rounds. Most of the men were in shorts and T-shirts right out of the sack from their coops.

"What the hell's happening?" one man shouted.

"Nobody knows, but we got shitfaces all over the place shooting at us," somebody said. The Security Alert Team leader left the armory open, and ran up a ladder for the deck above. He met no one on the ladder.

Another dozen more men raced to the armory and grabbed weapons and scattered. Now firing could be heard from several parts of the ship.

Forward, the Kenyans ran into a pair of sailors who had been smoking at the rail and watching the lights on the Mombasa waterfront fifty yards away. When the warning gongs sounded, the two sailors turned and ran for their General Quarters posts. They didn't make it. Two Kenyan rangers fired one round each of double-aught buck from their shotguns. The two sailors caught most of the slugs, slammed over the low railing, and splashed into the harbor below next to the pier.

The ship was silent for a moment, with only the gentle sound of the Mombasa Bay waters slapping the steel hull. Then two American sailors ran out of the passageway on the port side from the quarterdeck. Both men carried shotguns. Two more Kenyan rangers stormed up the brow from the pier. Damage Controlman Second Class Krokowski brought up his shotgun, surprising the Kenyans.

"What the hell you guys doing?" Krokowski bellowed. The Kenyans shrilled something in Swahili and lifted their rifles. Krokowski fired first, killing one of the Kenyans. The other invader triggered his AK-47 on full automatic, and Krokowski and his buddy spilled backwards on the deck, their weapons skittering away from them. Both the sailors were critically wounded. The Kenyan ran up, fired one round into the head of each American, and rushed down the deck.

Shots sounded from the forward part of the ship. Gunner's Mate Third Class Mondes charged around the 1 Mk 13 Mod 4 missile launcher for the surface-to-surface missiles on the forward main deck with an M-14 in his hand. He heard firing down the starboard side and ran that way. Mondes saw two sailors shot down, and he screeched in protest.

"What is this, a goddamn war?" he roared. Six Kenyans ran toward him and he got off a burst of six shots. He saw two of the Kenyans go down before he felt a hammer blow in his side and then another in his chest and knew he was falling. He hit the missile launcher base and went down. The last thing Mondes saw was a Kenyan soldier standing over him as he stared up at an ugly black rifle muzzle. He never heard the fatal shot.

Twenty men jolted awake by the General Quarters alarm in their aft coops berthing compartment stumbled around hunting clothes. A few got pants on and ran out the door before two Kenyan soldiers ran in and one blasted a shotgun round into the overhead. One of the Kenyan attackers spoke English.

"Down on the deck on your faces!" he bellowed. "The first man who moves gets shot dead."

The General Quarters gong kept sounding through the ship like a racing heartbeat. It sent dozens more men up ladders and reaching for helmets.

Two officers were gunned down as they charged into CIC, the Combat Information Center, where the missiles were controlled.

The firing shotguns brought Commander Joseph Goddard, CO of the *Roy Turner,* awake with a jolt, only to stare into the black bore of an Uzi submachine gun.

"Captain Goddard, I believe," Colonel Maleceia said softly. "I have just captured your vessel. If you would be so kind as to get up and dress, I'll put you with the other prisoners of war."

Commander Goddard shook his head to clear it. He came awake slowly these days. He heard more firing on board his ship. He nodded, started to slide out of the bunk, then whipped up the 1911 Colt .45 automatic he had slept with every night of his life for the past twenty years and snapped off a shot. It missed the huge colonel. The Uzi chattered and six 9mm rounds blasted into Commander Goddard's chest and belly, slamming him into eternity on his bunk.

"Too bad," the colonel said. "It's a shame to mess up such a fine bunk that way."

Six chief petty officers had been enjoying their weekly Sunday night poker game. The General Quarters blast surprised them, and two headed for the door to the enlisted mess. The Security Alert Team Leader jerked the door open and pushed in three shotguns and a Beretta.

"We've got Kenyan rangers all over the ship," he yelled. "Use these best you can." Then he ran out and up a ladder.

"Whoever they are won't be long getting here," Gunners's Mate Second Class Andy Johnson said. "They must know where this place is." He had one of the shotguns and pushed five rounds into the magazine.

"We'll blast a dozen of them before they touch us,"

Parachute Rigger Second Class Joe Lawler drawled. He loaded his shotgun and aimed it at the door. "Hail, in Tennessee we got shot at all the time. Damned revenuers never could hit their own assholes."

Outside, rifle butts hammered on the metal door.

Johnson moved up beside the dogged-down bulkhead door and waited. He saw the lever turn. A minute later he stormed away.

"Dynamite," he roared. Johnson swerved behind a heavy metal rack. The explosion that came moments later was muffled, but the locking bolts on the inside of the door snapped and blasted into the compartment.

Someone outside pushed the door open slowly. Johnson crawled forward. When the bulkhead door was six inches open, Johnson lay near it on the deck and threw a hand grenade through it into the passageway.

The blast 4.2 seconds later echoed through the ship like a warning gong. When the rumbling died down, the chiefs heard one man screaming outside.

A moment later, a flashbang grenade rolled into the compartment and went off with five furiously loud detonations and then six flashes of light so brilliant that a hand over the eyes kept out only a little of the intensity.

The six men reeled from the grenade. The explosion in such a contained space magnified its effect by three times. Johnson lay on the deck bleeding from his nose and one ear.

Lawler sat against the bulkhead shaking his head, blind and not able to hear a thing.

Three submachine-gun-toting Kenyan Rangers stormed through the door and kicked away the shotguns, then systematically shot all six chiefs to death.

In the Communications Center, Gunners Mate Second Class Art Brachman had just signed on the Internet to send an E-mail to his wife back in Portland, Oregon. He had the first two lines of his flash mail done when he heard the booming report of a shotgun. He knew the sound. He cut the lights in the center. Only the greenish hue of the consoles and screens gave off any light. He unlocked the crypto vault and pulled out the 9mm Glock Model 18 pistol with a thirty-three round magazine they kept there. He cranked back the slide, chambering a round, and had thirty-two more slugs to defend himself with.

The Captain had cautioned them yesterday when they tied up. He'd said almost anything could happen in a jumpy, wild-assed place like Kenya, so they should be ready. Only a few chiefs had had any liberty that night, and that was Cinderella liberty. Most of the 206 officers and men were still on the ship.

Somebody ran past the Communications Center room door. Then Brachman heard the steps come back. Brachman swore at himself for not throwing the steel bars on the door, which was always locked. He heard the handle turn; then a half-dozen rounds from a weapon slammed into the door lock and the steel panel swung open. The terrible muzzle of a shotgun poked through the opening.

Brachman fired four times a foot above the shotgun. The sound billowed around the small communications room, and Brachman knew he couldn't hear much. He saw a body slam backwards against the side of the door, then pitch forward. The scattergun clattered on the deck.

Brachman grabbed the weapon. The dead man was black—did that make him a Kenyan? He didn't recognize the green uniform. Brachman took the shotgun and looked at it in the glow of the screens. Simple. A five-round pump weapon fully loaded. He dropped to the floor, pushed over the dead man, and crawled to the open door. Brachman took a quick look down the passageway. Twenty feet down someone fired at him with a rifle. The round missed. Friend or foe?

He poked his head out for a second, saw the green uniform in the passageway, and pushed out the shotgun and fired one round at the approaching figure. The Kenyan ranger flew three feet backwards as he died on the way to the deck.

Brachman wiped sweat off his forehead. What the hell was going on? Bad guys all over the place. Where was the security team when you needed it? He heard more boots pounding down the passage. He searched the dead man's pockets and found four more shotgun shells. Quickly Brachman refilled the magazine and edged up to the door.

Three black men in green uniforms worked slowly toward him from the bow. He waited until they were within fifteen feet, then reached out and fired once. He looked out and saw two men down and the third retreating. Brachman's second blast of double-aught buck channeled in the passageway's steel walls, blasted into the running figure, and smashed him to the deck.

Brachman pulled back the shotgun, wondering if he should push in two more rounds. Before he decided, a submachine gun muzzle poked in the door and fired.

As soon as he saw the blue-steel barrel, he knew he'd never finish that E-mail to Jody. Brachman jolted sideways and tried to find the Glock.

Before he touched the small weapon, a six-round burst of 9mm lead slashed into his left leg, bringing a scream of anger and pain. A second later, four rounds of the next six-round burst caught Brachman in the side of his head and ripped off large chunks of his skull and brain.

Back on deck, Colonel Maleceia took reports from his remaining lieutenant. His best officer had been killed. He'd lost twelve men so far, and the fight wasn't over. He owned the bridge, the quarterdeck, Main Control, the Combat Information Center, the engine room, the Communications Center, and one of the two enlisted crew's berthing quarters. A dozen men had barricaded themselves in the last berthing compartment. He figured they were heavily armed.

"You told me that the crew's weapons would all be locked in the armory," Colonel Maleceia shouted at his last officer, Lieutenant Nigoru. The man took a step back. He knew the colonel's physical power, and his political muscle as well.

"That was our best intelligence, sir. We have the situation almost resolved. Another ten minutes."

"Fool. In another ten minutes we could all be dead." The colonel took a swing at the younger man, who dodged back.

"I'll go personally and dig out those last men, Colonel."

"Do it, Nigoru, or don't bother coming back," Colonel

Maleceia said in his native Swahili. The younger man lifted an Uzi and ran down the passageway.

"Where the fuck did the attackers come from?" Torpedoman's Mate Third Class Lew Klement whispered from where he lay beneath the bottom bunk in his mid-level coops. He winced when he moved his right arm, which had taken a shotgun's wildly ricocheting double-aught slug.

"I heard some big three-hundred-pound son of a bitch of a Kenyan officer killed Mathews on watch at the brow and the OD and they swarmed on board." It was Quartermaster's Mate Second Class Clifford "Jonesy" Jones. He always knew everything going on on board.

"How good is that bitch of a door?" Hospital Corpsman Second Class Jugs Wilson asked. He'd just wrapped up Klement's wounded arm.

"As strong as a Japanese mama-san's whorehouse door," Jonesy said. "Last about two minutes. You'll have lots of work to do in here shortly, Doc."

Klement watched the door. All the lights were out except one far back. The door wasn't a watertight-compartment type. One stick of dynamite would blow it right off its hinges.

As he thought that, Klement heard voices outside. One shouted in what sounded like an ultimatum, but Klement couldn't tell if it was in English or Swahili. He'd been doing some reading about Kenya ever since he'd heard that they would stop here. This was supposed to be a damn goodwill call, for God's sake.

The blast at the door came as a surprise. Klement thought he could see the metal door bulge. Then the hinges came off, slashing through the air like shrapnel.

The front three men in the quarters had the only weapons. Klement had a shotgun and a full five-round magazine.

Doc Wilson carried a .45-caliber automatic. The only weapon Jonesy could find was a flare gun with three rounds. At close range one of the flares could burn halfway through a body.

The three sailors were on the floor under the triple-deck bunks, which was below the dynamite blast that tore through the metal door and pitched it aside like a used tissue. Six Kenyan rangers stormed inside all firing automatic weapons.

Jonesy targeted the first man deliberately and hit him with the flare gun's magnesium round in the stomach. The round didn't penetrate, but it glued to the man's shirt and burned at two thousand degrees, putting the man down shrieking for help. Before Jonesy could target another Kenyan, two AK-47 rounds plowed into his chest, spinning him around under the bunk into death.

Klement fired his shotgun the moment the rangers ran through the door. He shot three times as fast as he could work the pump. The double-aught buck cut down three attackers before a round from one of the enemy guns drilled cleanly through Klement's forehead dumping him to the side, dead in an instant.

Doc Wilson pumped out six rounds from the .45, firing as fast as he could, before one of the heavy slugs caught him in the leg, another in the chest, and he slumped dead before he knew it.

The wave of attackers swarmed over the three on the floor. One man kicked the flare gun away and it was over. They took the rest of the men prisoners and had them all lie facedown on the floor. Quickly the Kenyan rangers put plastic hand restraints on the U.S. sailors. They were all bound by the time Lieutenant Nigoru arrived. He wiped a bead of perspiration from his forehead and marched the prisoners of war to the main deck.

Colonel Maleceia stood grim-faced as he watched the prisoners lined up on the bow. They had been brought in from all over the ship. The colonel turned to Lieutenant Nigoru.

"I want to know at once how many enemy are dead, how many alive, and how many wounded. Do it now."

As he spoke, five large buses rolled up to Pier 12 just below the brow. The drivers stopped the rigs and turned off their lights.

A few moments later, after conferring with two sergeants, Lieutenant Nigoru hurried up to the large Kenyan.

"Colonel, sir. My report shows that we have found twenty-eight Americans dead and a hundred and sixty captives lined up here who are not seriously wounded."

Colonel Maleceia nodded. "How many alive but with bad wounds?"

"We're not sure yet, Colonel. We've found twelve so far."

"That's only two hundred, Lieutenant. They had a full complement of two hundred and six officers and men. Where are the other six?"

"We'll find them, sir."

"Don't bother, we don't have time. Kill the wounded."

The black lieutenant hesitated. "Colonel, sir. Did I understand you correctly? We are to kill the badly wounded?"

Colonel Maleceia's face worked, and his eyes blazed with a such fury that the young officer shrank back.

"Shoot them in the head at once, Lieutenant, unless you wish to join them." The junior officer saluted smartly, and took two steps away. "Lieutenant, after you shoot the wounded, throw all the dead overboard."

2

Sunday, July 18

0135 hours
Dockside at Pier 12
Mombasa, Kenya

Seaman Greg Goldman stood in the bow lineup beside Radioman First Class Chuck Inman. Goldman scowled as he looked around. Lots of the men lived through the attack, but where were the wounded? He whispered the query to Inman, who shook his head.

"No wounded. I heard shots when we came past some compartments. Now it's just us and the KIAs."

"Bastards!" Goldman whispered. "They'll get theirs."

"Silence," a Kenyan sergeant bellowed. He walked along the line, but evidently couldn't figure out who had been talking.

Colonel Maleceia paced in front of the American sailors. He said something to an officer and left the ship.

The English-speaking sergeant screeched for attention. "Time to move to your new quarters. No talking, no lagging, or you'll end up in the bay. Move out now a line at a time to the buses on the dock."

Goldman looked down at the shorter Inman. He shook his head. Nothing they could do now. Maybe later. Maybe.

A hundred yards away, three Navy chiefs lay in the wreck of an abandoned building just in back of Pier 12 and watched

13

their shipmates marched off the *Roy Turner* and into the buses. They had had a little drinking party at a dockside bar, and had been almost back to the ship when they'd heard the firing on board. All wore civilian clothes since the Kenyan authorities had requested no U.S. uniforms be worn on Kenyan soil.

"Gonna be hell to pay," Gunner's Mate First Class Pete Vuylsteke growled. "Didn't think them fuckers would try to take over the whole damned ship."

Electrician's Mate Second Class Olie Tretter, a black man who sprawled beside the gunny, swore softly. "Them damned bastards shot up the old *Turner* pretty fucking good. You hear a lot of shotguns?"

The third sailor, Hospital Corpsman Second Class Rafe Perez, shot a stream of tobacco juice into the rubble. "Hell, yes, scatterguns, AK-47's, and something else. Always tell the Forty-seven by the high-pitched snarl." Perez shook his head. "What the hell we do now?"

"I sure as hell ain't gonna volunteer to get on them buses," Tretter said. "Most likely heading for that prison we heard about in town."

Vuylsteke, the ranking man of the trio, looked at Tretter. "You think you can find somebody to help us hide? Know damned well Uncle Sam ain't gonna let his ship be hijacked for long. Be a task force steaming in here in two or three days to blast this place apart and take back the old *Roy Turner*."

Tretter laughed. "Hell, you think 'cause I'm black I got kin here in town or something? Yeah, I talked with some of the natives tonight. Especially that one lady with the big tits who went topless. But hail, I ain't no diplomat."

"Weapons," Vuylsteke said. "Perez, you still carry that piddling little Thirty-two strapped to your ankle?"

"Never without it."

"So, we've got a start. We stay in deep shit here until the assholes out there hustle all our men off the ship. Then we slide out of here and find somewhere that we can eat and sleep for a couple of days. Two days, maybe three tops. By then Uncle will have about a thousand Marines in here to take back our ship."

Perez shook his head. "How the hell us two white guys gonna hide in this black country?"

"Didn't say it would be easy," Vuylsteke said. "Our man Tretter here is going to make it happen. What do we do first, Tretter?"

Tretter grinned. It wasn't often these two top hands asked him anything. Then he sobered. "From what I heard yesterday, some hairy-assed colonel staged a coup and took over the police and the radio, TV stations and the airports. He already had the army in his back pocket. So looks like this colonel is running the whole damn country."

"He figured the *Turner* would be a threat to him?" Vuylsteke asked.

"Who the hell knows," Tretter said. "I heard some guys talking who said this colonel is a huge guy, six feet five and three hundred pounds. Not a man to be pushed around."

"You understand this Swahili shit?" Perez asked.

"Not a word. But half the country can speak English. It's one of two official languages, so that'll help. What we have to do is find some friendlies who will cover for us."

"How?" Perez asked.

Tretter watched the last of the American sailors board a bus, and all five buses pulled out. They could see green-clad Kenyan troops on their ship. All had automatic rifles or shotguns.

"Must be leaving a squad or two to occupy the old tub," Vuylsteke said. He looked at Tretter. "So how do you find us some friendlies?"

"First I go back to that little bar—no, a different one. I can pass here, man. I buy somebody a drink and get him talking. Maybe I can find someone not happy with the colonel."

"We all should go," Perez said.

"No. I had to explain why I was with two white guys before. The ship. They knew about the *Turner*. Now they'll know she's been captured, so you white American sailors should have been captured too. I got to go by myself."

Perez bent down to his ankle, and a minute later came up with the .32 revolver with its tie-down holster. "This might come in handy. I don't have any more rounds. Didn't think the hell that I would need any."

Vuylsteke came back from the front of the abandoned building. "Looks like all of the army has gone except for the guys on board. Too many for us to take with our peashooter. Time for us to haul ass. Where to, Tretter?"

Tretter shook his head. "Right now I don't have the slightest idea."

3

Sunday, July 18

0800 hours
Coronado, California

Lieutenant Blake Murdock heard the ringing. Some giant ship was about to ram his forty-two-foot sailing boat in the middle of the Bahamas, and there was no possible way to avoid the collision. He did everything he could think of to get away from the huge freighter rushing toward his fragile craft, but he couldn't, and the ringing came again and again and again.

Murdock jolted upright in his bed.

Not the Bahamas.

Coronado, California. The phone had provided the ringing sound effects for his dream. Thoroughly awake by this time, Blake reached for the phone. His voice wasn't up to speed, however. He garbled out a hello and listened.

"You sleep all day out there in Lotus Land, Lieutenant Murdock? Hell, it's almost noon in Washington. The birds are out, the sun is shining, and it's going to be one fine day. This is Don Stroh."

"Figures," Murdock mumbled.

"You been listening to the news? It's all over CNN. I don't know how those newshounds get their stuff so fast. We've only had it since nine last night ourselves. You still with me, buddy?"

"Yeah. My body is awake, but my brain is still trying to outrun somebody in the Bahamas. What's all over CNN?"

"About one A.M. Sunday Mombasa, Kenya, time, a colonel who'd staged a military coup attacked and captured the frigate *Roy Turner,* which was tied up at a dock on a goodwill call."

"Yeah, now I'm listening. So?"

"Get your boys together fast. Uncle wants his ship back. Third Platoon will go in and get it. Be ready to load at North Island Air Station as soon as possible. Bring your sixteen men, personal gear, personal weapons, plus the fifty-caliber sniper rifles, and most of the ammo and goodies that you'll need."

"We have a hunting license?"

"The best kind, straight from Uncle Sam himself. He wants this taken care of quickly and with the more noise the better. He's got a carrier task force steaming that direction. I'll meet you in Riyadh, Saudi Arabia. You'll get a satellite printout of all we know about the situation."

"Who led the coup?"

"An old friend of yours. Remember Umar the Great?"

"Umar Maleceia, the huge guy? He was Kenyan, wasn't he. We put him through some tough sledding at the special training program we ran for certain of our allies."

"He loves you too. He pulled the coup. Start gathering in your chicks. I know this is Sunday morning. You don't fly out of North Island until four o'clock this afternoon. Gives you eight hours."

"I should have twenty-four. I think some of the guys went to Baja fishing."

"Hook them back and get them ready. I've got a hot lunch date, then I'm flying out of here. See you in Saudi Arabia."

They hung up.

Murdock flopped down on the bed, then popped right back up. The first thing he did was call David "Jaybird" Sterling, Machinist Mate Second Class and the Platoon Chief. He would know where most of the other fourteen men were. They'd get who they could, and send the strays over by a later plane. They'd done that before, but Murdock didn't like to do it.

He got Jaybird on the second ring. "Circle the wagons, we got a job to do," he told his chief by way of greeting.

"When?"

"We fly out of North Island at sixteen-hundred. We need sixteen live bodies. Spread the word. I'll be at the office in half an hour."

Murdock downed a cup of instant coffee, then drove to the SEALs' home base just south of Coronado on the Silver Strand in the U.S. Naval Amphibious Base. He called Lieutenant (j.g.) Ed DeWitt, his 2IC, leader of the Second Squad, and caught him at home.

By 1000, eleven of the sixteen men were on hand working on gear for the trip.

"We're still five guys short," Jaybird said, coming into the commander's office.

"Who?"

"Magic Brown, Adams, Red Nicholson, Lincoln, and Holt."

"Put one man on each one and have them track them down," Murdock said. "If they can't find them by fourteen hundred, have them get back here. Who went to Baja?"

"Brown and Red Nicholson, both fishing nuts. Don't even know where they were going. Not much below Ensenada, I don't think."

Murdock scowled. "Yeah, The Matzalan Fish Shack. Give them a call. Nicholson liked the guy that ran it. He used to go down there every weekend. Remember, he used to talk our ears off about the good fishing down there? You might hook them at that Fish Shack."

"Where the fuck we going, L-T?" Operation Specialist Third Class Joe "Ricochet" Lampedusa asked as he came in the door when Jaybird left.

"It make any difference?"

"Hell, yes, we take mucklucks or suntan lotion?"

Half the crew brayed with laughter.

"Make it suntan lotion and desert cammies. Any other dip-shit questions?"

The SEALs razzed Lampedusa, and went back to work packing their gear and cleaning weapons.

Murdock watched his men. He had finished his packing and cleaning and oiling his weapon, an H&K MP5SD4 specially custom-fitted for the SEALs. These were good men. He'd lost one on the last mission. He hoped he didn't lose any this time.

The Navy SEALs carried a ton of macho mystique with them that was becoming known more and more outside the service. Mostly they were famous for their training course—the six-months Basic Underwater Demolition/SEAL regimen. Over the years, the name had been shortened to BUD/S. It was rougher and tougher than any other training course in any military force in the world.

Every man who came to the BUD/S training center in Coronado was a volunteer. Most didn't know just how tough the twenty-six-week training schedule would be. Physical fitness and training dominated the first part of the schedule. Some of that involved lifting eighteen-inch-thick telephone poles on the shoulders of seven SEAL trainees. They might hoist it overhead and hold it, hoist it partway up, or put it on their shoulders and do a five-mile run.

They trained with eight-man inflatable boats in the surf, learning how to get them through the Pacific Ocean breakers, and how to get them back in without dumping everyone into the water.

They took ocean swimming as a matter of course, doing five- and seven-mile swims in the open sea with and without fins, and with and without underwater breathing apparatuses.

By the time the SEALs came out of BUD/S training, they were so accustomed to the water that it had become their second home.

The basic lesson in all of the training was teamwork. SEALs operated in eight-man squads. Every man relied on every other man to protect his life. Teamwork became so ingrained in SEALs that in combat situations they functioned automatically, taking the right action and making the right decisions. If they didn't, one or more of the team could die.

Navy officers go through the same training as any other SEAL. They have no rank when they enter a BUD/S class. They lift the logs, run the killer obstacle course, work the boats, get sand and water thrown on them during exercises and classes, and generally accept all of the rugged training procedures the other men do.

There is one officer-related requirement. Any officer in any SEAL trainee class is expected to test better than the rest of the class. All this helps mold a strong bond between enlisted, and their SEAL officers, and to a large degree breaks down the "officer country" psychology of the military. A lot of regular Navy officers don't like this aspect of SEAL operations.

SEAL officers say when you're trusting your life to the SEAL behind you in a life-or-death firefight operation, it doesn't matter what rank or rate he has. All that matters is that he can do his job, protect your back, and run a successful mission.

One thing about SEALs that Murdock had always questioned. The SEALs, like all enlisted men and women in the Navy, carry a rating, a work specialty like Hull Technician or Machinist's Mate. These ratings simply don't apply in the SEALs' operations. They have an entirely different kind of job and specialty.

To the Navy, however, these men still must study their manuals and take tests twice a year for promotion in that job specialty. This also bugs most of the SEALs.

In training and after it, most SEALs move toward a combat specialty that interests them and suits their talents. One man may be an expert on weapons, another communications, one parachute rigging, and somebody else electronics. All are slotted in where they can do the most good and still maintain their basic job: hitting hard with maximum firepower, killing the enemy, capturing the objective, and getting out without the loss of any men.

Losses. Six men from SEAL Team Seven, Third Platoon, had been wounded and one killed in the *Firestorm* mission.

Murdock had taken a bad arm wound. Now all but one of
the wounded had recovered during the two-month training
period, and were back in service. One man was still in the
hospital, and Greg Johnson had died of his wounds and was
brought home.

That meant two new men who were qualified SEALs had
been needed in the mix, and had had to learn to work with
their new buddies. Murdock had brought in Torpedoman's
Mate Third Class Les Quinley the first week back from
China to replace Johnson. Quinley's explosive talents would
come in handy.

Murdock wasn't sure when or even if Scotty Frazier
would be out of the hospital and fit for duty. He'd waited a
month. Frazier's "slight side wound" had turned ugly before
he got to Balboa Park Naval Hospital in San Diego, and
he'd been on the critical list for a week. After a month,
Murdock talked to Frazier's doctor, crossed Frazier's name
off the roster, and brought in a new man.

He'd picked Ted Yates off the available list. Yates already
had his Trident, the badge of honor of the proven and tested
SEALs who had seen covert-operations duty. He was
twenty-four and a Bos'n's Mate Second Class. He would
help lend a little maturity to the Second Platoon.

Now the men had trained together for a solid month,
including an interminable week at the Chocolate Mountains
gunnery range out near Niland. They'd slept on the ground
and lived on MREs, Meals Ready to Eat, for six days.

It had been almost as bad as Hell Week during BUD/S
training, when the new men were up continuously for four
days and got only four hours of sleep. It was right after that
tough week that a lot of the trainees laid their green SEAL
helmet liners with the class number on them next to the
quitting-bell post on the "grinder." They then were out of
the program and went back to the regular Navy. Many times
half a beginning class washed out. One famous class had
had every man quit before the six months were up.

Sixty-eight miles south of Tijuana along the Baja California,
Mexico, coastline, Eric "Red" Nicholson, Torpedoman's
Mate Second Class, hooked a fish and let out a rebel yell.

"Hell of a good bite," Red brayed. "Took that anchovy and dove straight down. Fucker is still taking out line."

"Not a yellowtail then," Martin "Magic" Brown, Quartermaster's Mate First Class, said. "Yellows don't sound that way. Bet you twenty bucks it's a bluefin tuna."

"No bluefins in the Ensenada Bay this time of year," Red said. He had his six-foot fighting pole lifted to an eighty-degree angle, and the bend was tiring out the fish below. A moment later, the line stopped whining off the spool.

Red grinned and lowered the rod slowly, reeling in as he went. Then he pumped up the pole gently and reeled down again.

"Gonna take you all day that way, Red. Hell, horse him in."

"You black guys don't know shit about fishing. I got it on a twenty-pound line, man. You playing with thirty. I got me enough yellowtail here to feed me for a month."

"Bluefin, dumb-assed honky, which is better eating anyway," Magic said. He changed bait, cast out into the bay, and let the six-inch-long anchovy run as far as he'd go before he tired. Every ninety seconds, Magic changed bait. They'd been doing that since dawn and had only two fish.

Magic saw the skiff coming out from shore. More fishermen. Maybe they would help chum up some good-sized blues. The skiff came straight at them, and Magic put his hand on a new toy he'd just bought, a new Para Ordinance P12–45. It held only ten rounds in the magazine and one in the chamber, but it had a smooth, easy feel. Handguns for civilians are strictly illegal in Mexico, but he wasn't about to cross the border without some protection. He'd heard too many stories about Mexican banditos ambushing unwary gringos.

Red kept working the fish.

"I'm getting him up," Red shouted. "You got that gaff?"

"You said we wouldn't need one," Magic shot back.

The skiff came straight on and was fifty yards away. The voice came over the water clearly.

"Señor Brown. I have urgent message for you from a Mr. Blake."

"Oh, hell," Red said.

"Shit, there goes the fishing."

Red had the fish showing color by then, and he got it close enough to the boat to identify.

"Yeah, a bluefin," Magic chortled.

Just then the frantic fish made one last surge for the bottom, and broke the line. "Oh, damn, Peter Pan," Red bellowed. "Knew I shouldn't have tightened up on that drag."

The skiff came alongside. An Indian-dark Mexican man in his twenties grinned at them. His English was better than most down that way.

"Sorry to hurt fishing. The man said you come home right away. Mr. Blake said you give me ten dollar."

Brown laughed. Sounded just like Lieutenant Blake Murdock, their ever-generous leader.

"What's the message?" Red said, handing the man a ten-dollar bill.

"He say get your ass back to base now. Big fly time tonight at eight bells. No, he say sixteen hundred, *Sí*, sixteen hundred. What time that?"

"Not much time left is what it is," Magic Brown snapped. "Get that motor started there, sailor, and let's head for shore. We must have ourselves a piece of the action some damned place out there in the big fat world."

Jaybird dug Ross Lincoln out of McP's Bar in Coronado, which was run by an ex-Navy corpsman who had served in Nam. He was better at telling stories than he was at serving beer. Lincoln was in a bullshitting contest with him, and the loser on every head-to-head story had to chugalug a mug of beer without breathing or stopping. Lincoln had lost six times in a row. It took them two hours to sober him up, and by that time they had his gear and his weapons packed for him.

"That leaves Holt and Adams," Jaybird said at 1200. "Holt took off Friday night solo. No idea where he is."

Lincoln looked up, holding his head. "Holt? Said something about a weekend with that bimbo he met at the Too

Late Club. Francine, something like that. Said he gave her phone number and address as his next of kin."

Jaybird snapped his fingers and went to see Lieutenant (j.g.) DeWitt. He'd have the next-of-kin data for all his men.

Holt showed up an hour later. He couldn't walk. Two men from his squad had to go bring him in from the taxi. He'd be lucky to be sober by the time the plane took off.

Nobody knew anything about Adams. He lived off base the way the rest of the platoon did, and nobody had been to his digs.

"Isn't Adams the one who's always listening to those old songs from the fifties and sixties on KJOY?" Murdock asked.

Lieutenant (j.g.) DeWitt nodded. "Yeah, Adams is a big-bands nut. Always listens to that station."

"Isn't there a DJ on there who used to be a SEAL? Loudmouth Larry?" Murdock asked.

DeWitt checked his watch. "Yeah, he's the one Adams talks about. Don't know when his shift is, but I'll see what I can do." The officer vanished to a phone, and came back five minutes later.

"Loudmouth wasn't there, but I talked to another guy, Sawtooth, and explained the delicate situation. He said he can cover us. He'll do a dedication and tell baby-chick Adams to head back to the nest. If Adams hasn't passed out, he should hear it."

An hour later, they heard from Adams. He was on his way in.

Lieutenant Blake Murdock checked every man before the platoon boarded a truck for a run through Coronado and out to the U.S. Naval Air Station North Island. He'd read the six pages of background on the Kenya situation that had come faxed from Don Stroh and his buddies at the CIA in Washington, D.C. He didn't understand much more than what Stroh had told him on the phone. He put it simply to the men as they waited on the flight line for the long-range Air Force Starlifter transport jet to have its final preflight check.

"We're going to Kenya, about halfway down on the

Indian Ocean side of Africa. They've had an elected government there since they gained their freedom from British rule back in 1963.

"This is the land of Jomo Kenyatta and the famous Mau Mau uprising and slaughter of whites. Two days ago an Army colonel took over the country and has declared himself dictator. Army strength there is set at about twenty-six thousand, but with little airpower and not much of a Navy.

"We go in and recapture a frigate that the colonel hijacked about twenty-four hours ago. Our target is in Mombasa, the country's only port. We recapture the ship, free the crew, and get the hulk back to sea. Sounds like a walk in the park."

"Them Mau Mau were prime-assed killers in their day," Magic Brown said. "Hey, I'm no relation."

"Where we get supplied?" Jaybird asked.

"We'll land on a carrier that, with its task force, is steaming down that direction right now. We can get all the firepower we need from the carrier. We're taking four folded IBSs with us just in case. Everything else we get from the carrier's supplies and armory."

"How do you rescue a four-hundred-fifty-three-foot-long ship?" Kenneth Ching, Quartermaster's Mate First Class, asked.

"We'll be talking about that on the way over," Murdock said. "Looks like we're cleared to board. Let's move."

Ten minutes later, they had settled into the spartan facilities of the Air Force Starlifter strategic jet transport plane, the C-141. It had a top airspeed of 556 miles per hour, and four big Pratt & Whitney TF33-P-7 turbofan engines to do the job. It could also be refueled air-to-air if needed.

The big plane had a crew of five, and could haul 155 paratroopers or two hundred non-jumpers. That meant the sixteen SEALs were rattling around in the big plane. Most of them sacked out on the floor and on their equipment packs.

"You sure they got us a big enough plane?" Jaybird asked.

"They wanted to be positive we had room enough for all of your ego, Jaybird," Lincoln jibed.

"Speed is the factor, guys," Murdock said. "We can go almost three thousand miles in this bucket without stopping at your local Texaco station."

Murdock watched his men. He was a career Navy man. Annapolis, a ring-knocker, single, and thirty years old. He stood six-two and kept his weight at a solid 200 pounds. He'd done some Gulf War work, been a SEAL for six years, and had been leader of the Third Platoon of SEAL Team Seven for just over two years. In that time they'd completed five major missions.

Murdock was the son of Congressman Charles Murdock, longtime member of the House Military Affairs Committee. He grew up in posh Fort Royal, Virginia. He went to Exeter, and then to Annapolis over his father's objections. His dad wanted him to go to Harvard, get into government service, and then run for his own congressional seat from Virginia when the old man finally decided to give it up.

Murdock wouldn't go for it, and earned his appointment to Annapolis instead. He almost got married once. Her name was Susan, a bright, vibrant girl who was Jewish, much to his father's discomfort. She was killed three days before the wedding that was to take place right after his Annapolis graduation. It happened in a car accident as she was on her way to see him.

Now the SEALs were his life. He grinned. He had met a girl a few months ago in Washington, D.C., who had made him stop and think about getting serious again. But they had put it on hold. She'd hoped that in a year he'd have his fill of the SEAL excitement and be ready to settle down at some posh military job at the Pentagon. He snorted. Fat chance.

Murdock called his men together.

"At least we know our route. We'll be going over the Pole and drop in on London. From there we touch down at Cairo, probably for more fly juice, then on to Riyadh, Saudi Arabia. Don't ask me about which countries we can fly over and which ones we detour around. Not my problem.

"In Saudi Arabia we'll pick up our old friend Don Stroh,

who is our CIA control on these pleasure cruises. For you two new men to our little family here, we are currently on a string for the CIA. Any dirty little job they don't want anyone to know that the U.S. has a hand in, they give to us. Not sure that this one will be all that covert, since CNN had the story of the hijacking all over the airwaves about six hours after it happened.

"We'll be getting more details on the harbor at Mombasa, which I hear is a good one and over three miles long. Plenty of dock space courtesy of our British friends, who built up the port in the fifties and sixties.

"From Saudi Arabia we'll be changing planes into the more familiar C-2A Navy Greyhound, our old reliable COD Navy turboprop transport. The Greyhound will land us on our home base, some carrier now steaming south just off the Somali Republic coastline heading for the waters off Kenya. As usual, the carrier has its normal protective task force. Any questions?"

"Yes, sir, L-T." It was Torpedoman's Mate Third Class Les Quinley, one of the replacements who'd come on board after the Chinese picnic. "Does this shitbird bad-ass Kenyan colonel have a name?"

"Right, Quinley. He's Full Colonel Umar Maleceia. He was a major last time I met him at a special training program in the States. He was a student there. Which means the U.S. trained him in the latest and best in weapons, communications, and tactics. Which he is probably putting to good use right now. Anything else?"

"Sir?" An airman stood at the edge of the SEALs. He had a piece of paper in his hand. "Lieutenant Murdock. I have some correspondence for you from Washington."

Murdock nodded, and the airman brought the papers forward, gave them to him, and retreated.

Murdock looked at the top sheet, read a few lines of it, and groaned.

"Gentlemen, our mission has just changed. Our Colonel Maleceia has just expanded his operation. Two hours ago he attacked the U.S. Embassy in Nairobi, the Kenyan capital. Now we are ordered to defend and if necessary recapture the embassy if it falls. The estimate in this report is that the embassy can't hold out more than about twelve hours. So our first mission will be on land at the embassy in Nairobi, which is about three hundred miles north of Mombasa."

"Damn long swim, L-T," Quartermaster's Mate First Class Kenneth Ching said. The SEALs all laughed.

4

Sunday, July 18

0512 hours
Ruined building, waterfront
Mombasa, Kenya

Gunner's Mate First Class Pete Vuylsteke woke up first. His back hurt where he had slept on the hard floor. He poked Perez beside him, and looked around for Tretter.

"Where the hell's the black kid?" Vuylsteke whispered.

Doc Perez rubbed his eyes. "Last time I saw him he was snoring over there. He sure ain't there now."

Vuylsteke looked through the broken window. "Damn near daylight outside. We gonna be safe in here? Where the hell is Tretter?"

They heard something at the edge of the broken-down building, and both dropped flat on the floor. The sound came closer; then Tretter stepped around the crumbling wall and waved.

"Hey, the two sleeping beauties have awakened. I should give you a medal already. Gents, I've been out and about on this fine day, and I bring back food.

"Had one hell of a hard time out there faking it. Nothing is open yet. Went down one street and looked in every small shop. Got to another street and saw a woman in an alley. She came my way. I waited and talked to her.

"She pegged me right away as an American. Clothes, she said. She pulled me into a doorway and we talked. Turns out she was looking for her milk delivery somebody forgot to bring.

"She said she wasn't at all sympathetic to the new military rule. She knew about our ship getting hijacked. She said the U.S. Navy would blow up half the town in two days to get the ship back.

"I asked her if she could help hide three of us. She frowned and said maybe. If I could help her. Hell, I said anything, we'd help her do whatever she wanted.

"So I found this fine little mama who says she'll help hide us, but, like, we have to play the game with her."

Tretter put down two plastic sacks. Inside were two loaves of bread, a small jar of jam, a dozen hot dogs, and three bananas. He pulled out another jar, a larger one, that contained some dark brown strips.

"Kippered fish, gents. A real delicacy. I didn't ask her what kind of fish. You dig?"

Already Perez had eaten one of the bananas. Vuylsteke had pushed two of the hot dogs inside a cut-off strip of the round loaf of bread, and had his mouth full.

"What's our security?" Perez asked as he broke off a chunk of the bread.

"This mama has a small place and neighbors. Nobody moving around when I was there. She says she can help us, but we got to help her."

"I smells me some trouble," Perez said.

"Oh, she said she heard the word last night. If any of the soldiers occupying Mombasa spot any U.S. sailors running around, they have orders to shoot to kill."

Vuylsteke waved his sandwich. "Yeah, figures. What does this broad want?"

"First she said I had to smuggle her on board our ship when we get it out of here. I told her not a chance. Then she said we had to get her a visa to come to the U.S. where she can be a recording star. She's a singer."

"Evidently," Vuylsteke said.

"I said easy. Just apply at the embassy in Nairobi."

"That do it?" Perez asked.

Vuylsteke waved his hand and pointed to the far end of

the building. They could hear voices. Then somebody pushed over some boards and they clattered on the floor.

The three sailors gathered up their food, and edged behind a half-torn-down wall. The voices came closer. A few moments later they could see two black policemen in khaki uniforms. Neither one had a gun. Both had night-sticks. Now the sailors could hear the English words.

"They tell us to search the place so we search," the taller one said. "Otherwise we get shot. These guys have no brains."

"How long will this coup last?" the shorter one asked.

"Who knows. We be careful until then. Maybe the United States will come in to rescue their ship. Who knows?"

The two policemen stood there a moment, then turned, and walked back the way they had come.

"We searched it. We tell them we searched the whole building and didn't find a thing except rat droppings."

"Yeah, that's good. Rat droppings." The smaller man shook his head. "Only, you can tell them, not me."

The sailors breathed easier as the two policemen went out the way they had come in.

Silently Tretter motioned for the other two sailors to follow him. They went to the near end of the building and Tretter looked out. It was daylight. Tretter rummaged around near a broken door until he found what he had left there. Straw hats, large and floppy.

"Put these on to cover those American heads. Keep your hands in your pockets and maybe we can fake it up two blocks. Hope not a lot of folks are awake yet."

They put on the hats and Tretter nodded. "For God's sake don't rush. We're almost on the equator here and it's gonna be hot as hell in an hour or two. Just mosey along. I've got the peashooter in my pocket if we need it."

They ambled across the dusty street to the alley and moved up it. A door banged somewhere ahead, but no one was there by the time they reached the spot. They saw no one along a second garbage-filled dirt alley that showed the backs of a few old buildings on both sides. They went across a wider dirt street to an alley, and paused inside in some shadows.

"Halfway up the alley," Tretter said. He scowled at them. "Don't gawk at this lady. She's half Arab and half Kenyan. She talks in English and sometimes Arabic, and some Swahili thrown in. Just take it easy."

"Hey, she can speak Hindustani for all I care," Vuylsteke said. "Can she save our swabby asses from that wigged-out crazy colonel?"

"Yeah, I think she can. The Army killed her brother. A lot of the Kenyan people look down on the Arabs and the Arab mixtures. She's not a happy camper."

"She got a big place?" Perez asked.

Tretter gave him a snort for an answer, and they meandered on up the alley. Then in a blink they were gone. All three had stepped into a dark doorway that opened to a knock. They went up wooden stairs to the third floor, and then down a hallway. The person who led them was a small woman, no more than five feet tall, with long straight black hair and dark clothes.

She opened the door at the end of the hallway and slipped inside. Tretter waved the other sailors in. The woman closed the door and faced them. She was tiny and slender and had a creamy brown complexion. She wore no makeup, but her eyes glowed a deep brown. She wore a long black skirt and black blouse. Her face was grim.

"So, United States Navy sailors. I help you, you help me, no?"

They nodded.

"The Army kill my brother. I want you kill three Kenyan Army soldiers for me. Three for one, my family tradition."

"I don't know, lady," Vuylsteke said. "We do that, and the whole fuc—the whole damn Kenyan Army gonna be down here looking for us." He was the senior man. It was his call.

She shrugged. "You think about. I live alone. Have two rooms. No close friends. Work at place across town. You stay here. Be quiet. Tonight I show you how to kill Army soldiers and not get caught."

"Oh, guys, this lady's name is Pita," Tretter said. "It

means the fourth-born, but she says she was only the second-born. Pita, this is Vuylsteke and Perez."

"Am pleased to meeting you. Now must go see my mother."

"Pita, is there anything to drink?" Tretter asked. "Water, coffee. We're all dry as hell."

Pita frowned for a moment, then brightened. "Yes, I have Coca-Cola. You like?"

5

Sunday, July 18

Ambassador Harrington G. Jerome watched out his second-story window as the gunfire continued to rake the U.S. Embassy. This was totally outrageous. The embassy was United States soil. How dare this renegade colonel fire upon them.

His First Secretary, Frank Underhill, rushed in, blood dripping from his right arm, which hung useless at his side.

"Sir, we have only our twelve Marines. I'm afraid most of the rest of us don't even know how to fire a weapon. The gate is holding for now. The Marines drove our big truck against the steel gate, but they say they can't be sure how long it will last."

"Yes, Frank, thank you. Keep all of the civilians out of the line of fire. Thank God for the wall around the compound. Otherwise we would have been overrun the first hour. Have that arm tended to at once. We can't afford to lose you."

"Yes, sir. I'll do it. We've held out four hours already. Maybe we can keep them away until night. They won't continue to come at us in the dark, will they?"

Ambassador Jerome remembered his days in the infantry. Night attacks were always the best for those attacking.

"Don't worry about it, Frank. Just keep things together.

Remember, if they do break in, your first act is to burn all papers and destroy the encrypto machine. Be sure of that."

"Yes, sir. I understand."

Below on the ground floor, three U.S. Marines stood beside a broken-out window. They had set up a light machine gun there and had a dozen belts of ammunition ready. From time to time the gunner sent five-round bursts over the top of the wall.

"There's one," Sergeant Wilson snapped.

An M-16 on single-shot barked once, and the figure trying to flip over the top of the concrete block wall jolted as the bullet hit him and he spun off the top of the wall and fell outside.

"Keep it up here," Wilson said. "I'm checking the north wall. That's their best attack point."

Sergeant Wilson ran through the embassy with his M-16. He had fatigue pockets stuffed with six spare magazines for the rifle. A window on the second floor on the north-facing side of the embassy had been opened before it could be shot out. A Marine stationed there raised up and looked out at irregular intervals, then quickly dropped out of sight. Twice rifle rounds had slashed through the window a fraction of a second after he'd ducked.

"Still there, Sarge," Private Marshall said. "Must be fifteen or twenty of them. Don't know why they don't come on across."

"They aren't sure how many guns we have in here," Sergeant Wilson said. "They think they know, but nobody is willing to be the first one to bet his life on it."

"So, is it a stalemate?"

"Only as long as they want it to be, Marshall. They have at least two armored personnel carriers out there and maybe five hundred men. One of those personnel carriers could probably punch a hole in our concrete-block wall. Not even sure if it has rebar in it."

A grinding and clanking brought both Marines up to the window for a quick look.

"Now we've got real trouble," Sergeant Wilson said. "We

have any of those RPGs left, or did we burn them up in practice?"

"Should be four of them in the basement," Private Marshall said.

"Go down and get them and bring them all up here. I'll man your post. Run, damnit. That's a tank out there grinding along toward us. It could smash its way through that wall like it was flypaper, rebar or no rebar. Move it."

The Marine took off on a run. Sergeant Wilson lifted up and fired a burst of five rounds out the window at the wall. All of the rounds hit the inside of the blocks, but the Kenyan soldiers on the other side would get the message. He had to buy a few more minutes. He jolted up, looked out, and came down in one move.

A rifle round slapped into the outside of the wall near the window. The tank was halfway across the open field north of the embassy wall. This time, when Sergeant Wilson fired, he lifted his sights to aim at the tank. Then he paused just a fraction of a second to see if any of the six rounds hit the tank. He couldn't tell. He jerked his head down, and two chunks of hot lead blasted through the open window a microsecond later.

Where the hell was Marshall? The fucking tank would be on them any minute.

Marshall panted up to the window with four Rocket Propelled Grenades. They were self-propelled and had little back-blast. Quickly Sergeant Wilson put one of the devices on his right shoulder, checked the sight, then pulled the tab to arm the grenade. He moved up to the window, aimed the grenade out it and in line with the tank, and fired.

The rocket whooshed away, leaving a burning cloud of smoke behind it. Half-a-dozen rifle rounds hit the window and came through it, but Wilson had dropped down just in time. Long before the smoke cleared away they could hear the tank. The round hadn't stopped it. Wilson wasn't even sure if it had made a hit. He sent Marshall to a window down the hall with two grenades and told him to fire at the tank if it smashed through the wall.

"Aim for the fucking tread. That's about the only way we can stop it."

As he spoke, a blast shook the north wing of the embassy. It must have hit just below them. Sergeant Wilson lifted up and looked out the window. The tank's gun, maybe a .75-caliber, still smoked. They had fired a round at the embassy.

The next time he looked out, Sergeant Wilson saw that the tank was too close to the wall to fire over it. That wouldn't last long. He looked out the window now every three or four seconds. He took no incoming fire. The snipers must be off the wall.

A moment later he saw the ten-foot concrete block barricade bulging. Then cracks showed, and a second later one large section of blocks crashed down inside the compound. The tank's gun swiveled around to point to the front again as the tank clanked and rattled as it crawled over the broken and bashed-in blocks, then stopped just inside the compound.

The tank's machine gun chattered, and the window frame above Wilson shattered as half-a-dozen rounds hit it and rained glass down on him. The last grenade.

Wilson armed it, checked the sight, lifted up, and in another quick move aimed, fired, and ducked. This time he wasn't quite fast enough, or the marksman outside had been firing already before Wilson had launched the small missile.

The AK-47 round glanced off the rocket launcher, tumbled as it smashed forward, and dug into the right side of Sergeant Wilson's mouth, then slanted to the left and slashed through the top of his mouth into his brain. He slammed backwards, and died before he knew if his round had hit the tank.

One window down, Private Marshall saw the sergeant's round explode on the left tank tread and blow it off the rollers. The tank was dead in the water. Then the big gun swung around, and Marshall got off his round aimed at the small driver's window slots in the front. He saw the round hit and explode, but he wasn't sure of the damage.

He fired his last RPG round as a dozen Kenyan troops ran

through the hole in the wall. The grenade splattered four of the soldiers into spare body parts, and put down three more. Then Marshall picked up his M-16 and fired out the window. He couldn't understand why Sergeant Wilson wasn't firing.

Downstairs at the front window, the Marines kept the machine gun chattering aimed just over the wall. The men there heard the tank and the RPG rounds, but they didn't know the tank had crashed through the wall.

Two green-shirted Kenyan soldiers worked along the front of the embassy building, tucked in close so no one inside could see them. One crawled the last twenty feet, lay on his back, and pulled the pin on a hand grenade. He tossed it into the window where the machine gun chattered, then ran back the way he had come.

Private Anderson saw the grenade come in. Four-second fuse, he thought. No time to run. The small hand bomb bounced once on the wooden floor; then Anderson dove on it, shielding it with his body as it exploded with a mind-numbing rumble.

The machine gunner's eyes went wide as he stared at the man on the floor who had just saved his life. Then he bellowed in fury and angled his weapon to the north, where he saw the movement of green uniforms. He fired until his last belt ran out, then grabbed an M-1 and kept blasting away at the oncoming Kenyan soldiers.

Ten minutes later, it was all over. Ten of the twelve Marines were dead. The other two had been knocked unconscious by the concussion of the .75-caliber rounds and captured. Four of the civilian employees of the embassy had been killed by gunfire. The Kenyan troops backed the truck away from the main entrance and opened the gates.

A weapons carrier drove in, and Colonel Maleceia stepped out. Two of his officers had found the ambassador, and brought him to the front of the building.

"Mr. Ambassador. This embassy is closed and all your rights are nullified. This is no longer United States soil. You all are prisoners of war, and will be treated as such. Any resistance by you, or any of your people, will bring immediate execution. Do I make myself perfectly clear?"

Ambassador Jerome nodded. Tears ran down his cheeks. "I understand, Colonel. None of my people will resist in any way. Already four of the staff have been killed along with ten of the Marines. You have no right. . . ."

The ambassador stopped as Colonel Maleceia snapped up his head. "Careful, Mr. Ambassador. What room is large enough to hold all of your people?"

"The formal dining room."

"Not good. We'll put everyone in that large room in the basement. I don't want you to be too comfortable. We'll see what your government will do to ransom you. How many people do you have left alive, Mr. Ambassador?"

"Forty-two alive and fourteen dead. Fourteen that your men killed when it wasn't necessary."

"Don't criticize me, Jerome."

"Do you know what you've done? The whole weight and power of the United States will bear down on you. You can't possibly live for more than a week. You are a monster and a dead man. You have violated every diplomatic code of conduct of behavior ever invented."

Colonel Maleceia growled, and drew his weapon from the holster on his right side. He lifted the automatic, stepped forward, and shot the ambassador in his right eye. Ambassador Harrington G. Jerome jolted backward and died in a sprawl on the front steps of the embassy.

"Clean up this mess," Colonel Maleceia barked. "The rest of you round up everyone inside and take them to the big room in the basement, the one with the steel doors and no windows. We don't want anyone to escape."

Ten minutes later in the locked basement room, one of the Marines still alive used strips of cloth to wrap up Frank Underhill's shot-up arm. He had lost a lot of blood, but he knew that he would live. There was so much to do. He was in charge now. He shivered when he remembered how matter-of-factly that madman had executed Ambassador Jerome. Terrible.

He made sure the six others who had been wounded were

tended. All were non-life-threatening but one. Madelyn, a secretary and code clerk, had taken a ricocheted bullet in her chest. Evidently it had missed the vital organs. But she was pale and lying down.

The basement room was smaller than Frank remembered. With forty-two people in it—no, only forty-one alive now—there would barely be room for everyone to lie down on the floor. He had no hope for food, water or toilet facilities. There simply were none.

An hour later, Colonel Maleceia had figured out the radio in the communications room. He didn't bother with the code-books that he found partially destroyed. He would broadcast in the clear. It would bounce off the satellite overhead and be picked up in Washington, D.C., as clearly as if he'd phoned from down the block. He hadn't spent all of his time at the U.S. military training center working on tactics. His radio and electronics capability was considerable.

First, he broadcast a warning that an important message would be coming. He gave his name and new position as ruler of Kenya.

A frantic message came through in the clear to the embassy asking if all was well. They knew it was not. Maleceia ignored it.

His message was brief.

"To the United States of America. This is a notification and a warning to the people of America. First, I now hold one hundred and sixty of your sailors from the *Roy Turner* and forty-one members of your diplomatic staff at the former U.S. Embassy in Nairobi. These hostages will be humanely treated pending your acceptance of my conditions.

"The United States of America will pay to the nation of Kenya the sum of one hundred billion dollars in gold, food, merchandise, jet fighter aircraft, naval ships, and in credits around the world that Kenya can draw upon, for the release of these two hundred and one individuals.

"There will be no attack or threat of attack on Kenya soil

by U.S. forces. Any such attack will result in the execution of one hostage for every hour of any such attack.

"The United States has forty-eight hours to start delivering the gold, the merchandise, the ships, and planes as demanded. If this schedule is not met, one hostage will be executed and the video beamed to the world on television every hour until delivery starts.

"There is no alternative. I know of the wealth and squandered goods and riches in the United States. The people of Kenya are starving for such goods and food. It will be delivered on schedule or the dire measures will be carried out.

"This is General Umar Maleceia, Premier, President, and Commanding General of the great nation of Kenya, ending his proclamation."

General Umar Maleceia toured the ambassador's private quarters and bounced on the bed. He chuckled.

"I will sleep here tonight," he told his aide, a major who had taken advanced lessons in kowtowing.

"Yes, General," the major said, recognizing the new rank the colonel had granted himself.

Maleceia smiled at the man. "You'll go far, Major. What was your name again?"

"Ralston, General. An English name my parents liked when I was born."

"Too bad. Yes. Now, the kitchen. Send for the chef. Bring him from the basement. Tonight I will feast on roast duck or maybe a roast turkey dinner with all the trimmings like we had twice a year in Texas. Yes, a roast turkey dinner."

Five minutes later, the cook, a smiling little Italian man from the Bronx, explained the problem.

"General, sir. We have no turkey, no duck. I can prepare a feast for you from some chicken breasts, stuffing, mashed potatoes, giblet gravy, cranberries, peas and carrots, with fluffy dinner rolls and strawberry jam."

General Maleceia frowned. "I can't make a turkey appear. All right, the chicken dinner. You have an hour. Now get to it."

Back in the ambassador's suite, he broke open the locked

liquor cabinet, selected a fine scotch, and poured himself a shot. That was so good he had two more. He didn't offer any to the major.

"Oh, yes. Now, Major, we visit the hostages below."

In the basement room, the general looked over the people. Some were still crying. He selected a young blonde girl he guessed was a secretary, and a slightly older redhead who looked to have some fire. Both were young and slender.

"You two, go with the major."

The women pulled back. The First Secretary, Frank Underhill, now in charge of the embassy, started forward.

"At ease, all of you," said the general. "I'm not going to shoot these hostages. There's some secretarial work I need to take care of. Both you women can read and write, I assume?"

They nodded.

"Very well, go with the major."

Upstairs in the ambassador's suite, the general closed the door, dismissed the major, and pushed the women into the bedroom.

"Now, ladies, I want both of you to undress without a lot of tears or anger. As they used to say in Texas, you might as well relax and enjoy it. One way or another you're going to get fucked. Clear?"

"You have no right. . . ." the redhead began. His look of anger and rage cut her off.

The blonde girl began crying softly.

"No," Maleceia thundered. The roar stopped her weeping. Slowly both disrobed. They turned their backs as they took off their underwear.

"Turn around," the general demanded. They did, and he smiled. "Nice, extremely nice. I like big tits. You'll enjoy tonight. I've never disappointed a woman in my entire life." He watched them both, then moved first toward the blond woman.

"You have a name?" he asked.

"Sally," she said so softly he could barely hear.

He faced her, and she shivered. The redhead behind him moved forward without a sound. He had taken a stance with his feet apart in front of the much shorter Sally, and reached both hands for her breasts.

Marilee Zilke, a C-2 Field Agent with the CIA, moved the last few feet silently and kicked with her right foot as hard as she could. Her foot scraped past his thigh, and slammed into General Maleceia's crotch with crushing force. Only his thick military pants saved him from a shattered testicle. He lunged forward, almost lost his feet, then righted himself, and bent over for one long agonizing moment. Marilee darted forward, swung both of her hands made into one fist at the back of his neck, and drove the big man to his knees. She was about to kick him again when he turned, lifted his pistol, and fired six rounds into the CIA agent. She jolted backward three steps and crashed to the floor. He fired once more into her head, and turned to the weeping Sally.

General Maleceia could hardly talk. He pointed to the bed, and Sally sat down on it.

"No more trouble," he squeaked out. Sally had never seen a human being die before. She had shrieked in horror when the bullets hit Marilee. Now she couldn't utter a sound.

The general pulled off his clothes, and stared down at the softly weeping secretary from Elbow Bend, Wisconsin.

"Like I said, little lady, I've never disappointed a woman yet."

6

Monday, July 19

1513 hours
Wahhabi Air Base
Riyadh, Saudi Arabia

Third Platoon had landed at Wahhabi ten minutes ago. There was a rush on, but Murdock led the SEALs in a ten-minute double-time workout around the edge of the taxi strip. Then they loaded into the U.S. Navy C-2A Greyhound, a two-engine turboprop cargo plane that had the ability to land on an aircraft carrier.

The plane took off as soon as the SEALs had buckled in. Don Stroh had gone on the jog with them, and had been talking with Murdock. Now he motioned to one of the Navy airman on the ship, and he brought out box lunches for all seventeen of them from the base galley.

"Not much, gentlemen, but something to last you for a couple of hours." The airman passed around chilled cans of Coke, and the SEALs grinned.

Later, Stroh called the SEALs around, and waved at the familiar faces and the two new ones.

"Another walk in the park, gentlemen. The President is really pissed about this one. We train this mountain of a man, and he goes back home and grabs control of the army and then takes over the whole fucking country. Promotes himself to general.

"You know he knocked over the *Roy Turner*. Then he

47

assaults and captures the U.S. Embassy in Nairobi. That just isn't done anymore. Not after Iran. So we move in and get some payback. He's asking for a hundred billion dollars in goods and materiél. Ransom. I guess he hasn't heard that the U.S. never pays ransom no matter who is kidnapped or taken hostage. That demand was B as in billions. The United States does not pay for hostages, not even two hundred of them. We also don't send bundles of goodies to dictators.

"We'll be landing on the aircraft carrier USS *Monroe* in about three and a half hours. She's steaming south along the Somalia coast. Kenya is just south of Somalia. The captain of the carrier tells me he should be off Kenya or within chopper-infiltrating distance at about two A.M. tomorrow morning."

Murdock took over. "Don, we've kicked this around during the past twenty hours, and the only way we can see to get in and get out of that embassy is with choppers. We'll need at least three, maybe six. That means protection to keep any snipers down and out of business until we can get in, take over the place, get our people freed and on board rescue choppers. The birds will probably have to come in one at a time. Then we get the choppers safely in the air and head for the carrier."

Stroh rubbed his face. He was the CIA contact between the platoon and the President. He outranked everyone from admirals right up to the Vice President.

"I talked with Captain Prescott of the *Monroe* about an hour ago," Stroh said. "Given the three hundred miles between the coast and Nairobi, his thoughts were along the same line as yours. There'll be no trouble getting cooperation from the admiral. His ship is at your disposal. I'd guess he got a special call from the President."

Murdock took in what the CIA man said, and looked at his crew. "All right, let's plan this puppy from the ground up. What do we have to work with, the Seahawk?"

Jaybird spoke. "The SH-60 Seahawk is an ASW chopper, but if they take out all of the missiles and depth charges, it should be able to carry twenty-five hostages with no luggage.

The Seahawk has a range of seven-hundred-eighty-one miles at four-thousand-feet altitude, with auxiliary fuel. So the three hundred miles to Nairobi and back is no problem. We'll need two of them to exfiltrate the forty-one hostages."

Magic Brown spoke up. "So to keep it all coordinated, we need another Seahawk to transport us in with all of our goodies, and to get us out of there without a lot of bullet holes in our hides."

"That leaves our assault on the compound," Murdock said. "My guess is that this colonel-general will keep the hostages in the easiest place to contain them: a basement room if there is one. Meaning we won't hit any friendlies when our gunships strafe hell out of the place to dislodge the crew that the fat man leaves there when he moves on."

"Does this task force have any Cobras on board?" Miguel Fernandez, Gunners's Mate First Class, asked.

"Not on the CVN, but there should be an amphib ship along in the fleet," Murdock said. "It's got a bunch of them. We've used them before. Only problem is they don't have the range. They top out at four hundred miles max. We'll have to go with something else."

"What about a pair of F-14 Tomcats?" Joe Douglas asked. "They can't fire their missiles, but they can use their twenty-millimeter cannon."

Murdock pointed his finger at Douglas. "Yeah, sounds about right. We'll talk with the flyboys about it."

Stroh rubbed his face with one hand. "Damn, sounds too simple. Does Kenya have any air capability at all?"

"You're the one who should know that," Murdock said. "Give your buddies in Langley a call and ask them. Whatever air they have, another pair of Tomcats riding a wide shotgun circle around the embassy should be enough to handle any trouble."

"I'll ask them when we get a list of things," Stroh said. "Now, we need to know how to find this embassy. It's on 2249 R Street North West. Remember, Nairobi is a town of just over two million people. We don't want to blow up the wrong compound—say, strafe the hell out of the French Embassy."

"The pilots will know how to find the place," Jaybird said. "That's their job. So we're in on the ground. What weapons do we take, our MP-5's and the M-4A1's?"

Magic Brown chimed in. "We'll still need the sniper rifles and the MGs. Sounds like our usual weapons."

Murdock looked at Ed DeWitt. "Ed?"

"Regular shooters plus four fraggers for each man. It's close-in work. Kill House stuff. The MP-5 will do fine, but we won't need the suppressors. Get more range that way."

"Agreed," Murdock said. "We all have our regular weapons, and a double load of ammo. We can get any more we need from the carrier's supply and stash it on board our chopper. Don't forget the forty-mike-mike grenades. Our side arm will be the Mark 23 again. This time we won't have that hellish long silencer, so be glad."

"Looks like a regular shoot-and-scoot operation," Red Nicholson said.

Murdock turned to Stroh. "My guess is the President doesn't want to wait another day on this. We get on station at 0200. Does he want us to jump on those choppers and head inland right then? The Seahawk will do about two hundred mph. That's an hour-and-a-half trip if we're right at the coast. If we're a hundred miles off the coast of Kenya when we launch, it'll take us two hours.

"Stroh, talk to the skipper of the *Monroe* and see if he has three Seahawks and at least four F-14's we can use. Then find out how far we'll be from Nairobi at 0200."

Stroh had been taking notes. He nodded, stood, and hurried up to the cockpit.

Murdock looked at his crew. "Let's see if we can get some shut-eye. We'll need it. We can't make any more plans until we know for sure we can get the choppers we want."

Monday, July 19

1848 hours
USS *Monroe*, CVN 81
Indian Ocean off Kenya
The Greyhound COD landed on board the carrier after dark, and caught the two wire.

"Any landing you can walk away from," Murdock said as he supervised the unloading of the cargo plane, and moving all of the SEALs' equipment, ammo, and collapsed IBSs to a spot where they could be loaded on one of the Seahawks.

A white shirt, a safety guide, led Murdock and his men off the flight deck and into a mess hall where a hot meal waited for them: steak, spare ribs, or fish, and all the trimmings.

Murdock sat across from a three-striper who said his name was Commander Lewis.

"We've made all the arrangements you asked for, Lieutenant. We have a new position for you. As of 0200 we will be about forty miles off the northern part of the Kenya coast. That's three hundred and thirty-five land miles from Nairobi. Flying time to your target in the Seahawk is about an hour and forty-one minutes.

"First we thought of the Sea Knight. She hasn't got that kind of range. They top out at about four hundred twenty miles. The Seahawk is the right bird. We've stripped down three Seahawks for you, the SH-60B. They're ASW hunters. We've taken out the torpedoes, most of the armament, and the missiles. We'll move in to the three-mile limit and the Seahawks can get you there and back with a load of twenty hostages."

"The KIAs, sir?" Murdock asked.

"The dead will have to wait, Lieutenant. We don't expect this coup to last long. We've got plans."

"The Seahawks it is, sir." Murdock looked at Don Stroh, who had his mouth full of steak. "Stroh, what about the timing?"

"Just got a signal from the White House. We are to begin the operation at the earliest possible time. Meaning as soon as we get on station about 0200."

"Commander, what about the F-14s?" Murdock asked.

"Yes, we'll go with the Tomcats. No missile firing but they can take a load of twenty-millimeter rounds and give you good close ground support."

"Are they ready to roll?"

"They will be ready when you are, Lieutenant. We'll send

the Tomcats out well after you leave here so they can be on target and give an almost continuous attack starting fifteen minutes before you arrive at the embassy."

Murdock stood. "Men, chow call ends in five minutes. At 0200 we'll be in the air. Let's move it."

When the SEALs got to the Seahawks, the one the SEALs would ride in had been loaded with all of their gear and ammo except for the IBSs, which were stored. Murdock saw the F-14s roll out and two get positioned. They wouldn't take off for an hour yet. The Seahawks would be near the target when the Tomcats strafed the place with the 20mm cannon.

Murdock settled back against the side of the chopper and thought it through again. Yes, they had the best scenario. They had an hour-and-forty-one-minute flight. By the time they got there, the compound would have been pounded by the Tomcats for ten or fifteen minutes. The SEALs' chopper would set down inside or on the street close to the embassy, and his team would charge in and take out any Kenyan soldiers left there alive.

The other two Seahawks would wait for an all-clear signal to come in to pick up the hostages. The first twenty would go out in the chopper the SEALs arrived in.

Murdock saw four of the SEALs sleeping. Good. Nobody was wound up tight. This should be a walk in the park.

An hour and a half later, he was in the cockpit of the chopper looking down at the U.S. Embassy grounds. A Tomcat swept down, fired a salvo of 20mm rounds, and slanted up and away. The radio chattered.

"Slowboy, that you? Sweepers ready to retire and circle. Be available for any special targets."

"Sweepers, this is Slowboy, we're approaching. Any more visitors?"

"We'll watch for any mounted reinforcements coming in by land. Expect no air. Our last run completed. Good hunting."

The Seahawk pilot looked over at Murdock. "Get ready, Lieutenant, we're going in. See down there in the spotlight? There's an area just this side of the main building where I can set down. Close, but I can make it. You want us to hold or take off?"

"There'll be some damn angry rebels down there. You scoot, and come back when you see a red flare. Shouldn't take long. Looks like the Tomcats did a good job."

Three minutes later, the tricycle landing gear on the Seahawk touched the Kenyan dirt inside the enclosure, and the crewman jerked open the side hatch. Murdock hit the ground running, and heard the rest of Third Platoon right behind him. That was when they took the first enemy small-arms fire.

Tuesday, July 20

0341 hours
U.S. Embassy basement
Nairobi, Kenya

Frank Underhill heard the jet plane roaring past again, then the explosions above. He wondered if there would be anything left of the embassy. For the past fifteen minutes the jets had been attacking the rebels above who defended the grounds. None of the Kenyan soldiers had tried to enter the basement room.

Underhill and the two Marines had barricaded the doors, and put a two-by-four through the large handles of the doors. They opened inward. The two-by-four would need to be broken to get the doors open. At least no Kenyan could rush in and machine-gun them all.

Underhill's shot-up arm hurt like fire. He tried to forget about it. Two women clung to each other. They had been that way since the strafing began. He saw several people with their eyes closed and their lips moving as they fingered their rosary beads. The woman with the bad chest wound had quietly died about an hour ago. There was nothing they could do for her except hold her hand.

Somebody was going to pay.

"Mr. Underhill," someone said beside him. He looked up at the big Marine. "Sir, you think we should open the door yet?"

"No. Not until the firing stops. What's happening up there, Sergeant?"

"Well, the strafing is done. They were bigger rounds than machine guns. Maybe twenty-millimeter cannon. Makes a nasty mess if it hits someone. Then I'd think, with the jets pulled up, some assault choppers would come in. Only I don't know where they'd come from.

"Course the jets came from somewhere, maybe a Navy carrier. So they would have some choppers. Could be a detachment of Marines from the carrier."

They heard the stutter of automatic fire from above. Someone pounded on the basement doors and fired some rounds at it, but the steel door held and wasn't penetrated by the rifle slugs.

The Marine sergeant nodded. "Oh, yeah, the guys on top have auto M-16's, or maybe some other automatic weapon. Bet they give them Kenyan GIs a bad time. Wish to hell I was up there with an M-16 and about twenty magazines. Damn!"

A woman wailed in the far corner, and Underhill went over to try to calm her. He hoped that he could.

Lieutenant Murdock sprinted to the stub of a block wall, and dove behind it. He heard rounds going over his head. Single shots. Good. He saw Magic hit the ground down about ten feet, and a moment later Ron Holt skidded in beside him. Holt was the radio operator for the platoon, and carried his ever-present radio. It was the AN/PRC-117D. It was extremely compact at fifteen inches high and eight inches deep. It weighed only fifteen pounds, and was the most sophisticated tactical radio in the world. They called it the SATCOM.

It could send and receive UHF satellite communications on the SATCOM. That meant it could reach literally anywhere in the world. It could use UHF line of sight to talk to the Tomcats or the choppers above. With VHF or FM, it could use the bands that most of the world's armies use.

Changing bands was easy as flipping a switch and deploying the right antenna. Its power could go from ten watts maximum down to .1 watt to reduce enemy interception. An encryption system was embedded in the hardware, and the crypto keys could be changed daily by punching in a new set of numbers. It could transmit in voice, data, or video, and with a special interface could even link into the worldwide cellular telephone system.

Murdock could talk directly with the CIA in Washington or the President.

Murdock saw winking flashes of weapons firing ahead coming from the front and side of the embassy. He hadn't seen anyone shooting out of the embassy windows.

They worked their attack plan. Ed DeWitt and his Second Squad would circle around to the back and clear that area. Then they would charge inside the building, flushing anyone inside out the front door. Murdock and his squad would eliminate any hostiles in the front of the building, and be ready for anyone trying to get out that way.

Murdock saw the rest of his squad spread out along the near side of the building and this wall. He motioned at the three men he could see, and waved them ahead. They ran with assault fire at the windows as they charged forward and jolted against the end of the main structure.

Murdock whispered into the filament mike perched below his lower lip. It connected to the Motorola MX-300 each of the SEALs wore for instant communication. They each had an earpiece, and a wire down the back of the neck through a slit in the cammies and plugged into the Motorola unit secured to the combat harness.

"Ed. Progress," Murdock said.

"Couple of stubborn boys back here." He heard more firing of the M-4A1's, then the *karumph* of a fragger grenade exploding.

Murdock looked at the front of the embassy. In the faint light he could see some pockmarks from the 20mm. In the dark he couldn't see much, but the soft moonlight helped. A figure bolted from the front door and darted toward the open steel front gate in the block wall.

Two three-round bursts brought him down in the dust of the courtyard. He didn't move.

Fire erupted from two windows along this end of the second floor. Murdock lifted his MP-5 Heckler & Koch submachine gun, and sent four three-round bursts into the first window. He heard the heavier sound of the M-4A1's with the sliding buttstock pounding away. For a moment there was no more firing.

Murdock surveyed the land. He had to move across an open space to get to the protection of a pair of cars. They would give him a perfect field of fire on the front door and half of the windows facing the street.

Murdock used the radio again. "Horse, can you cover the front door?"

A moment later Ronson's voice came back. "If I move about five yards toward the street. Just a minute."

Murdock figured his thirty-round magazine was more than half full.

"Yeah, I got it," Horse responded. "Cover for you ready."

"I'm moving to those old cars. Now, Horse."

The H&K 21A1 machine gun blasted off six rounds to Murdock's left. The Platoon Leader and Holt came out of a crouch and jolted forward, sprinting the fifteen yards for the pair of parked cars. Both cars had been hit by 20mm rounds, Murdock decided.

Half way there an automatic rifle opened up from the second story window. A spray of hot lead drilled the ground just in front of Murdock and Holt.

Behind him he heard the 7.62 mm NATO rounds slamming out of Horse's machine gun. By then Murdock had hit the dirt behind the tire-flattened cars and caught his breath. Holt skidded in close behind him.

A dark figure ran from a door half way down the building. Magic Brown saw him, brought down the 6 x 42 telescopic sight, found the target and fired the H & K PSG1 sniper rifle without the suppresser. The 7.62 NATO slug slammed into the figure's chest and jolted him into the dust.

Murdock heard more firing from the back of the building. He hit the mike again.

"Ed, need any help?"

"No. We've got two men inside. One pocket of three bad

guys don't want to give up. Lincoln is moving up on them with a pair of fraggers."

"Keep it wired."

Murdock saw more winking flashes from the second story. It might be harder than they thought to drive these guys out. He had no idea how many there were.

He flipped down his NVG. They turned the night into a soft greenish hued dusk. He scanned the face of the two story embassy and spotted a man coming out a window on the far end on a rope. He figured the range, 80 yards at the most. They all had taken the sound suppressors off their MP-5 submachine guns for more range. They were good without the silencers for 150 yards.

Murdock sighted in and fired a three-round burst, then another. The man shook when the last three rounds hit him, and spun off the rope. He jolted hard into the ground. Murdock watched him through the NVGs, but the Kenyan didn't move.

Jaybird Sterling charged along the stone front of the embassy. He was so close no one inside could see him. He ducked under first-floor windows, and came near the front door. Just then a machine gun began hammering away out the front entrance. Murdock and three other shooters put a hail of fire into the opening, but the weapon kept slamming bullets out at eight hundred rounds a minute.

Murdock ducked as the rounds drew slow stitches across his protective car. Jaybird had gone flat on the ground next to the building near the front door when the MG started firing. Then, as the friendly fire tapered off, he crawled forward, pulled a fragger from his harness, and jerked out the safety pin. He squirmed another few feet, then rolled the grenade into the front-door opening.

It was 4.2 seconds later when the hand bomb went off. Sandbags toppled, and the machine gun on a tripod tipped over with its smoking muzzle on the floor. The gunner sprawled in death with one arm blown off and his chest tattooed with shrapnel.

For a moment all firing stopped. Then, in a rush, three Kenyan soldiers charged out the front door heading for the

open gate. Jaybird put one of them down from behind with
his MP-5. Kenneth Ching nailed the second one with three
rounds from his M-4A1.

Doc Ellsworth dropped the third one with a throaty blast
from his Mossburg pump action shotgun throwing out
double ought buck.

The radios spoke to the 16 man SEAL team. "Rear
secured, we've moving inside," DeWitt said. "Haven't
heard any firing on the second floor lately. We'll move to
the top and clear it as we come down. You can be sure it's
a bad guy target if anyone comes out the front door or a
window. We'll stay inside."

7

Tuesday, July 20

0352 hours
U.S. Embassy
Nairobi, Kenya

Lieutenant (j.g.) Ed DeWitt waved at his two most experienced men, Scotty Lincoln and Miguel Fernandez. Both had traded their usual weapons for MP-5 submachine guns. They had lots of experience training in the Kill House back in California. Both men wore NVGs, and flipped them down and nodded.

Fernandez went in the rear door first, angling to the right. He saw nothing move in the green-tinted world. It was a storeroom of sorts on the ground floor.

Before he could move, Lincoln bolted in and covered the other half of the room.

"Clear," Fernandez whispered into his throat mike.

A door led off to the right, and another one to the left. Lincoln took his side, and Fernandez went to the right. Fernandez dropped to the floor and looked around the doorjamb from ankle level. The room ahead was a meeting space, with tables and chairs. Something moved on one of the tables. A man lying flat. Fernandez stared at the figure through the night-vision goggles. The man lifted a weapon.

Fernandez hosed him down with two three-round bursts, and saw him take the 9mm rounds and roll off the table. Another form down the way sprinted for the far door, and made it before Fernandez could bring his weapon around.

He checked the rest of the room area by area. No more bad guys. "Second room right clear," he said into the mike. He came to his feet and sprinted for the next door. Three rounds came through it and he dove to the left, and skidded against the wall three feet from the opening.

He pulled a hand grenade from his harness, popped the safety pin, and threw it into the room. The explosion brought a pair of screams that trailed off. Then silence.

This time he looked around the side of the door about three feet off the floor. Inside was an office with two desks. Two bodies lay sprawled in the aisle between the wooden desks. A form lifted up beside a filing cabinet and fired three rounds from what Fernandez figured was an AK-47. The rounds missed.

Fernandez sighted in on the side of the cabinet where he had seen the Kenyan and waited. Almost a minute passed, but Fernandez held his sight. Then the Kenyan leaned quickly out from steel filing cabinet, but before he could fire, Fernandez nailed him with three rounds from the "room sweeper," and the Kenyan slammed to the rear with half his throat shot away.

The SEAL ran into the room with his MP-5 ready, but he found no more living Kenyans. He hurried to the far door and looked around the doorjamb. He saw a figure lunge up from behind a line of file cabinets and throw something.

A grenade.

It hit once in front of the door, bounced true, and Fernandez tracked it through the open door on his nightscope. He caught the hand bomb, and in the same motion threw it back the way it came. He jolted against the wall outside the room, and a second later the grenade went off with a blast.

Fernandez heard no human sound from the room. He edged around the door again and looked. File cabinets against the walls, some down the center of the room. He saw a bloody head on the floor halfway along the files. A moment later he touched his mike.

"Clear three right," he said.

Lincoln's hurried call came just after his message.

"We may have a problem in room two my way. I hit a staircase, and somebody is up there covering the whole damn room but gives me no target."

"Hang tight," Fernandez said. "I'm out of rooms and on my way."

A minute later, Fernandez slid to a stop beside an open door. Lincoln was by the other side. Fernandez checked through the door, and jerked back at once. Two slugs drilled through the air where he had been.

"He's got some night vision too," Lincoln said.

"What's in the room?"

"Stores, looks like lots of food and office supplies. No good cover down there. Except maybe that stack of what looks like boxes of paper halfway down to the left."

Fernandez took a look from head height. "Yeah." He put a slug into the boxes and jerked back. They never even wiggled. "Cover," he said. "You spray that stairwell top and I'll get to the boxes. That'll give me a good angle to shoot straight up the stairs and nail the bastard."

Lincoln pushed a fresh thirty-round magazine into his MP-5 and nodded. He poked out the muzzle and pounded off three rounds, then adjusted and nodded at Fernandez. Twelve rounds on full auto slammed into the top of the staircase as Fernandez charged the fifteen feet to the stack of cases of paper, then rolled to a stop below them out of sight of the stairway.

Lincoln kicked six more rounds up the top of the stairs. Then Fernandez added his firepower, with the advantage of the angle. He slapped twelve rounds out of his weapon, and heard a scream from up the stairs.

Fernandez saw a hand appear at the top of the stairs holding a grenade. Before it could be thrown, Fernandez drilled the arm with three rounds, and the small bomb dropped out of the Kenyan's hand and three seconds later exploded.

Fernandez looked back at Lincoln and nodded. He sent covering fire up the stairs until he felt Lincoln slide into place beside him.

"No response up above," Lincoln said. "Might just have solved our little problem."

Fernandez used the mike again. "L-T, we could use about four good men in here. The stairs is ours."

Moments later Adams, Lampedusa, Bos'n's mate Ted Yates, and Quinley ran into the room and found cover.

Quinley had a shortened pistol-grip shotgun with no stock or much of a barrel, and five rounds of double-aught buck.

"Quinley," Lincoln said. "You and me up the stairs. Side by side. You've got the left. Blast at anything that moves."

Quinley pulled down his night-vision goggles, and the two ran for the stairs and up them.

Quinley fired one round upward as they hit the bottom step. When they got to the top they dove to the floor and surveyed the scene. Just in front of them lay a green-clad Kenyan ranger with his head half blown off his shoulders. His AK-47 lay just beyond his stiffening fingers.

Ahead they saw a long hall with lots of doors opening off it.

"Shit," Lincoln said. "We got to clear every fucking one of those rooms." He touched his mike. "Bring up the troops," he said. The other four SEALs ran up the steps and went flat on the floor at the top.

"Rooms to clear," Lincoln said. "Two men to each room, just like in training. We do three rooms at the same time. Move out."

The first three rooms contained no enemy troops. The next three had two men in one who didn't get off a round before they had half-a-dozen 9mm slugs in their vital organs.

Fernandez looked at the last two rooms. The doors were farther apart. So far they had found only sleeping quarters for two to three persons.

Fernandez motioned to Quinley, and they took the far door. Lincoln and Adams had the near one. The other two pointed outward as security.

On signal they kicked in the doors and charged inside.

Fernandez saw it was a three-room suite. Maybe the ambassador's. The main room was clear. They swung open another door and found a bathroom. Adjoining it was the master bedroom. Once inside the bedroom, Fernandez swore. One woman lay dead on the big bed. She was naked, and her breasts had been sliced off. The other woman, a redhead, lay on the floor, naked as well, with several big-caliber slugs in her body.

"Gonna be hell to pay," Quinley said.

Fernandez nodded. "Hope to hell I get to do the collecting."

Lieutenant Ed DeWitt ran into the room, and shook his head. "The bastards."

He went out to the hall. At the end of it there was another corridor at right angles. There were only six doors on this side. Before they got into the line of fire from down the hall, DeWitt sent a three-round burst down it.

Two weapons answered him.

"One came from the second room on the right," Quinley said. He had been flat on the floor peering around the wall. "The other one was farther down.

"They don't have NVGs," Quinley added. "If they did they would have seen me."

"How in hell do we get down there and not get ourselves shot to hell?" Fernandez asked.

"I'll go," Quinley said. "Hey, I'm the smallest one here. I'll take fraggers and crawl down there along the wall. You guys give me some cover fire three feet high. I get to the second door. Must be open or they couldn't fire out of it. I cook a grenade for two seconds, then throw it in, and two seconds later, whammo."

"Could work," DeWitt said. He touched his mike. "Front side, we've got a holdup here on the second floor. We're working it out."

"Need any help?" Murdock asked.

"Negative, front side. Hang on."

They fired from the wall opposite the one that Quinley crawled along. Bursts of three rounds, then single shots, never in any pattern. Some shots went to the third and fourth doors too.

Quinley had almost gotten there when a rifle poked out

the second door and slammed off six rounds well over his head. Most dug into the walls. Nobody got hurt. Quinley surged ahead before the door could be closed, and let the arming handle pop off a grenade, held it two seconds, then threw it into the second room.

The explosion came almost at once. Quinley jolted forward, came to his feet, and surged into the room with his MP-5 chattering. A few seconds later, he waved out the door with a thumbs-up. Three SEALs used assault fire and stormed down the hallway to the second door and rushed inside.

Lincoln led them. Now he checked the hall. They weren't sure which door the second sniper had used. DeWitt had cleared the first room, and Yates and Lampedusa cleared the third room. They had three ahead of them.

"It was either the fourth or fifth door," Quinley said. "Sure as hell wasn't the last one. All that's left is four and five."

"One man on each side of the hall," Lincoln said. "Same procedure. I'm on one side, Willy Bishop on the other. Same thing Quinley did. Give us some cover."

Two more SEALs ran into room two, and were ready for support fire. Lincoln nodded and dove to the far wall, and Lincoln took the near one. The SEALs laid down the covering fire. One weapon poked out of door four, but jerked back in when the fire concentrated there.

Lincoln had that side. By the time he got there the door was closed tightly. He fired three rounds into the locking area, kicked the door open, and sprayed the inside of the room with 9mm whizzers.

Return fire blasted through the door. Lincoln had fired from low and to one side. He tossed in a fragger grenade, and when it went off, he was up and charged inside. No shots came from the room.

DeWitt and the others cleared the last two rooms, and they relaxed.

"Second floor clear," DeWitt said into his mike.

"Nobody exited the joint," Murdock said. "Good work. You moving downstairs for the first floor?"

"Roger that."

The Second Squad went down the far steps quietly and with caution. They cleared three doors and found no one home. They went through the kitchen, the infirmary, a library, and six more offices. There were no more Kenyan rangers in the compound.

"Clear all," DeWitt said. "Where the hell are the hostages?"

"We found a door with stairs leading down," Willy Bishop said.

"Let's do it," DeWitt said.

The stairs were clear. In the basement they saw two small rooms had doors standing open. Big locked double doors led to what must be a larger room just beyond the smaller ones.

DeWitt tapped on the steel door with the butt of his MP-5. He waited. Three taps came back. DeWitt tapped again, three quick raps, then three slow ones, then three fast ones. Dot-dot-dot, dash-dash-dash, dot-dot-dot. SOS in Morse code. They heard a cheer from inside. More noises came as the doors were evidently being freed so they could be opened. One door swung open slowly, and a lone man stood there with a bandaged left arm.

"Lieutenant (j.g.) DeWitt at your service, Mr. Ambassador."

First Secretary Frank Underhill let the tears roll down his cheeks. "Thank God," he whispered, then pulled both doors open wide. "Thank God for the United States military forces."

"Hostages freed," DeWitt said in his mike. "Call in the choppers, Murdock. Time's a-wasting."

The SEALs had never received a warmer welcome. Every one of the hostages hugged the SEALS, and the women kissed them on the cheeks and didn't want to let go of them.

"The two women Colonel Maleceia took away?" Underhill asked. DeWitt took him aside and told him what they had found.

"The redheaded woman was our CIA agent. I'm sure she put up a fight. She'd know the time to pick. Damned shame.

Both fine women, both of them." He paused a moment. "We're taking out our dead, of course."

DeWitt shook his head. "Sorry, but we don't have the capacity on our aircraft. We'll be back soon to claim them. We won't leave them here for long. You have the U.S. Navy's word on that."

The wounded were led up first. DeWitt picked out twenty people, including the wounded and the distraught, and kept them inside on the first floor until the big Seahawk chopper landed and the dust cloud blew away.

The SEALs spread out as security around the landed Seahawk as the civilians ran to it and climbed on board. Underhill declined to go on the first bird.

Just as the first Seahawk took off, Holt ran to Murdock. "Better listen to this, L-T. I switched to the pilot's frequency."

"Roger that, Sweepers. You have two incoming blips about eighty miles out."

"Slowboy, we figure they're Kenyan jets. Arms unknown."

"Sweepers, just lifting off number-one Slowboy. Suggest you splash the bogies if they don't ID."

"Just had clearance from Home Plate to do that. No change in their course or speed."

Murdock frowned. Eighty miles. In the age of jet interceptors that was like bayonet fighting. Say the Kenyan jets were old, could only do only a thousand miles an hour. That was still seventeen miles a minute. In five minutes they would be here. He needed probably fifteen minutes to land, load, and launch each of the last two choppers.

DeWitt's voice came over the Motorola. "Hey, Boss, we've got three bad-guy weapons carriers heading our way. Not more than two blocks down the street. Can't be sure, but looks like they have fifty-calibers mounted on top."

8

Tuesday, July 20

**0353 hours
U.S. Embassy compound
Nairobi, Kenya**

Radar Intercept Officer Lieutenant Satterlee checked his screens in the back seat of the Tomcat high over Nairobi. "Cap, we're tracking on both the targets. We have a weapons-free order yet?"

"Soon, my boy, soon. Stay on the first target." That was the front-seat jockey of the Grumman F-14D Tomcat, Lieutenant Commander Harley Allison.

"Still tracking," RIO Satterlee said. "Range sixty-five miles. We'll go with a Phoenix launch if we get a chance. The bogie might turn tail and run when his radar picks us up."

"A chance, but we hope he doesn't."

The AIM-54-C Phoenix is unique in U.S. armaments. It's a 985-pound missile with a range of over 120 miles and a speed of just over Mach 5. In the U.S. arsenal it can be fired only by the F-14 Tomcat with its advanced AWG-9 radar-guidance system. The Tomcat's radar was a set-to-track-while-scanning system, and could lock onto six separate targets and guide missiles simultaneously to all six locations.

"Range fifty miles, Cap. I see no indication of enemy radar locking on us."

"Just got a weapons-free signal from Home Plate. Sat, let one fly."

"That's a fox three from Eagle One," Satterlee said, giving the aviator's code words for a Phoenix launch and his own ship's ID.

Satterlee hit the launch button, and the Tomcat bounced higher as it dropped the half ton of missile from its belly. The Phoenix ignited at once under the Tomcat, and jolted forward at more than three times the speed of the Tomcat, leaving a contrail streaming after it.

"Missile away," Allison said. He brought the Tomcat into a hard climbing turn, then pushed the wheel forward, slamming his bird downward toward the Kenyan countryside below. It was a maneuver designed to shake an enemy missile if one had been coming at them.

Then Allison put the bird in a hard climb.

On the ground, Murdock took the mike from Holt. "Sweepers, this is Ground. We could use some help down here. Anybody listening?"

"Eagle Two, I'm with you, Ground."

"We've got three half-track weapons carriers coming up from the north toward the compound. You won't be able to see them, but they're about a block out along that north-south street that runs right along the compound. Welcome them if you can. We need another twenty minutes here minimum."

The second Seahawk had set down in the compound, and Murdock fought the cloud of dust. He wiped his eyes and spat twice.

"Eagle Two, you copy?"

"Roger that, Ground. Yes, I have the road. I'll make my run away from the compound. Don't expect any miracles with the twenties."

Almost before the transmission ended, Murdock heard the jet coming in. Most of the sound on a jet goes out the rear burners, but they give off a sound wave in front as well as they rip through the air at an operational speed of 1,342 knots per hour. The Tomcat flashed over the compound at less than a hundred feet, firing repeatedly at the vehicles a block away. Then it swept up, vanishing in the night sky.

"DeWitt, that do any good?" Murdock asked on his Motorola.

"Scared two fucking months' growth out of me," DeWitt answered. "Looks like one of the rigs is dead in the water, the second one is wounded. Here comes the third one. Wish we had our own fifty."

DeWitt brought three of his men up with the M-4A1's, and had them start lobbing HE 40mm grenades out of the M203 launchers under the barrels.

Ted Yates set up his H&K-21A1 on top of the wall, and began blasting the confused half-track men with the 7.62mm rounds from the machine gun. Six men went down before the rest ran for cover in neighboring houses and stores. The third weapons carrier turned forward, and the .50-caliber machine gun stuttered, slamming the big rounds into the block wall.

Yates slid off the top of the wall and hunted for a better-protected spot. Adams, Bishop, and Lampedusa all worked their .40mm grenades on the half-track. They switched to Willy Peter, and the white phosphorus blazed white trails across the top of the carrier, and brought some wails of anguish as the intensely burning phosphorus burned straight through wood, leather, canvas, and human flesh.

When the dust cloud eased, Jaybird Sterling had the last twenty-one hostages waiting to run from the front door to the Seahawk. The last one on board was Underhill. When he was sure all of his people were safely inside the bird, he stepped in, and the craft jolted into the air and raced toward the coast.

The next Seahawk came down almost immediately. The dust from the takeoff hadn't even cleared.

Murdock was on the Motorola. "DeWitt, get your men up here. We've got transport. I say again. We have transport. Fall back to my position south of the main building to our LZ. Move, move, move."

All the men in the Second Squad heard it. Bishop got off one more shot, and saw his WP land just in front of the slowly moving half-track and spray the engine, cab, and body with the burning chemical. Then he ran for the side of the main embassy building, and down to where he could see the Seahawk with its big top rotor swinging around.

"Twelve, thirteen, fourteen," Murdock counted. "Where are the last two?"

"We need Jaybird and Magic Brown," DeWitt said between gasps for air. He'd sprinted 150 yards, and the last batch of air had been loaded with dust.

Jaybird materialized out of the dust helping Magic Brown, who limped badly. Eager hands pulled both on board.

"Go, go, go," Murdock bellowed. A crewman slammed the side door shut, and the bird jumped off the ground like a frightened deer.

"You still set for the flyboys?" Murdock asked Holt, who sat on the floor of the chopper beside the L-T.

Holt nodded, and handed Murdock the mike.

"Eagle Two, this is Ground."

"Have you, Ground. Is your last Slowboy off the deck?"

"Roger that, Eagle Two. Off and moving. Thanks for the twenties down the road. You saved our bones back there. That last weapons carrier was bearing down on us."

"All in a night's work."

"What happened to the two jets coming in?"

"Eagle One splashed one out about sixty miles. His buddy turned his afterburner on and gunned back the way he came. We have no IFF on them. They didn't respond to our friendly signal, so we know they weren't the good guys."

"Thanks again. You going home?"

"Going to do a little cover work until you get wet; then we'll break it off."

Murdock gave the mike back to Holt, and moved among his men checking them. They had some scrapes and gouges. Nothing Band-Aids wouldn't cure. Then he looked at Magic Brown. The corpsman on the chopper worked on Brown's leg.

"Sir, this man took a round through his thigh. I don't know how he even walked, let alone ran. Said he got it early on. Don't think it hit a bone, but the doctors will tell us that for sure. He's going to be resting up for a week or so."

Magic Brown snorted. "Hell, little scratch like that won't slow me down none. Got me some work to do. We still got to get that fucking ship back in U.S. hands."

The corpsman grinned.

Murdock shrugged. "Hey, he's not your ordinary sailor. This man's a SEAL. Usually bullets bounce off Brown. Don't know what happened this time."

Magic Brown gave Murdock a thumbs-up. Then the morphine worked its magic and he dozed.

In the middle chopper, a corpsman looked over two slightly wounded embassy people. Nothing serious. Then he checked Underhill's arm.

"Sir, have you had any medication?"

"No. None available."

"I'll give you a shot of morphine. That's a serious arm wound. We'll have the doctors ready for you when we get in. A little under two hours and we'll have you on board the carrier. Your other people are all in good shape. About half of them are sleeping."

First Secretary and Acting Ambassador to Kenya Frank Underhill nodded wearily. He hardly felt the injection. So many of the embassy people had died. They had to go back and get them. Had to. They just had to. America didn't leave its dead for the butchers to desecrate. Had to go back and get them.

Then he slept.

9

Tuesday, July 20

0628 hours
USS *Monroe*, CVN 81
Indian Ocean off Kenya

Six of the hostages needed medical attention, but First Secretary Frank Underhill was not among them. He was in the Carrier Intelligence Center talking by SATCOM to the State Department in Washington. He told them what had happened, and how the Ambassador had been murdered. He asked for instructions.

Below in the hospital, Murdock watched the doctor treat Magic Brown's leg wound.

"The round missed the bone, which is good," the doctor said. "I'd suggest at least a week of limited duty. That means stay off that leg until it gets a chance to do some healing. You're a SEAL?"

"Yes, sir."

"Then you're grounded for two weeks." The doctor nodded at Murdock, who was still in his dirty cammies, and left.

"Two weeks?" Brown asked. "He's got to be kidding. When do we go back after that ship?"

"Not sure, but the ship won't be next. We've got a hundred and sixty sailors somewhere in a jail. State still has some contacts in the Mombasa area. They're trying to find out where the colonel stashed our guys. Then we move."

"I'll be ready by morning," Brown said. He shook his head and blinked. "They give me a shot?"

Murdock grinned. "Something's got to knock you out. You have a good sleep, and we'll talk tomorrow."

The hostages had been given quarters, showers, clean uniforms if they wanted them, and the option of having dinner or sleeping. All but one went for the midnight supper. Murdock's men were fed in the crew mess, and then hit their own berths.

Murdock went topside with Don Stroh to find out if they had an intel yet on where the crewmen were being held in Mombasa.

Stroh leaned back in a chair and scowled. "Murdock you look like hell warmed over. How long you been up now, thirty-six or forty-eight hours?"

"Long enough. Any news from Mombasa?"

"State made contact with a newsman there they use now and then. He has a SATCOM radio. Said he warned State about the coup almost thirty-six hours before it happened. He's trying to find out where the sailors are. Most likely in the Indian Ocean Prison on the outskirts of Mombasa. Remember, that's a big town, over six hundred thousand."

"He give any time when he might have the information?"

"Said he just didn't know. Might be a few hours, might be two days. He doesn't want the colonel to come calling and blow his head off."

"Right. We can use some sleep anyway, and some more food in the morning. You wake me up the minute we know the location so we can start planning."

"Choppers again?"

"Not sure. Depends how far from the bay it is. We can get ashore in the IBSs. But if it's ten miles to the lockup, we don't want to walk. We'll see. Remember, give me a call if you get the location."

Murdock found his sleeping quarters, showered, and flaked out on the bunk. He was sleeping before he knew it.

Tuesday, July 20

1630 hours

Murdock got up, showered, ate dinner, and then went to the room that Don Stroh had taken over as his headquarters. The CIA man worked on a third cup of coffee.

"Nothing yet. Hey, it's been slow over there onshore. He should get something tonight. D.C. said he'd give us a call here direct."

Murdock waved. "Going to check on my men."

He found them cleaning weapons, checking equipment, and grousing about it. Jaybird had them toeing the line. Ed DeWitt came in with a sour expression and a cup of coffee.

"Don't think I slept an hour. I kept seeing those two women that the colonel slaughtered. He's got to go down. Wouldn't mind doing that job myself."

Murdock agreed with him, then brought the men up to date on the next step.

"The crew off the *Turner* is our next target. We're not sure yet where they are or how we go get them. We have the IBSs and all the choppers we need. There must be some fast launches we could call on too for close-in work in that bay. First, we need more information."

"How's Magic?" Fernandez asked.

"Mean and lean. I'm surprised he isn't down here."

"I checked him this morning," Lieutenant DeWitt said. "He was boiling because they took away his uniform. He's only got that little white robe that ties in back." The men roared with laughter imagining Magic making his escape bare-assed.

"Think he'll be with us on the next op?" Jaybird asked.

"The round took about two inches of meat, missed the bone. If Brown can walk, we'll play hell to breakfast to keep him out of the next run. We'll wait and see. Lot depends how soon we saddle up."

"We could start some planning," Jaybird said. "Like what we do if the place they have the guys is right on the bay, or if it's five miles inland."

"Shoot," Murdock said.

For the next hour they kicked around ideas about what to do and how to do it. It could all be wasted effort, or they might have a foundation to work on when the word came down.

A half hour later Don Stroh came into the big room where the SEALs were quartered, and at once the place went quiet.

Stroh looked around. "Hey, I didn't kill anybody. What's going on?"

"Any word?" Murdock asked.

"Words, yes, but not the right ones. Got two messages for you, though. On paper." He handed two sheets to Murdock. They had come straight from the encryption machine. The first was from the Secretary of State.

Murdock read it out loud. "Lieutenant Murdock. SEAL Team Seven. Congratulations on pulling our people out of Nairobi. Excellent work. Tell your men well done. We wish you success on the rest of the mission. The whole State Department congratulates your team." Below he read the name of the sender: "Mable L. Thorndyke, Secretary of State."

"What the fuck, somebody noticed," Red Nicholson said. "Usually we're the deepest darkest secret in town."

"True," Stroh said. "But this one wasn't exactly covert. Some talk of getting you guys some ink on this one. What's the other one, Lieutenant?"

Murdock switched the pages and looked at the next message. He glanced at the bottom of the page first. It was over the name of the President.

"Lieutenant Murdock and SEALs, Third Platoon, SEAL Team Seven," it read. "Please accept our sincere appreciation for the outstanding job you and your men did getting the forty hostages away from the rebel Kenyans and safely back to the carrier. We commend you, and offer you the thanks of the entire nation—even though the American people probably will never realize the service you performed in their name.

"I know your mission isn't complete there, and we and the White House family and staff wish you a safe and successful completion of your work. Thanks again." The typed name on the paper was "Wilson Anderson, President."

"Who's that one from?" Ken Ching asked.

"Just some guy in Washington," Murdock said. They yelled at him until he held up his hand. "Okay, just don't get swelled heads. We got much work to do yet."

He read it aloud, and when he finished, the men were quiet.

"Well, somebody knows that we exist," Ron Holt said.

"Oh, Washington knows about you," Stroh said. "The President and the Director of the CIA are most aware of you and your work. That's why you're on that special string that goes from the President to the Director of the CIA and down to me and then to you. Congratulations. Now, what were you doing? Didn't mean to interrupt." He grinned. "The hell I didn't. I'm getting back upstairs to wait for that damn radio to start talking to us."

When he left, Doc Ellsworth looked at Murdock. "L-T, how long you think it will be before we know our target?"

"My guess, sometime tonight, and we'll go in as soon as possible. That means we wrap this and have some sack time right after chow. I don't want any of you falling asleep on me with bullets flying around."

Sunday, July 18

0613 hours
Pita's apartment
Mombasa, Kenya

Olie Tretter watched the Kenyan-Arab woman go out the door and close it. They heard her lock it from the outside. Tretter let out a long breath.

"Man, I have been at sea too long. That is one fine mama."

"She's finer yet if she can save our fucking tails from the locals," Vuylsteke snapped. He regretted it at once. He hadn't slept well last night on those boards.

"Easy, guys," Rafe Perez said. "She looked cool to me.

She hates the colonel and his Army. Looks like she will keep our secret hoping we can help her."

"Sure, kill three Kenyan Army guys," Tretter said. "Hell, that would bring a company of troopers down on our heads."

Vuylsteke took a long drink from the Coke. He'd come halfway around the world to find a can of Coke in this hot, dry, and definitely hostile place. He had to think. The woman had saved them so far. She would be in big trouble if the Army knew they were hiding in her apartment. Maybe she'd keep on hiding them.

"Look we've got no big fat choice here. The ship is captured and has a ton of security on board. The Army is in the streets, so I guess this place is under martial law. If that damn colonel can count, he knows not everybody got back on board the FFG by curfew."

"Oh, yeah," Tretter said. "He must know. So he'll send some troops into this area to hunt for us."

"Maybe." Perez said. "Depends on what else he has going. My guess is that Uncle Sam ain't gonna take kindly to having his ship shanghaied. Gonna be some action down here shortly."

Vuylsteke drained the Coke and looked in the other room. A bedroom with a single bed. It had been made up.

"Right now, I need a snooze. Keep it quiet. No radio anybody can hear outside the walls. Station might have some English reports on it. Wake me up at noon and we'll talk it over again. I'll be halfway human by then."

When Vuylsteke woke up about 1400 that afternoon, the other two sailors were sleeping. Tretter was stretched out on some pillows on the floor. Perez was sprawled in an easy chair. He roused them, and asked about any news on the radio.

"Couldn't find any," Perez said.

Vuylsteke took the small battery-powered radio and searched the dial. Halfway down he found some news in English.

"The People's Military Committee has announced that it

is now in total control of the nation. The members urge calm. All facilities and functions of the government will continue. Police will be in place. All aspects of our usual life will go on with no change.

"General Maleceia will address the people on this radio station and the national TV network. All citizens are urged to listen. His press secretary says there will be important announcements made."

"Sure there will, like turn over all of your teenage daughters to the Army and send us all of your money."

Vuylsteke turned off the radio. "Money. Tretter you changed dollars into shillings, didn't you?"

"Yeah, I got about twenty-five hundred left. What was it, about sixty shillings to the dollar."

"I bet Pita doesn't make much at her job. Some cash would come in handy for her. Might also save our Navy asses."

"Yeah and give her some some shillings to buy some food with," Perez said. "We gonna eat her out of this place in another day."

Tretter yawned and pulled on his shoes. "So, we gonna help this broad kill them Army guys?"

"Don't see how we can," Perez said.

"Or maybe it's the only thing we can do," Vuylsteke said. "Hell, we saw those murdering fuckers butcher our guys on the *Roy Turner*. We got some payback to do."

"With one five-shot thirty-two peashooter?" Tretter asked.

Vuylsteke found another Coke in the small refrigerator. Only one more left. "Got an idea that Pita wasn't talking about shooting anybody. She wouldn't have a gun. She doesn't know we have the little shooter. She has something else in mind. Let's see what it is first. Hell, it might be we need to stay hid here for a week. We better take care of the lady."

Perez looked at Tretter. "Hey, goof-off. Just 'cause you black, don't get no fucking ideas about the girl."

"Me? No way. I like women with big tits. She ain't got much up on top. You saw her. Hell, we're just friends."

"Keep it that way," Vuylsteke said. "Remember, I'm senior here and I'm in charge of your bodies."

"Yes, suh, Boss Man," Tretter said in his best Down South poor-black-trash voice.

Perez chuckled.

It was after six that evening when Pita knocked on the door, then used her key and came inside. She had an armful of groceries.

"Told them I was laying in supplies for a week," she said. The men took the two sacks and put them on the kitchen counter.

"More Cokes," she said, smiling. "First I feed you, then we get outfitted and we go kill ourselves some soldiers."

10

Tuesday, July 20

1730 hours
USS *Monroe*, CVN 81
Off Mombasa, Kenya

Lieutenant Blake Murdock sported a grin as he walked into
the training room the SEALs had been given to use for their
planning.

"Damned signal came in," Jaybird said, watching his
commander.

"Roger that," Murdock said. The fifteen other SEALs
gathered around the eight-foot table as Murdock sat down
and spread out a paper in front of him.

"Our man in Mombasa says it's confirmed, the one
hundred and sixty men and officers from the *Roy Turner* are
being held in the old Indian Ocean Prison. It was supposed
to be torn down a year ago. Colonel, now self-promoted to
General, Maleceia released over three hundred civilian
prisoners there and dropped in our citizens. The place is
fortified by at least a company of Kenyan rangers.

"Our spy says the rangers are handpicked, and specially
trained by the colonel for his elite palace guard. They can
fight.

"In their army a company is about a hundred and twenty
men. They have machine guns, AK-47's, as well as shotguns, and at least two mobile fifty-caliber MGs.

"The target is situated about three hundred yards from the

end of an inlet of Mombasa Bay. The water just peters out into a marsh that's great for concealment, but hell for moving through."

"When, L-T?" Jaybird asked.

"When we're ready. I suggested in two hours. Let's make it 2000 to be sure."

"We going in with our IBSs?" Horse Ronson asked.

"That we should kick around. Mombasa is an island almost six klicks long. The deepwater port, Kilindini, is on the west side of the island. As I read the satellite pictures we have, the prison is situated directly across from the main port docks. The bay is more than a klick wide there, and the prison is on a small inlet on the west side on the mainland."

Murdock spread out a dozen satellite photos showing the area.

"We'd come in from the sea down here past this little place called Likoni?" Ed DeWitt asked.

"Looks like it," Doc Ellsworth said. "Then how far to that inlet, half a klick?"

Lincoln studied it and checked the printed mileage line. "Like maybe two and a half klicks."

Fernandez eyed the beach area near the small Likoni settlement. "How big is this place, and can we stash our IBSs along there? Do we motor right up to the back of that jail or swim in underwater? We need more input."

"So how do we find out? Send in a recon team?" It was Al Adams asking.

That was the way it started. Murdock watched, moderated, prodded, and encouraged. He always liked to have input from his men on a mission. Some of the SEAL commanders didn't work this way, but he'd found that men who got a chance to help plan an operation understood it better and were more enthusiastic about making it work.

If it didn't go right, they died.

They worked over the ingress and egress, how they would attack the prison, and then how to get the Navy crewmen out of there and back to the carrier. Eventually, they solved the small problems, tackled the big ones, and had a plan.

Murdock wrote it all down, and went out the door.

"He's checking out the plans with the CIA," Holt said.

"Yeah. Stroh'll probably bump it up to his boss, and maybe all the way to the President," Joe Lampedusa said.

"Oh, hell, no," Bishop said. "The President just gives us a go or no-go on a mission. He doesn't get into the how. What does he know about tactics, the situation, and the terrain?"

Murdock showed the plan to Stroh a few minutes later.

"You can do this?"

"Yes, if you can be sure the help and transport is on-site when we need it."

"No F-14's to soften up the rear entrance?"

"Not this time. We want three or four F-14's to blow shit out of the front entrance. That will suck all of the defenders to the front and give us time to storm in that rear door. From then on, it's flying by the seat of our pants and hoping that our luck holds. I'd rather surprise them, get our men out, and be halfway to the water before they know we were there. Nothing else is going to work against what could be a hundred twenty defenders."

"I'll check with the XO, but I don't see any problem. You have all the ammo, weapons, and explosives you'll need?"

"We could use another five pounds of TNAZ."

"What?"

"The new explosive that's stronger than C-5."

"You've got it. Timing?"

"Get away from here in our IBSs at 2000. We're, what, four miles offshore?"

"About."

"We'll want the carrier to be directly off the mouth of Mombasa Bay at 2000."

"I'll talk to the XO. Should work out okay. The President says it's your ship right now. What Murdock wants, Murdock gets."

"Good. We'll need some chow now. Then get the IBSs inflated and figure how to get down to the water."

Yeah, damn long jump."

"You have some better satellite shots of this prison?"

"Wondered when you would ask. An even dozen. Not a bad-looking place—unless you want to break in."

They spread out the pictures. One was a long shot of the whole structure. Murdock figured it was six to eight hundred feet long. Maybe half that wide. It was built in a rectangle with a courtyard. Closer shots showed two entrances, a front and a back. The rear way in was closest to the inlet from the bay.

Murdock grunted as he pushed the pictures together. "We've got some more work to do."

"Take it easy. I don't want you guys to burn out before we get that ship back."

"You've got pictures of the ship too?"

"Right, and we'll have more before it's time to worry about her. Let's get the crew out first."

Five minutes later, Murdock spread the satellite recon photos across the SEALs' worktable.

"Sweet Jesus, that's a big sucker," Fernandez said.

"So let's figure out how to bust in," Jaybird said. He pointed at the rear entrance. "We decided to go in this way. Still looks best. Do we get an attack on the front entrance from the fly-guys?"

Murdock said they did.

"We have a close-up on those gates?" someone asked.

Magic Brown came busting in the door. "Damnit, you fuckers are hard to find. This is one big rowboat."

"We love you too, Magic," Murdock said. "You get a medical clearance to leave that bed?"

"Hell, no. Looks like we got some action. We got a go on finding the Navy crew yet?"

Murdock watched Brown walk to the table. The same gait, the same hint of a swagger. He wouldn't limp now if it killed him.

He stared at Murdock. "I'm going, I'm going. Don't try to keep me back. I won't hold up nobody. Fact is, I think you got to have my fifty sniper baby along. Where's my gear?"

By 1800 they had the last of the detailed planning done. Every man knew what he'd do to get inside the prison. From there it would be a matter of playing it by ear. They had no intel where the Navy crew might be in the big place.

"Our informant says the place must be empty except for the *Roy Turner* crew," Murdock said. "We find them, then bust back out of there."

There were a few more questions, then Murdock held up a hand.

"Enough of this. We chow at 1830, and we should be shoving off from this tub about 2000. It'll be dark by then, but not cold. We're almost on the damned equator. We'll wear our desert cammies and take all of our goodies, including the belt .45 but without the silencer." He looked at his men. "Okay, let's chow down."

Magic Brown kept working on his gear. He had stripped the .50-caliber, and was cleaning and oiling it. He looked up as Murdock squatted beside him.

"Hell, L-T, I've been eating for the past sixteen hours."

Murdock nodded, went back to his quarters, and made sure that his men would get fed.

Tuesday, July 20

1930 hours
Pita's apartment
Mombasa, Kenya

Pita stood by the small kitchen table. She wore a silk blouse with wild black-and-orange patterns. The top button was halfway to her waist, and she showed an inch of cleavage. Her black pants were skintight and outlined her sleek legs. Her long black hair had been brushed until it shone and flowed down over her shoulders. Her lipstick was a sultry red, and a touch of rouge highlighted her soft brown cheeks. She tapped her fingers on the table.

"Enough," she said softly. "I know you hope American Navy come soon and fight and capture ship. Not for two, three more days. I let you put Pita off for two days. Now three days you here. Tonight we go out and kill bad soldiers. We all go kill soldiers or you find another place to hide."

Vuylsteke stood and nodded. "Okay, Pita. We owe you

that much. But how in hell do we kill a couple of their rangers and they don't come looking for us?"

"Pita show you. Now faces, hands."

She took out some cream and began rubbing it on their hands so they were darkened to an even light brown.

"Now, you do faces. You two wear hats, you no look like funky Americans."

Perez was almost that color already. He snorted, but applied a little of the brown makeup, then put on more.

Tretter grinned at his two shipmates. "Remember, you guys, you wanta look black you gotta have this brother walk, kind of loose-jointed, you know, bro?"

He ducked as Vuylsteke took a swing at him.

"Pita, you have guns, knives, maybe a hand grenade or two? What do we use to kill these dogfaces with?"

"No guns, too noisy," Pita said. She reached in a drawer near her small sink and pulled out a piece of quarter-inch rope. It was three feet long and at each end was a four-inch loop. "This work nicely."

"A garrote?" Vuylsteke asked.

"Shit, you done this before?" Tretter asked.

"No, of course not." She paused, lifted her brows. "Yes, once. Man tried to rape me. Surprised him from behind. Not too hard to do when man is drunk."

Perez grinned. "Gonna be an interesting night."

She put their hats on, checked them, and then led the way out of the apartment. It was fully dark by then. They went down the same alley they had come up three days ago, along the first street toward the waterfront, then stayed a block from the waterfront until they came to a row of small drinking houses.

"Lots soldiers," she said.

"Only three of us," Tretter said.

She shushed him. "Tretter and me go inside. I bring out one horny soldier. Let him feel me. I say sex in alley. He be half drunk and come down alley with me. We do him there, put in trash box."

Vuylsteke squinted and watched the small woman. She

was serious. She must have thought it out in the past three days. Yes, it would work.

"You going back in there for number two and three?" Perez asked.

"No. Go to next bar. Same way. Come." She placed them thirty yards into the alley behind the gin mill. It was as dark as a fifty-foot ocean night dive.

"Stay," she said.

Tretter handed Vuylsteke something and left with Pita. Vuylsteke knew what it was, a six-inch steak knife from the kitchen. He showed it to Perez.

"Yeah, I got me a butcher knife, too. Who's got my thirty-two?"

Vuylsteke said he did, and they waited.

At the door, Tretter knew why he was with Pita. No unescorted women were allowed. They went in. Then she drifted away, sat at a rough bar, and within five minutes had soldiers in uniform sitting on each side of her. She whispered something to the smaller of the two, and slid off the stool and headed for the door. The larger Kenyan ranger swore in Swahili, and the smaller one went out the door two steps behind Pita.

Tretter waited a full minute, then left his drink and went outside. Pita wasn't in sight. He ran to the alley and looked down. He saw only three shadows. Someone grunted, then gave a short, sharp cry before it was all silent again.

Tretter moved up slowly, and saw the two sailors lift a body and drop it in a big trash box. They threw some cardboard boxes in on top of it.

Vuylsteke had blood on his hands. He touched Pita.

"Enough," he said. "An eye for an eye. One body for one body. That's all we help you with. We're going back to your place. We can get away with one kill. Three and the Army would be down here tearing half the buildings apart looking. We listened to the radio. It says there are ten U.S. sailors missing from the captured ship. We can't afford an all-out search. They'd shoot you as well as us if they found us in your place."

She pulled away from his grasp. Tretter saw the determination in her face. "Hey, Pita. I think the big guy is right. You have your revenge. No sense getting yourself killed. Let's go back and see what happens the next couple of days. We still want to get you that visa to America. Might even be able to get enough cash together for an airline ticket one way to New York."

Her face remained angry, then faded to stern. After a few moments she turned and walked back toward her apartment. They moved with her, three shadows trailing behind in the dark street.

In her apartment again, the four looked at each other. Vuylsteke washed the blood off his hands. Perez took out the butcher knife and began washing blood from it.

Pita screamed. She rushed him and knocked the knife from his hand, then grasped the handle, leaned it against the floor and the cabinet, and stomped against it with her shoe. The blade snapped in half.

"No enemy blood on one of my knives," she said, her voice wavering with anger. "I'll never use that blade again. Throw it out. Throw it into the alley."

Perez had jumped back when she grabbed the knife. He looked at Vuylsteke, who nodded. He picked up the two halves of the knife and went out the door.

"In my country, no knife that has touched enemy's blood can ever be used for anything else. It killing knife. Not used in kitchen. An old custom." She sighed. "Maybe we not as civilized as we think."

11

Tuesday, July 20

Murdock had checked over each man in his squad, as had DeWitt. Everyone had double the usual load of ammo for his weapon. Magic Brown would have the drag bag for the big M88 .50-caliber sniper rifle.

They had their extra ammo and gear in waterproof equipment bags that were stashed in the IBSs and lashed down. Murdock paced the deck near where they would launch the Inflatable Boats Small.

"I'm forgetting something," he said half to himself.

Holt looked up. "Hey, not me, L-T, I'm here."

Murdock chuckled. "Indeed you are. We're going to need lots of communications if we make this one work right. We brought a backup SATCOM, didn't we?"

"Yeah, we always do. Never needed it before."

"We just might this time. Get it from our stash of supplies and put it in a tow bag. We can have a spare if things get hot. Maybe let somebody in Second Squad carry it."

"Yeah, L-T. Be right back."

Murdock checked everyone again. Then he looked over his second in command, Ed DeWitt.

"Now you check me out, DeWitt," Murdock said. He did. Murdock paced. He wasn't nervous. Not really. Or maybe he was, but just didn't realize it. He'd been here and done this a few times before. He still had an unsettled feeling. Anything could go wrong. That was why he wanted the second radio.

"Who's worked a radio before?" he asked the rest of the platoon.

"I have," Willy Bishop said.

"Good. You worked the AN-PRC-117D?"

"The SATCOM, sure."

"You're elected. You'll pack the second SATCOM in case we need it. You'll be backup. It will be preset to the air-cover frequency."

"Yeah, no sweat."

Holt came in with the radio, and Murdock told him to take it to Bishop. They talked a minute.

"L-T, it's time," Jaybird said.

Murdock nodded. "Let's get these tubs in the water and move out."

They launched from a small platform hanging down from a hatch just above the water. The Indian Ocean was almost calm.

Three minutes after their 2000 target time, everyone and all the equipment was loaded in the two IBSs and they pushed away from the mountain of a ship.

"It always looks so damn big from down here," Fernandez said.

"It's fucking huge, always has been," Ted Yates said, then looked toward shore.

They were a little over four miles out, just beyond visibility from land. Murdock had been given a course to set with his plotting board, and angled that way. The two boats kept close to each other, never more than ten yards apart, as the muffled outboard motors purred. They could move the IBSs at a top speed of eighteen knots.

These IBSs had the smaller thirty-five hp engine, and with an eighteen-gallon fuel tank they had a range of sixty-five nautical miles.

Murdock led with Horse Ronson on the tiller. They kept the speed to ten knots as they approached land. That would drop to five or less as they entered the harbor. These IBSs, also called CCRCs or Combat Rubber Raiding Craft, were black and inflated in pockets so one rifle bullet wouldn't sink them. At night they were hard to see, invisible to the best radar. With the dark-clad SEALs low in the craft, they could slip into most harbors without being spotted.

After fifteen minutes of powering toward shore, Murdock figured they had covered about two and a half miles. Now they could see a few shore lights along the mainland. The city of Mombasa was mainly on an island over six miles long and half that wide. The channel they wanted led up the left or west side of the island. They would stay in the middle of the channel to avoid detection.

"Any sign of the harbor entrance?" Murdock asked Red Nicholson, who angled his NVGs that direction.

"Small cluster of lights on the left," Red said. "Then, what looks to be farther away and to the right, a whole shitpot full of lights. That must be the end of the island with an ocean frontage."

"Right. So we head for that cluster of bright ones on the left. That must be Likoni. If there's much harbor activity there, we may want to swing right more into the channel to go around it."

Murdock wanted to check the SATCOM radio link, but he knew it worked. Holt had tested it just before they left. They might be able to talk directly with the carrier on another frequency. Holt had checked that out just as they went into the water. Relax, just relax, he told himself.

Ten minutes later they could see the spit of land that stuck into the Indian Ocean and the dark channel between it and the brightly lighted Mombasa Island on the right. They could make out more lights and activity in the small settlement of Likoni, but stayed in the middle of the channel to avoid any night-running pleasure craft docking there.

They slowed to five knots and worked closer to the shoreline, which was relatively unpopulated right here and mostly covered with trees and brush.

"Another two and a half klicks and we should see the little bay off to the left," Jaybird said.

They all wore the lightweight desert cammies, tan with dark brown and light brown splotches, and the usual jungle boots with their black socks folded down over the tops and laces to prevent snagging. SEALs don't wear hard helmets. Each man picks his own type of headgear, from the floppy soft hats with brims also called "boonies," to black stocking watch caps, or a wide headband, or maybe a bandanna pulled up and tucked in. They all had on the back padded fingerless gloves that protected the backs of their hands and snapped tightly around their wrists.

They wore their combat harnesses fitted with pockets to match the type of weapon they carried. The machine gunners carried 600 rounds, and the M-4A1 men all had a mixed group of 40mm rockets. Ron Holt had his radio on his back, and each man carried a web-belt-holstered H&K Mark 23 .45-caliber pistol with a twelve-shot magazine. It weighed a ton and had a long suppressor that could be added. They'd left the silencers on the carrier.

They watched the shoreline creep by. Five knots was slower than walking. Jaybird said he could swim faster than this, so he was invited to jump overboard. He declined.

"There it is," Murdock said, looking through his night-vision goggles. "Bear left in another fifty meters. Everyone get your eyes on."

The men all put on their NVGs and watched the shoreline come into sight in all of its pale green wonder.

"Nobody looking at us I can see," Jaybird said.

The SEALs all had their Motorolas on for instant communications.

Murdock touched his mike. "Let's lock and load quietly."

Each SEAL charged a round into the chamber and pushed the safety on. They were ready.

They came around the small point to the inlet and saw that it angled slightly due south. Murdock used the mike again. "Stay sharp, you guys. Figure we have maybe half a click up this inlet. Then the prison is three hundred yards away."

He looked at Holt. "How's our time? Fire up that Tomcat frequency and see where our bird friends are."

"Time, we're at 2052, about three minutes early from our ETA."

He spoke softly into his microphone. "Tom Birds, this is Water One."

"Water One, we're about ten klicks off shore. Ready when you are."

"Give us another seven minutes, Tom Birds. That's a mark. Then lay your eggs out front. That's a south-to-north run on the front gate."

"Roger that. Have your time mark. All plotted in with some really wild twenty-mike-mike rounds out of our Vulcan. Each one of us has six hundred and seventy-five rounds. You'll hear us in about six and thirty."

Holt had the speaker on low, but Murdock heard it all.

"Goose it a little, Horse, let's get up there. We don't mind waiting a bit for our flying friends."

The speed picked up to seven knots, and they sailed up the middle of the five-hundred-yard-wide inlet.

"I've got the prison," Jaybird said. "Lots of lights up there about eleven o'clock."

"Right. Horse, let's slow it down and move to the left and hug the shore. I don't see any buildings." The shoreline here was dark green with brush and small trees.

They came to within fifty yards of the end of the inlet. A small stream meandered into the bay. There were no reeds or marsh at the end. So much for their good intel.

"Take it all with you," Murdock said into the mike. The men were not to leave any equipment or ammo in the IBSs.

"Stay dry," Jaybird whispered into his mike.

The first IBS angled for the shore twenty yards from the small creek. Jaybird felt the rubber bow touch shore, vaulted out of the boat to dry land, and tugged the craft forward another three feet. The SEALs arrived dry.

"Deflate?" Jaybird asked Murdock. It was one point they hadn't covered.

"No, they'll know we're here, and we can't take out a hundred and forty men in these two tubs."

The other IBS grounded, and the men got ashore. By that time the First Squad had spread out five yards apart. Red

Nicholson took the point as usual, followed by Murdock, his radioman, Holt, dogging his heels.

When the Second Squad formed, Murdock moved out with his seven men. They had come onto a ten-foot beach, behind which was a tangle of growth of brush and small trees. The SEALs moved into the brush for cover and went slowly forward. They worked their way through the brush, and came out in a stretch of small trees that covered them but let them move more quickly.

Murdock could see the lights of the rear of the prison through the trees. They had another two hundred yards to go. He figured they were behind schedule. He touched his mike.

"Double it," he said. At once the SEALs began jogging forward. Magic Brown swore softly as he dragged the twenty pounds of the .50-caliber sniper rifle and ammo. He snorted, but knew that he had asked to bring it.

Murdock and his squad broke out of the end of the trees, and saw that all growth had been cut to the ground for a hundred yards beyond the prison wire. They went to ground. Jaybird crawled up beside Murdock.

"No searchlights along the walls, L-T. Not even many lights. No trouble getting up to that first wire with a casual walk."

"Quinley ready for the wire?"

"He is."

"Let's give our top-deck boys a couple of minutes," Murdock said. "I'd like to have all eyes inside looking out the front when those multi-barreled cannon rounds hit them in the front gate."

Just then they heard the eerie sound wave pulsating ahead of a jet fighter. Then came the stuttering sound of the cannon fire hitting the front of the prison, and then the roar as a plane Murdock figured must be an F-14 Tomcat slashed overhead in a climbing turn.

Moments later another F-14 made a strafing run with the Gatling gun-type 20mm Vulcan rounds slamming the prison's front gate.

"Move it," Murdock barked, and the sixteen men lifted up

and ran for the first set of wire fences that guarded the rear of the prison.

Quinley was ready to use wire cutters or primer cord designed to look like a pencil-thick roll of high explosive. The cord came in a roll, and you took off as much as you needed. It did the cutting job quicker, but also attracted more attention.

Quinley tossed Willy Bishop a pair of foot-long wire cutters as soon as they bellied down at the wire. It was triple-layered and twelve feet high, but with a regular soldered pattern.

"We'll use the wire cutters," Quinley said. "A lot quieter." Quinley began cutting upward on one side, and Bishop moved over three feet and cut upward as well. In thirty seconds they had opened in the wire fencing and bent up a doorway five feet high. The SEALs ran through the opening and angled for a concrete block wall with a small door in it fifty yards ahead.

Before they got there, another jet roared overhead. This one slammed another two dozen of the 20mm rounds into the front of the prison and slanted upward and away.

A small sentry position at the outside of the wall was not manned. The door in the wall was metal. Quinley unrolled his primer cord, made two circles around the door handle and its lock, and inserted a timer detonator. He waved the SEALs back twenty yards and set the timer for ten seconds. Then he ran.

The primer cord exploded with a shattering sound and impact. The lock disintegrated, and was blown into the prison yard. One side of the door itself tore off the top hinge, and pivoted downward on its bottom holder until it slammed into the ground on the inside.

The SEALs moved up to the door cautiously. Murdock looked inside past the smoke from the explosion. Two Kenyan rangers shook their heads trying to get their hearing back. Murdock cut them down with a three-round silenced burst from his MP-5. He saw no other defenders.

Murdock touched the throat mike. "First Squad inside. Second Squad hold at the door."

Red Nicholson jolted through the opening in the wall, followed by Murdock and Holt. They raced the fifty yards across a prison yard toward a pair of wooden doors in a two-story building with no windows.

A rifle fired at them from a catwalk along the top of the building. Nicholson hosed the area down with a half-dozen rounds from his M-4A1, and kept running. All eight men of the First Squad pressed against the main prison wall. Jaybird was closest to a door. He tried the handle. Locked. He leaned back and fired a burst from his HP-5. The 9mm whizzers pulverized the door lock, and it creaked open six inches.

Murdock ran up and kicked the door inward, then jolted back behind the wall. As he did, an automatic weapon blasted a dozen rounds from the inside through the door opening. Jaybird, on the other side of the door, pulled a fragger from his combat harness. He tugged the safety pin from the round and smooth M-67 hand grenade, and bounced it through the door.

Four seconds later the blast shattered the sudden silence. Jaybird and Murdock charged through the door. Murdock took the left side and swept the area with his NVGs. He found no enemies. Jaybird checked the right side, and cut loose with one three-round silenced burst.

"Clear right," Murdock said.

"Clear left," Jaybird said.

They were in a room thirty feet long and ten feet wide. It held boxes and some desks and looked like a storeroom. One door led out at the center of the rear wall.

"Come," Murdock said in his mike. "DeWitt, move up to the outside of the main building."

Jaybird tried the inside door. It was unlocked. First Squad got against the inside wall and out of the line of any fire. Murdock turned the door knob slowly, and swung the door outward.

A machine gun chattered in front of them, and angry messengers of sudden death slammed through the doorway. It was a ten-round burst, then a five, then a ten.

"We need a prisoner alive," Murdock said.

"You go talk to him," Jaybird said.

Murdock shrugged. "Next time." He pulled a fragger from his straps and let the arming spoon spin off the bomb. He held it for two seconds, then threw it through the door. Almost at once it exploded, and Magic Brown and Red Nicholson darted through the door into the next area.

They could hear the jets hitting again. The cannon fire rocked the old structure for a moment; then the birds were gone.

"Promised us ten minutes worth of shelling," Holt said. "They're about ready to go upstairs and ride shotgun to see if we need any help or cover."

"Clear right," Brown said.

"Clear left," Nicholson said on the Motorola.

"Let's take a look," Murdock said. "DeWitt, come into this room when we leave."

They faced a steel security door that blocked their way.

"About time they had some steel here," Murdock growled. "Get Quinley up here."

When the explosives man arrived, he looked at the door and the heavy metal bars on the rest of the entrance.

"Electric lock," he said. "Shouldn't be too tough. Locking bars into the steel sidebar. Sliding door. I'll have to hit all three weak points. Better get the troops back a ways."

He went to work with packs of TNAZ explosive. When he had it all positioned correctly, he inserted detonators in the pliable material, set them for fifteen seconds, pushed the timers to the on position, and ran back around the corner.

The three blasts went off almost at the same time, pounding through the hallway like a freight train out of control. When the sound and the shock wave had worked down the corridor, the SEALs checked Quinley's work. The lock was shattered. The two push rods were broken off, and the door had rolled back two feet. It wouldn't move any farther.

"Close enough," Murdock said. "Now, what the hell is behind the door?" It was a long corridor that could run from one end of the big building to the other.

The hallway had night lights glowing every fifty feet. The

NVGs came in handy in the low light. They could spot no one either way. One Kenyan lay crumpled around a machine gun to the left.

"Which way?" Jaybird asked.

"Which is the longest way?" Murdock asked him.

Jaybird shrugged. "We could split up. One squad each direction."

"No, no splitting," Murdock said. "We stay together unless we need a rear guard. How in hell are we going to find those sailors in this huge place?"

2215 hours
Pita's apartment
Mombasa, Kenya

They had spent the past two hours eating, and drinking wine that Pita had brought home. Two days before, they had given her all of the shillings they had left, 2,512. She had been surprised, pleased, and delighted. She had said she would buy some special food for them.

Now the wine was making everyone friendlier. Pita hadn't changed from her seduction clothes, and now and then her blouse slipped open a little. Vuylsteke tried not to look. Perez stared the other way. Tretter grinned at the flash of rounded breasts.

Just before 2300 the wine was gone. Vuylsteke yawned where he sat on the floor. Tretter sat beside Pita on the couch. She bent over and kissed him on the lips, and he growled softly. She stood, reached for his hand, and led him to the bedroom door.

Vuylsteke looked up and shook his head.

"By God, no, Tretter."

"Man, you got no rank on me here."

"Don't go in there. Could mess up our whole cover."

"Not a chance. Anyway, I figure this little lady has saved our asses for three days now. If she wants something in return, I ain't gonna be the one to turn her down."

"I'm warning you, Tretter." Vuylsteke stood.

Perez came to his feet and moved in front of Vuylsteke. "Hey, easy. Take it easy. It's Pita's call. None of our damned business. We're guests in her house, right? Now just cool it. You take the couch tonight, I'll sleep on the fucking pillows."

Pita smiled at them all, then caught Tretter's hand again, led him into her bedroom, and closed the door.

12

Tuesday, July 20

"We move left," Murdock said looking down the long corridor. "As I remember, the bulk of the building was to the left."

"We clear all these doors?" Jaybird asked.

"No, this isn't a prisoner area. We look for some stairs or an open area or cell blocks. Where the hell do they keep the bad guys in this place?"

They trotted down the corridor on the concrete floor. Four lights down they came to a stairway to the left. At the top of the one flight of steps, a steel security gate barred the way. Quinley had stayed close behind Holt this time, and moved up to the barricade without orders. This one was different.

It had double locks on a hinged door. Less secure than the previous one. Quinley applied TNAZ blocks, molding them around both hinges on the four-foot-wide door. The SEALs moved back down the hall fifty feet, and a moment later Quinley came racing down the steps and around the corner, putting his hands over his ears.

The explosions were sharper this time, and just as effective. The steel gate sagged to the side, blown off both hinges but still fastened with the lock. They kicked the gate open further and hurried through. Murdock motioned his

101

men along both walls, and he pointed at Red Nicholson, his scout.

Red went up the corridor, and around a corner. He was back in half a minute. "Bingo, L-T. We've got cell blocks up here, but they're all empty."

"How many?"

"A bunch. Extend to hell and gone to the left and right."

"No prisoners?"

"Nary a damned one, L-T, and two security gates like this one are wide open."

"Let's go have a look."

It was as Red had said. They jogged down the aisle in the center. The cells were open, but showed signs that they had been used recently.

Loudspeakers boomed.

"All prisoners, this is general lockdown. A general lockdown. No prisoner will be outside his cell. Any so found will be shot on sight."

Murdock scowled. Where the hell were the American prisoners? He put his men on double time, and they ran down the cell block. Twenty yards ahead, a stuttering machine gun sent a rain of bullets toward them. They flattened out, and four men in the front of the line of SEALs returned fire.

The lighting was faint in the cell blocks, but with their NVGs they spotted two Kenyan soldiers ahead working with a jammed gun. Red used his M-4A1 and cut down both men with two bursts. The SEALs ran forward.

The two Kenyans had guarded a cross corridor. This security gate was shut tight. Ahead they could see more cell blocks, but better lighted.

"Do it, Quinley," Murdock said. It was routine now. Quinley hit the gate on the hinges again, and the SEALs were through in thirty seconds.

When the sound of the blast died down and their hearing came back to normal, they could hear men chattering somewhere. They listened. English.

Murdock motioned his men down the corridor. Almost at once it opened into a catwalk over a huge room with two floors of cell blocks and guards patrolling below. Murdock hit his mike. The green-clad troopers were looking around after hearing the explosions. Some had cowered behind cover.

"Got them," Murdock said into the mike. "Looks like our guys. Go to the floor. Fire over the ramp. Watch for any ricochets into the cells. Those are our boys down there. Don't fire until we're at the other end. Then use the silenced shooters."

He left DeWitt's crew there, and with his seven men moved slowly and silently along the catwalk-like structure to the far end. It was about fifty yards.

They used the silenced MP-5's when Murdock turned them loose. DeWitt's crew nailed three of the Kenyan ranger guards before they knew what happened. Murdock's squad cut down four more on his end of the cell block.

A moment later every light in the cell-block area went out. Murdock grinned in the blackness. "Good, we use the NVGs. We can see them, they can't see us."

Murdock used the mike. "DeWitt, spread out your men to cover this area. I'll take my guys down some stairs I see ahead. Must be a control area here somewhere. We need it to get those cell doors open."

"Hey, you guys up there. Americans, right?" The voice came from below. A shot blazed in the darkness from below.

"Yes. Keep quiet so they don't shoot you. Stay cool," Murdock yelled. A round came his way, but missed. He moved his squad out to the door. He and Red went down the steps cautiously. They found two guards below bewildered by the blackout.

Red moved up on one and clubbed him with his rifle butt, and gunned down the other man. They dragged the dazed Kenyan back, but then realized he might speak no English. Murdock slapped him back to consciousness.

"Die in ten seconds or talk to us in English," Murdock snarled.

The man groaned, felt his head, and looked to where he could make out the vague shadows.

"Yes, English. Who the hell are you?"

"We ask the questions. Where are the cell-block control panels?"

"End of corridor to left. Not far."

"Good, you might live through this. How many soldiers and guards here?"

"Only fifty soldiers. Guards all run away."

"Let's go to the control panel. We can see in the dark. Lead the way. Remember, you yell a warning, you're dead."

The soldier nodded. They lifted him to his feet. Nicholson twisted one arm behind his back and held it, and let him walk ahead. They passed up sure shots on two guards down the corridor as they turned left into another smaller hallway. At the end, they came to a door. The man motioned toward it.

"Get them to open it," Murdock whispered. "Say it in English."

The Kenyan nodded. The black man pounded on the door. "Open up, open up! Orders from the commander!"

Nothing happened. He pounded the door again and yelled the same words.

Again, nothing happened. "Red, go bring up Quinley. This is another metal door, probably an electric lock. We'll blow it."

Murdock heard some of the 4-A1 rifles firing from where they had been. Good, only fifty defenders. Much better odds.

Quinley came puffing up with his extra load of explosives. He looked at the metal door through his NVGs.

"Lock looks too tough. I'll hit it and the two hinges. Three shots of TNAZ. Get back around the corner when she blows." He worked on the door as he spoke. He put timer detonators in each of the three chunks of explosive, all set for ten seconds. He got the SEALs back, then pushed in each timer, activating all three, and sprinted for the corner and around it. He had his hands over his ears. The other SEALs did the same, as did the captured Kenyan soldier, who was still with them.

The three sharp explosions were magnified by the narrow spaces. The sound, and a pair of shock waves, roared through the tunnel-like passages. This time they sounded like three 155's going off in your clothes closet.

Red Nicholson was first around the corner with his stubby rifle set for automatic. The door had been blown off both hinges and had pivoted inside still connected to the twisted locking mechanism. A stunned dark-green-clad soldier came out waving a rifle. Nicholson blew him backwards with a three-round burst and charged in after him. The dead Kenyan was the only man in the control center.

The lights were all still out. There had to be a master switch somewhere. Murdock looked at the control panels. All of the labels and directions were written in Swahili and in English.

"Jaybird, find the right buttons and open the cell doors," Murdock said. Murdock left Ken Ching to back up Jaybird and deal with the captured Kenyan, and took the other five men with him toward the cell block. Just as they rounded the corner, a squad of six rangers opened fire. The SEALs jolted back.

Ronson let out a yelp and then gritted his teeth.

"Check him, Doc," Murdock said.

Ronson had taken a round through his right forearm. Doc rolled back his sleeve, and put a compress over it.

"Hold that tight while I get some supplies," he told Ronson.

"Oh, damn. What's that, an AK-47 slug?" Ronson asked.

"Probably," Doc said. He pulled his pack around and took out some larger squares of gauze, and a short stretch bandage like an Ace. He sprinkled the wound with some antiseptic and healing powder, put on two new squares of gauze, and then wrapped it tightly with the stretch bandage and fastened it with a double-hook clip.

Murdock had been checking the aisle between the cells. He saw shooters on both sides, hugging the cells so any firing at them would endanger the sailors behind them. He pulled Magic Brown up.

"Do it. We need delicate hits. No misses into the prisoners. Those are our boys."

Magic tightened the sound suppressor on the short barrel of the new H&K PSG1 high-precision sniper rifle, and went belly-down at the corner. He angled the muzzle around, and checked through the 6 x 42-power scope.

"Bastards are firing at sounds," Murdock said. "They can't see a damned thing."

Magic's sniper rifle coughed through the suppressor, and they heard a wail of pain down the corridor.

Magic took his time finding the next victim. One Kenyan lifted up and ran away from them. Magic slammed one quick round at him. Then, with his eye on the scope, Magic nailed the man with the second shot, smashing him to the concrete floor, where he didn't move.

A sudden clanging sounded, and two hundred cell doors rolled back all at once. Magic watched the men pour out of the cells. Half a dozen overwhelmed each of the Kenyan soldiers still alive in the alley between the cells. One AK-47 blasted, but then all was quiet.

"Hey, sailors," Murdock bellowed. "Who's in charge of this outfit?"

Murdock watched through his NVGs as a man worked through the sailors.

"That would be me, Lieutenant Commander Wilson Judd. My compliments on your quick action. Our Captain is KIA."

The officer came forward. He wore no rank on his dungarees. He saluted the shadow in front of him, and Murdock took his extended hand.

"Lieutenant Murdock, with the SEALs. Glad we could be of some service. Afraid the dance has just begun. Have your men get any weapons they can find from the ex-guards and the Kenyan military. We'll need them. You have any idea how to get out of this mousetrap?"

The commander laughed. "Not a fucking clue. Just glad to see another American. How is the ship?"

"Don't know. First order of business is to get you and your crew back to the *Monroe*."

"You've got a carrier offshore?"

"And a whole task force. You're important people to the Navy, Commander Judd."

Murdock touched his mike. "DeWitt. Any reason we can't go back the way we came in?"

"Considerable. We're still in the balcony seats. In the corridor behind us are at least twenty-five angry Kenyans who are howling and bellowing and firing down the corridor. How about a detour or an alternate route?"

"Working it. DeWitt, get your troops down here." Murdock looked around. "Where's Nicholson?"

Jaybird had joined the party. "He wandered off when the cell doors came open."

"He'll be back. You have any wounded, Commander Judd?"

"Three or four, all minor."

"Get them up here and let Doc look them over. We may have a couple of minutes before my scout gets back."

The commander passed the word, and soon Doc had three men to check out.

"You have any KIA, Commander?"

"One. One chief had been on the nervous side, and he mouthed off to one of the guards. The bastard shot the chief four times."

"Not sure we can take him out with us. Depends on the route. There should be a stretcher around here somewhere. I'll have my men with the goggles look for one. If we can't take him out, we'll damn well come back and get him."

Red Nicholson came up and touched Murdock's shoulder.

"Sir, found another corridor that isn't covered. Not sure where it goes, but it's on the first floor."

"Even if it goes out the front of this place, that's better than facing those guns back there," Murdock said. "Take three men and check it out, and leave one of them as a guide at each turn. Move out."

Murdock began getting the sailors into some kind of order. Four of the men had found AK-47's with some extra magazines. He put them at the end of the sailors to be a rear guard.

Commander Judd separated the 160 men into groups and

had officers with each bunch. Murdock approved, and they moved out.

Commander Judd walked beside Murdock. "You wouldn't have an extra weapon, would you, Lieutenant? I feel naked."

Murdock unsnapped his Mark 23 pistol and gave it to the commander. "That's a forty-five auto with a real kick. Twelve rounds. Here are two spare magazines."

The commander thanked him, and they hurried down the corridor that Nicholson had found. At the first turn they picked up Ching. A tough-looking security gate there stood open. Evidently Jaybird had opened more than the cell doors in the control room.

At the second turn, they found Magic Brown. He still lugged the extra twenty pounds of the .50-caliber sniper rifle and ammo. Another security door had been swung flat against the wall.

Thirty yards down a dark corridor, they came to Red Nicholson, who was waiting. Murdock moved up beside him.

"Looks like we're working toward the front of the complex, L-T. Only trouble is we have a sandbagged machine gun set up on a tripod down there maybe fifty yards. He's got good protection. Doubt if our 223s or our NATO rounds would hurt him."

"How many men down there?"

"I've seen four. May be more. The weapon is aimed our direction like they know we're coming."

Murdock used his lip mike. "Magic Brown, get your bones up front. We need your talents."

Commander Judd eased up beside Murdock. "Problems?"

"One heavy machine gun and a whole shitpot full of sandbag protection."

Magic dropped beside Murdock. "You want the Fifty?"

"Amen." He told the black man the situation. He saw Magic grin in the darkness.

"No fucking problem, L-T." He pulled open the drag sack and unlimbered the big sniper rifle. A specially fabricated ten-round magazine was in place with the five-and-a-half-inch-long rounds.

"Sir?" Murdock said, looking at the full commander.

The officer nodded, and moved out of the way. Brown angled the big weapon around the corner with the bipod out front. He adjusted the Leupold Ultra MK4 16-power telescopic sight and settled in to take a shot.

Murdock moved the others back ten feet, and Magic Brown began doing his thing. His first round took out the man sitting behind the old-style .30-caliber heavy machine gun. Magic could only see half of his head and one shoulder. The round smashed through the Kenyan's left eye, and splattered half of his head down the corridor.

The booming sound of the .50-caliber round sounded like a 105 artillery round. Before the sound had echoed down the tunnel-like hallway, Brown had his second shot lined up. A foolhardy Kenyan had pushed his dead buddy out of the way and moved into the seat behind the weapon. This one looked around the side of the machine gun, and Magic fired again.

The perfect shot centered on the soldier's mouth, and blasted his head off his shoulders.

Half-a-dozen rifle rounds whistled past Magic, and he pulled back to the safety of the wall for a moment, then leaned around and worked the bolt quickly three times, slamming three chunks of hot lead from the magazine into the sandbags and anyone foolish enough to get in his way.

He paused a moment, then looked around the wall and checked his target through the scope. A dim glow back-lighted the position. Magic spotted one man working slowly back toward the light. The heavy .50-caliber round made him drop what he had been dragging, and blew the soldier a dozen feet down the hall and straight into any afterlife he might have.

"About it, L-T," Brown said.

Murdock motioned to Red, and the two of them aimed their weapons around the corner of the wall and sent full magazines of hot lead down the long corridor.

"Let's go," Murdock said. He rounded the corner, and

sprinted down the narrow hallway. He jumped over two sandbags, almost tripped over a body, and kept going with the First Squad of SEALs right behind him.

Murdock stopped at the light they had seen. It was an overhead ventilation shaft of some kind. There was no way to get up to it. Murdock waved them past, and Red took the lead. They came to a section with half-a-dozen doors off the main stem. They ignored them and moved ahead, weapons ready.

A pair of corridor-wide swinging steel doors blocked their path. Red edged up to them, and pushed one in four inches so he could look through to the other side. Machine-gun fire blasted into the door but missed the inch-wide hole, and Red fell back swearing.

Murdock squirmed forward. "You hit?"

Red shook his head.

"Forties," Murdock said. Red nodded. Murdock used the mike and told Adams and Lampedusa to get up front and break out their 40mm rounds.

They worked it systematically. One man edged the door open far enough to get his M-4A1 through, then fired a half a magazine of .223 whizzers down the hall. Meanwhile, the next man pushed his weapon through below that, and fired an HE 40mm round. As the lower man loaded a new round, the top man fired the last half of his .223's from his magazine.

Then the lower man fired another grenade. They worked the ritual for six grenades. The last one was a Willy Peter phosphorous round that exploded with the impossible-to-put-out sticky phosphorus that could burn through anything but metal, including human bones and tissue.

No return firing had come after the second grenade.

Murdock held up his hand to stop the action. They waited. A groan came from in front of them. Murdock hoped that the WP smoke would drift out of the hallway ahead of them.

He nodded at Ron Holt, who lay on the floor, and Holt pushed one of the swinging doors open with his MP-5. There were no incoming rounds. Holt held the door open as the First Squad raced over him and into the hall half filled with smoke.

They heard no firing from the front. Red Nicholson ran through the smoke, past three dead Kenyans, and to a door that swung half open. Fresh air billowed through the door, and outside he could smell the green countryside of Kenya.

A minute later, Murdock edged the door open wider. A bright moon bathed the landscape. He wasn't sure where they were, but they were at an outside door.

"Holt, get your ass up front," Murdock said into the mike.

"Right behind you, L-T," Holt said, grinning in the darkness.

"Crank up that box of yours and see if the flyboys are still up there riding shotgun."

Holt flipped two switches and took the mike. "Tom Birds, this is Water One. You still flying?"

The return came through at once.

"That's a roger, Water One. Cruisin' and snoozin'."

"We're almost out, may need some help."

"Can do. Give us a call."

"Time?" Murdock asked.

Holt punched the light on his watch. "It's just after 2235, sir."

Murdock took another look outside. "Road out there, and no inlet, so we're in the motherfucking front of this asshole place. We need the back, and we need to get wet."

Just as he started to push forward out the door, a chattering machine gun snarled and seven rounds jolted into the door slamming it all the way open.

The SEALs ducked back inside the building.

"Anybody hit?" Murdock asked.

"If somebody got hit he's dead," Holt snapped. They laughed. It was what they needed.

Murdock took a quick look out the door to the right where he had heard the machine gun. He saw it mounted on a three-quarter-ton-type military truck. Had to be a .50-caliber.

"Brown, get it up here. Got one more small job for you to do."

13

Tuesday, July 20

General Umar Maleceia stormed from one side of his large office in the military headquarters to the other. His dark green uniform shirt showed stains of sweat under the arms and down the chest. His eyes bulged as he stopped in front of his second in command, Colonel Jomo Kariuki.

"How could this happen? Our troops at the American Embassy have been slaughtered and the hostages have been taken away? How could you let this happen?"

"General, sir. They had fast jet fighters that attacked the embassy. Then they brought in large helicopters with troops in them, and the fighters flew cover. Two of our weapons carriers were destroyed."

"These same jets shot down one of our MiGs?"

"Yes, sir. We now have only *tatu*, just three of the MiGs left."

The phone rang. The colonel picked it up. He answered, listened for a moment, then held out the handset. "General, you better hear this."

"What? What is it?"

Colonel Kariuki pushed the handset toward the general.

"Yes, yes, what is it?" Maleceia listened a moment, then had the man on the other end repeat the words when static interrupted the telephone conversation.

113

General Maleceia pulled the handset away from his mouth and threw it and the phone across the room.

"Attacking us again! They are attacking the prison where I have the rest of my hostages! How can I demand money and goods from America if I don't have any hostages?"

Colonel Kariuki stepped back to be out of the rage pattern of his commander.

"Sir, we have five hundred seasoned troops in a camp just north of Mombasa. I can alert them now, and they can be at the prison in a half hour."

General Maleceia seemed not to hear his advisor. He swept everything off his desk. He threw a portable radio across the room, smashing a window. He kicked over his desk chair, and then sat down on the desk hard, his hands over his face.

"General we can send in troops from the camp north—"

General Maleceia looked up with a killing stare, and Colonel Kariuki stopped.

"I know where our troops are, Kariuki. In a half hour the attackers may be gone. Why don't we have more helicopters? Why not more than three jet fighters? I know. They cost hard currency, which we don't have. Yes, send the jets down to blast anything they see that moves around the prison. If we can't keep the hostages, at least we can kill them all."

"General, the report is that there is air cover for the raid. It is probably the F-14s, the same type plane we think shot down our MiG. Sir, they are much faster, with better missiles and far better radar than our older MiGs. Our pilots wouldn't stand a chance."

"Send them up now. They can be in Mombasa long before the troops can move across town in the trucks. Order it at once."

"Yes, General." The major went outside to his desk, where he made two phone calls. Three minutes later it was done. The three jets would be lifting off from their home base near Nairobi within fifteen minutes. They would be at Mombasa in another thirty minutes. It all depended how quickly the American raiders could rescue the sailors and get them out of the area. It all depended. He had no hope that the troops in their trucks would be of any practical use.

If the jets got to the prison in Mombasa before 2245, they might have a shot at helping. The colonel gave a short sigh. If they weren't shot down fifty miles from their target.

Tuesday, July 20

2240 hours
Indian Ocean Prison
Mombasa, Kenya

"Somebody has night eyes over there," Brown said. He had just cranked out another .50-caliber round that didn't find a home.

"Soon as I got off that first round, that damned truck jolted behind that offset in the front of the building. Can't even see the bastard now."

"But if we started sending men outside, he could pull out, fire off a dozen rounds, and slam back in hiding before you got off more than one shot," Murdock said.

He turned to Holt. "Call in the Tom Cats. We need some help."

Holt picked up the mike. "Tom Birds, got your ears on? This is Dry Water One."

"Oh, yeah, Dry Water. We've got company. Two more Cats to help. What's up?"

"Do a flyby at the front of the building. There's a vehicle with a fifty-caliber MG that has us pinned. We're at a door at the front near the west end of the place. Be right obliged if you could disassemble that fifty and not burn us out."

"Roger that, Dry Water. How far are you from the target?"

"Eighty yards, Tom Bird."

"Keep your heads down."

Two minutes later two jets came in on a strafing run, their 20mm cannon spouting bright flashes in the darkness. The front of the building took a pounding as the birds followed one another, then slanted up and away.

Brown watched through his scope. "Close, but no hits. Tell them to move it about twenty yards left."

"Tom Birds. Our spotter says no rubber duck. Adjust twenty yards your left for target."

"Thanks, Dry Water. We're a little blind up here."

On the next run, four Tom Cats thundered out of the sky at twenty-second intervals, and blasted the small truck into two million pieces. Magic Johnson laughed and folded up his bipod.

"I'd say we're free and clear, L-T."

"Holt, get on the horn to the carrier. Tell them we're moving out of the store with the goods. ETA the water, thirty minutes."

"Got it, L-T."

"Commander, get your men moving out and to the left. We'll ride shotgun for you. Can your men march?"

"No food for three days, but we can move, maybe not up to SEAL standards."

"We'll go at your pace, Commander. Let's do it now."

They came out the door in a ragged line, formed into a column of ducks, and worked down the front of the building for another fifty yards, then angled toward the brush that hid the finger of Mombasa Bay. It was too long a line, and Murdock was worried.

Holt thanked the Tom Birds that were in a holding pattern over the site. Then he picked up some flyboy chatter.

"Tom Bird One, this is Four. I have what could be a visitor from the north on my screen. Anyone copy it?"

"Tom Bird Four, I don't see anything. You and Three take a run up north for fifty miles and see what's out there."

"Will do, One."

Murdock looked at Holt. "What was that all about?"

Holt told him.

"Is Maleceia foolish enough to send more of his too few MiGs down this way?"

"Could be, could be a flight of geese."

The line of sailors moved slower than Murdock wanted. Two men had broken down and were being carried by a two-man hand-chair arrangement. They had roughly a half mile to go to a spot along shore where a pickup could be made. Murdock figured his men would be late. They had left the dead sailor in the prison.

Murdock heard the chatter of small arms before he saw anyone.

"Hit the dirt!" Murdock bellowed. The SEALs down the long line repeated the words.

Murdock looked at a slight rise to the west of the prison. He saw the headlights of a vehicle before someone remembered and cut them off.

"Ronson, get set up," Murdock bellowed. The machine gunner came out of the line, flopped on his stomach, and angled his H&K-21A1 toward where he had seen the lights.

"Wait for some muzzle flashes," Murdock said. The SEALs with long guns were down and ready.

Half-a-dozen flashes came and bullets sang around them. The SEALs poured fifty rounds into the immediate area. Ronson's machine gun chattered with five- and seven-round bursts until the one-hundred-round belt emptied. He fit in a new one and waited.

"Range?" Murdock asked Jaybird, who had been firing beside him.

"More than fifty yards, sir. I'd say about two hundred."

"Ching, Adams, Yates, Jaybird. Let's move up there. Long gunners, give us some cover. We'll be to the right for five minutes, then cease fire."

They moved out with their NVGs up, running low to the ground. Murdock led them. The land had been cleared here for two hundred yards and there wasn't much cover. Murdock hoped the men on the rise didn't have NVGs. The SEALs covered half the distance and went to ground. The SEALs below hammered out with the heavier rounds from the sniper rifles, MGs, and M-4A1's.

Murdock angled his men more to the right. He could see the small ridgeline, and a couple of minutes later they were to it. He looked over.

Down forty yards, he saw the enemy. Six Kenyan rangers fired over the small ridgeline with perfect cover. Until now.

Murdock brought his four men up so each had a free field of fire.

"Now," he said in his mike, and all five blasted the six men. The rangers were caught by surprise. Four of them went down in the first furious fusillade. One crawled toward the small truck. Murdock slammed six rounds into him before he made it.

Jaybird caught the last man trying to run up the hill. He blasted him with a three-round blast, and the man went into the dirt and lay still.

"Move the men out for the water," Murdock said into his mike. "Tell the commander to get his men off their asses and heading for the bay."

Murdock and the four SEALs jogged down the hill, angling to catch up with the rest of the group.

Holt touched Murdock's arm. "L-T, the flyboys are on again."

"Tom One, this is Three."

"Find anybody out there?"

"We've got three blips coming in fast from the north. Still over a hundred miles away. Closing at about six hundred."

"Those old MiGs again. Warn them to turn around, and get a radar ID."

"Roger that."

"Home Plate, you copy that?"

"Right. If they keep coming and don't acknowledge, you have missiles free. I repeat, Tom Birds, your missiles are free."

"Roger that, Home Plate. You copy, Tom Three and Four?"

"Right. They're still coming."

Murdock looked at the shadowy line of men. He wanted to run up and carry each one. No food for three days would take a toll on them. They had been functioning on adrenaline, but that was burning off. They still had a quarter of a mile to go, and there was a small ravine in front of them they had to cross. Bad news.

"Holt, tell the carrier we're running late. Have them hold the transport offshore until we get better positioned. We need to be there waiting for them when they come in. They can't do it quietly, so it has to be fast."

"Will do, sir. They have the two LCACs off the coast now waiting for our go. They say it will take them less than eight minutes to get from two miles offshore into out inlet."

"That fast?"

"They do forty knots, L-T."

"We're nowhere near ready for them to be moving yet. Have them hold."

Murdock heard something. At first he thought it was a plane, but the jets were well overhead. Then he caught it: truck engines. The sound came from the hill where the six men had been. The sound came closer, then stopped.

The first sailors were in the ravine. It was the only cover around here. The trucks had to mean more troops from somewhere in Mombasa. The prison troops had had time to call for help.

"Get all the crew in the ravine," Murdock yelled. "We've got company."

"SEALs, get these men into the ravine," Murdock said on his radio mike. "It's the only cover anywhere around. First Squad break to the right and form up. Second Squad go left so we can get some cross fire on these assholes. Move. Take the suppressors off the MP-5's to get more range."

Two searchlights came on, shining from the ridge above, and began to sweep the area. Magic Brown lifted his H&K sniper rifle and blew out both of them with two quick shots. The lights hadn't touched the last of the sailors, who dropped into the ravine and out of sight.

Murdock had his men in an assault line when the first of the troops came over the small ridge that had been protecting them.

He used the Motorola. "See them? Let's give them a real hot SEAL welcome."

Sixteen weapons opened up on the surprised Kenyan troops. They had no idea where their enemy was. Fire laced into the ranks from both sides and they dropped to the ground. A few fired at the gun flashes on both sides.

A Kenyan machine gun opened up, firing at DeWitt's

squad. Six of his weapons concentrated on the MG man, and he went out of business quickly. For a few minutes there was no leadership among the men on the ridge.

Murdock had no way of estimating how many there were. He'd seen maybe twenty different weapons firing. For the number of trucks he heard, there should be a lot more ground troops than that.

Then just to his left, fifty yards from the first soldiers, another group of Kenyan rangers hit the ridge firing. The rounds weren't aimed at anyone. They couldn't see anyone. They simply fired down the slope.

Murdock's men concentrated on the new targets. Answering the SEALs' fire came a scattering of rounds, and Murdock heard a sharp cry to the left.

"Holt, that you? You hit?"

He got only silence.

Murdock crawled five yards to where he had last heard from Holt. The radioman lay on his back, the SATCOM radio half torn off his shoulder pack.

Murdock felt Holt's back and side, but didn't find any blood. He slapped the radioman's face gently. Holt shivered, then shook his head and blinked.

"What the hell?"

"Your radio just became a casualty. You hurt anywhere?"

"Sore as hell in my back and side. Maybe the round hit the radio and that damn SATCOM hit me and knocked me out."

Murdock unstrapped the radio and dropped it on the ground. He hit his Motorola mike. "DeWitt, we just lost the SATCOM. Get Willy Bishop to warm up his contact with the planes. We can use some close ground support on this puppy."

The men on the ridge kept firing. Murdock moved his men twice, and told them to hold fire so the Kenyans couldn't find them and have a target.

Two minutes later DeWitt came on the Motorola. "SATCOM contacted the F-14's. They see the firing, want a flare and a red smoke on the target. They'll be here in three minutes."

"You shoot the flares in two minutes," Murdock said.

It was a long damn two minutes, Murdock decided. Then the white flare burst over the Kenyans and a red smoke hit among them, and within seconds two F-14's came down in rapid order blasting the Kenyan troops with 20mm rounds.

"Fire at will," Murdock said into his mike, and all the SEAL weapons opened up again.

One more jet came sweeping in, blasting the men and probably the trucks behind them just as the flare burned out, and Murdock nodded. He saw two fires burning behind the ridge. Two trucks to the torch. The Kenyans would be lucky if they had enough men left for one truckload.

Engines roared, and the remains of the truck troops motored away in the direction they had come from.

"Back to the ravine," Murdock said.

It took them fifteen minutes to get the tired sailors on their feet and out of the safety of the ravine. Two more had to be carried now as they moved down the slope toward the inlet three hundred yards away.

Murdock didn't believe that it took them ten minutes to move the three hundred yards. Just as they hit the trees near the water, he told Bishop to call the LCACs circling offshore.

"Tell them we're on the beach ready to board," Murdock said.

Bishop came up to Murdock. "Message sent, sir. They said they have three craft and will be on-site here in eight minutes. How fast are those air-cushioned boats anyway?"

"The LCACs can do forty knots when they're in a rush, which they will be. We're going to put fifty-nine men on each boat, so it will be damn crowded, but the ensign from the boats said it will work."

Commander Judd came up. "Three craft coming in?"

"Yes, sir. Time to split your men into three groups. We'll load fifty-four of your men on each of the air-cushion boats and get the hell out of here."

"With five of your men, that's almost sixty men to a boat," Judd said. "Where will they put us?" Then he shrugged. "They must know what they're doing. I'll split up the group."

Murdock told DeWitt to put his squad on one of the hover-craft, saying he'd split his own squad between the other two. Then the SEALs spread out, all facing toward the prison, as a rear guard to wait for the boats.

Murdock had wondered about the air-cushion craft as well. They had almost no cargo space, were only eighty-eight feet long, and topside were covered with ducts and fans and blowers. He hoped the sixty men could find a place to hold on.

Murdock heard the jets overhead. They'd be there until the landing craft were tucked up to the carrier four miles to sea. What could go wrong now? Maybe the Kenyan Navy. They had talked about the patrol craft the Kenyans had. The question was how many of the ships had gone over to the colonel in the coup. They heard some of the ships had simply put to sea to wait out the confusion.

On the carrier, they had been most worried about the two Kenyan fast-attack craft with missiles. They were the Nyayo class, 186 feet long, and could do forty knots. They carried SSM:40T0 Melara missiles with radar guidance and 210-kilogram warheads.

The F-14's would be watching for them.

Bishop came up and gave Murdock the listen/talk hand-set.

He heard the fighters overhead.

"That's a roger, Bird One. The three bogies are still on course, now about fifty miles and closing. They have ignored our ID calls. They definitely are not friendlies."

"This is Home Plate. Tom Birds, your weapons are free. Splash two. I repeat. Splash two."

"This is Tom Bird Three. I say lock on. I have a fox three from Tom Bird Three." It was the aviator's code for a Phoenix missile launch.

"This is Tom Bird Four. I have lock on. I say a fox three from Tom Bird Four."

"Two Phoenix birds away and homing," Tom Bird Three said.

A moment later. "I have splash on bogie three."

"Splash on bogie two."

The air was quiet for a moment. "The third target has just turned and is heading back the way he came. Looks like the fun is over."

"Well done, return to your cover assignment," Home Plate said.

On the ground by the inlet, the SEALs heard the whine and roar of the air-cushioned craft two minutes before they saw them. Three of the craft raced forward at a surprising speed, making a huge spray of water and foam as the ducted air fans beat air into the water to keep the craft lifted off it, while fans in back slammed them forward. Suddenly they cut power and slowed dramatically before they drove directly on the beach from the water, scattering sand and sticks from the air blowers. The engines idled down, and the front ramps lowered on both craft.

Commander Judd had the men in three groups on their feet waiting. They moved on board like well-trained combat troops. Murdock gawked in surprise. He got his men on the second and third craft, saw DeWitt get his squad aboard, and then the ramps came up. At once they roared off the beach into the water and slammed down the inlet toward the bay. The LCAC boats hadn't been on the sand more than a minute and a half.

Their only armament were 12.2mm machine guns. Murdock told Magic Brown to get out his fifty just in case they needed it. The sixty men crowded the rail and clung to the sides of air shafts and any spare spot they could find on a deck filled with pipes and tubes and compartments. Murdock saw why the specs said the boat was made to handle only twenty-four troops.

They entered the bay proper, and turned left in a gentle curve spraying water fifty feet. Douglas tailed Murdock wherever he went. His radio was still set to the aircraft, and a moment later they heard the landing craft's radio.

"Tom Birds, this is Cushion One. I've got lights and a wake coming up fast behind us. Can you see it? Left side of the island in the channel."

"Looking, Cushion One. Yes, have it. Looks like a fighting ship. Kenya have any big patrol craft?"

"Tom Birds, could be a fast-attack boat with missiles. We're ducks on a pond here. They match our speed."

"We can't see much on each flyover."

"Can you tell if they have missile launchers?"

"I'd say that's a roger," another voice came in. "Can't be sure. Can see what looks like a three-inch gun on the bow."

"She must be a thousand meters behind us. If she's got missiles, we're dead swimmers down here."

"How about a strafing run in front of her with twenties?" Bird One asked.

"Give it a try."

Murdock and the men watched as one F-14 slanted down and traced a fifty-yard line of 20mm rounds across the path of the speedy boat and not more than thirty yards off her bow.

"Got her attention, she slowed some." There was a pause.

"Nope, she's up to speed again, Cushion."

"Can you get a go-ahead to splash her?" Cushion asked.

"That's a negative, not unless we get some hostile action from her. Maybe she's an escort."

A moment later the Kenyan boat behind them began winking at them with what had to be rapid machine-gun fire.

"Hostile action, we're being fired on," Cushion shouted into his mike.

"Weapons free, coming around."

Murdock nodded at Magic Brown. "See if you can find their range."

Brown had been sighting in on the craft with the 16-power scope. He held his breath, refined his sights, and fired. He pulled the bolt back and rammed it forward and sighted in again.

"Oh, yeah, right in his basket," Magic said. He pounded off three more rounds, then took out the magazine and pushed in another ten-shot magazine filled with armor-piercing rounds. Three more rounds from Magic slammed toward the enemy craft over half a mile behind them.

"Why don't they use the missiles?" Murdock asked.

Brown shook his head, and went on firing. "Maybe they don't have any on board."

He fired six more times before three F-14's blasted down on a strafing run, and riddled the Kenyan boat with 20mm cannon fire. Murdock couldn't tell how many of the 20mm rounds hit the Kenyan craft, but it slowed and then made a sharp right turn, and almost plowed into the side of the mainland.

"That river rat down there is out of business," Tom Bird One said. "He took thirty or forty hits, and I think lost his bridge. He's dead in the water."

"That's a Roger, thanks, Bird One," Cushion said. "We're continuing down the channel."

Murdock slapped Magic on the back. "Glad the Kenyans didn't get their missiles working. Also wonder why didn't they use their twenty-millimeter gun on there that can spit out eight hundred rounds a minute."

"Hell, that's nothing," Magic said. "On a good day I can get off fifteen rounds in a minute."

They all laughed as the eighty-five-footer slashed along at forty knots heading down the last half mile of the bay toward the ocean.

The flyboys came back on the air.

"Cushion One, looks like you're free and clear. We see no more pursuit. We say negative on any more pursuit."

"Thanks, Tom Birds. You earned your day's pay. We've got about a hundred and eighty men on these boats who thank you."

They swept past the little village of Likoni on the point of land across from Mombasa Island with a roaring and a massive spraying of water from the air-cushioned crafts that would give the natives something to talk about for weeks.

Four minutes later, the three landing craft took turns pulling alongside a landing platform hung at a low hatch on the big aircraft carrier. Slowly and carefully, the hostage crewmen left the landing craft and walked onto the carrier. Six wounded had to be taken off by corpsmen on stretchers.

Murdock was the last man off. He shook hands with the

ensign on board the landing craft, and went up to the SEAL planning room, where he had told his men to meet.

The SEALs had sprawled where they landed in the big room. Murdock looked at Jaybird. "Casualty report."

Jaybird looked around. "Ronson for sure. Doc needs to look at Holt's back. He might have a cracked rib or two. We'll check on Magic Brown's leg. Anybody else?"

"Yeah," Red Nicholson said. He held up his hand. His spray-soaked desert cammie sleeve showed bright with blood. Then he fell forward flat on his face.

14

Wednesday, July 21

0220 hours
Pita's apartment
Mombasa, Kenya

"This is crazy," Vuylsteke said.

"Crazy or not, it's got to work," Tretter said. "There can't be more than a dozen or maybe two dozen troops on the *Roy Turner*. They're army guys, mud-kickers, for God's sakes. We know spots in the guts of the *Turner* where they'll never find us. We get on board and harass them and waste a few and hide out, and we'll be there to help capture the ship when the damned Marines, or somebody, swarms ashore to retake her."

"Yeah, real crazy idea," Perez said. "If somebody comes to retake her. What if they don't? Aw, hell, it sounds just wild enough to work. We can find weapons on board. We can waste a couple of them Kenya Army guys, and take their shooters. Hell, we might be able to capture the whole damn ship ourselves."

Vuylsteke scowled. "Hey, don't get carried away. First, how do we get on board? Second, where do we hide out? How many Kenyan Army men are on board? Hell of a lot of questions to get answered."

"We can't answer them here," Tretter said.

"So, how do we get on the *Turner*?" Perez asked.

"Pita said she'll help," Tretter said with a grin. "She'll be a decoy, get the deck guard to come down. She'll fake a fall, say she broke her leg. He goes down to the pier to help her. If nobody else's on deck, we rush out of the shadows, clobber the guy, take his piece, and get on board."

Vuylsteke worried it. "Then when he wakes up, we hope that this Army guy thinks some locals wanted to get his rifle."

"If he wakes up," Perez said. "I hear they killed over twenty-five of our shipmates. It was on the radio."

Pita came out of the bedroom. She had put the sexy blouse back on and only buttoned two of the fasteners. As she moved, the men could see flashes of both breasts.

"I'll wear this blouse and it'll come open a little," Pita said. She gave them a seductive smile. "I have listened to you. We can do it. If you kill one more of the sadistic Kenyan soldiers, I will help you."

"I keep my thirty-two," Perez said. "Things get hot at the ship, we shoot and run. We break up on the dock and go four directions, and get here on our own without being tailed."

"God, we really going to do this?" Vuylsteke asked.

"Why not?" Perez asked. "We can cut down the odds for whoever comes on board to retake the *Turner*."

"I'm in," Tretter said. "Let's get out of here and go kick some Kenyan ass."

"Hold it. What time is it?" Vuylsteke asked it.

"It's 0227," Perez said. "All them assholes will be sleeping except maybe two guards. Easy. We watch for an hour, find out their pattern. Then we take out one or both of them. Piece of cake."

"Easy for you, Perez, you got the piece," Tretter said.

"Yeah, and we'll have all the weapons we can use before daylight. Let's go and do it!"

Vuylsteke hesitated. "Pita, can you get some soldier off the boat and distract him?"

Pita smiled, unbuttoned the two fasteners on her blouse, and held open both sides showing her full, light brown breasts to them. She smiled and moved her shoulders so her breasts jiggled.

"Now you believe me?" Tretter asked.

Vuylsteke nodded slowly. "Oh, yes, I think those two will do the trick. I want a butcher knife to take along. You better get one too, Tretter, until we get some better weapons."

Twenty minutes later, the four of them sat in the shadows at the edge of the pier where the USS *Roy Turner* lay tied against the dock. They had seen one sentry on the ship, walking on this side, but he vanished now and then, maybe to work the far side.

After ten minutes, they had seen only one man on watch.

"Got to be another one somewhere," Tretter said. "How about the quarterdeck?"

They couldn't see into the quarterdeck, but watched it. Nothing developed. The steel gangplank had been moved away from the ship. The way the tide was now, the ship's deck was no more than two feet above the pier and nudged tightly against the concrete dock.

Pita and Tretter whispered a moment. Then she stood up from the shadows and limped badly as she moved into the soft glow of the ship's lights, working toward the vessel just in front of the squared-off helicopter hangar. She had almost gotten to the side of the *Turner* when the soldier they had seen with a rifle came running up with his weapon at the ready.

"What the hell you doing, woman?" the sentry called from the ship.

"Oh, I didn't see you. I fell over there, broke my ankle, I think. Can you help me?"

"How? Can't leave my post."

"Maybe somebody else?"

"Only one damn guard awake. The sarge is sleeping. What the hell?"

Pita opened her blouse. "You want me, I'll be glad to fuck you if you help me first. I need my ankle splinted or bandaged."

"Damn! I can't come down there."

"We can fuck right here in the shadows after you help me."

"Oh, damn." The sentry looked around. "Maybe just . . ." He looked along the deck, then jumped down the two feet to the dock and knelt beside her. She was close to the edge of the pier, and he had to put his back to the far side of the dock where the sailors waited.

Tretter began to move as soon as the soldier laid down his rifle and began to examine her ankle. Tretter ran forward like a shadow without a sound. The first thing the Kenyan ranger knew of any danger was when the side of a brick slammed down on his head. He slumped to the dock before he could cry out.

Pita pulled a knife from her skirt and stabbed the soldier, then sliced his throat.

"Into the bay," she whispered. Tretter searched the man's pockets and brought out three magazines for the rifle. Then Pita and Tretter rolled the body over the small berm and into the water between the ship and the pier.

When the soldier crumpled on the dock, the other two sailors ran for the ship. They both jumped on board, and pressed against the bulkhead near the quarterdeck door. Tretter kissed Pita and pushed her toward the shadows where they had hidden. She was supposed to go directly to her apartment.

Tretter jumped on board the ship with the dead ranger's AK-47 and three magazines of ammo. He pasted himself against the bulkhead just forward of the quarterdeck.

They had agreed to take a look at the in-port operational center and see if anyone was on duty, then do a quick look for another guard. If they found none, they would move to their hiding spot.

Perez took three steps to the quarterdeck door on the starboard side. They watched both ways. Nothing moved on the weather deck. They heard nothing. Perez edged his head around the opening until he could see into the passageway. Somebody had turned on the red lights, and he could make out the area. He saw no one. Then a moment later he spotted a figure leaning back in a swivel chair that Perez figured had been in the Captain's quarters.

The man in chair gave off a soft wheeze of snoring.

Perez had never killed a man. He set his jaw and waved the other two sailors forward, then slipped inside the quarterdeck and with soft, cautious footsteps approached the sleeping man. He had the revolver in his left hand, and in his right he held one of Pita's eight-inch-long butcher knives.

He took a deep breath, and surged forward the last six feet. He held the butcher knife like a saber, so it extended straight out from his hand. It gave him a three-foot-long lance. He drove forward and the knife hit the green shirt of the Kenyan ranger, glanced a quarter of an inch off a rib, and plunged into the sergeant's heart. The Kenyan almost woke up, his eyes blinked, and then he gave a long sigh as the last breath he would ever take came gushing out of his lungs.

At the same time his bowels emptied and his bladder gushed as all muscle control over them relaxed.

They had agreed to leave anyone they killed on the deck in place. Too much trouble and too much noise to try to get a body overboard.

Vuylsteke nodded at Perez as he ran up. He took an automatic shotgun from the big sergeant along with two U.S. Navy sacks of shotgun shells with the bandoleer-type loop that went over his head. Each sack should have fifteen rounds. They saw nothing else of value, and hurried down the passageway.

Midships of the quarterdeck companionway, they stopped at a ladder that descended one deck to where they could move on down to the auxiliary machine engine storage space just above the bilges.

The three crept down the ladder silently, made a turn, and a few moments later had continued into the bowels of the ship. They slipped under the steel grate just over the bilges. The grate held all sorts of spare compressors, pumps, valves, and other types of auxiliary engineering equipment.

The space between the steel overhead and their luxury quarters in the bilges was less than eighteen inches. They squirmed in and lay down, trying to avoid the small puddles of oil and water that had drained from above them.

"Damn tight," Vuylsteke said.

"Yeah, but safe," Tretter said. "No fucking Kenyan is ever gonna come down here. Even if they did, they could be standing right on top of us there and never know we were down here."

Above them, and all around the engine room, equipment hummed along doing its designed duty, which wasn't much now. Mostly there were generators maintaining the batteries, and a few bilge pumps.

Perez lay a short way from the other two. He was at the spot where there was one true access into the bilges under the platform. But only an experienced *Turner* crewman who was supposed to check that area every few hours would know how to find it.

"So we're on," Vuylsteke said. He was still senior noncom in the trio and felt some responsibility. "We get some sleep now and wait until tomorrow and see what kind of hell we've raised. Be damn nice to be a fly on the wall somewhere when they wake up and find both their watch guys dead as roadkill skunks in July."

Perez laughed softly. "Oh, yeah. Did you see how Pita did in that Kenyan ranger? Damn, if there's a fight, I want her to be on my side."

Tretter tried to find a comfortable spot. "Fucking hard steel is giving me fits. Perez, can you find any blankets or padding or anything soft up there in that engineering area that we can lay on? Hell, we got us fourteen, sixteen hours to stay in this place."

Vuylsteke waved at Perez. "Yeah, see what you can find. Nobody gonna be down here for hours, maybe not at all."

Perez groaned, but moved up to the grating. They could hear him walking around. Five minutes later, he came down with three blankets, two pillows, and a pair of flashlights.

"Damned engineers getting soft," he said. "I found them so I get a pillow. You guys can fight over the other one."

"Let's figure out what to do next," Vuylsteke said. "Is tonight a done deal, or do we go topside and make some more trouble?"

"How?" Perez asked. "We don't even know where the fuck these guys are bunked down."

"We could check the coops," Tretter said.

"Hell, they'll be in the Captain's cabin and officer country," Vuylsteke said. "How many you suppose are here?"

"My guess, two dozen," Perez said. "Not enough to defend the ship, but they won't expect an attack on her from the Navy since they got all of them hostages."

"Hey, just thought that we didn't see any dead bodies up there," Tretter said. "We figured there must have been a hundred and fifty of our guys got on the buses. Where the hell are the others?"

"Overboard," Vuylsteke said. "They probably tossed the dead and bad wounded into the bay." He paused, and they thought about that. "So, what the hell are we going to do next?"

"Still got a lot of night left—two, three hours," Perez said. "Let's go find some of these murdering shitheads and kick ass."

Wednesday, July 21

0310 hours
RX Military Headquarters
Nairobi, Kenya

General Umar Maleceia sat on the front edge of his desk in his large office. He looked at the clock, and then at the door. There were two sharp raps; then it opened, and four military police came in ushering a man still in his flight suit but without his hard helmet.

The man was strained and tired, and had a laceration on the side of his head. He'd had no medical attention. The pilot came to attention eight feet from his commander and snapped a salute.

"Captain Ngala Mawai reporting to the general as ordered, sir."

Maleceia stared at the pilot, who now showed signs of sweat on his forehead. The pilot lowered his salute when it was not returned, and stood at a braced attention staring straight ahead.

"Look at me," General Maleceia shouted.

Mawai turned, looked at the general, and blinked several times. His face worked a moment.

"Tell me about the attack," Maleceia said, his voice gentler.

Mawai relaxed a little. "General, sir. Three of us lifted off on your orders proceeding at top speed to Mombasa. About sixty miles from the coast our radar showed four enemy fighter aircraft in the sky with two coming toward us. Their missiles have much greater range and speed than ours do, sir, but we hoped to be able to get within range before they fired.

"Then we were lit up by the enemy radar, and a moment later my two wingmen's planes exploded with direct missile hits. We had no warning."

"Then what did you do, Captain?"

"I felt more of the radar on my craft, so I took quick evasive action to avoid being targeted. By then it was two superior fighters against me. I decided it would be better to return to base and have one MiG left rather than try to outgun the faster, better armed fighters."

"Who ordered you to return to base?"

"No one, my general. It was a tactical decision to save my aircraft."

"As well as to save your miserable life. Do you think you have served the new government well, Captain?"

"I have always served the government. It is my life. I do your bidding. I also rely on my tactical decision making for the safety of my aircraft for the glory of a greater Kenya."

General Maleceia turned his back on the pilot, reached for a cigar from his desk, snipped off one end, and lit it. Only after several puffs did he turn around. He gripped the long cigar in his mouth so tightly he almost bit it in two. In his right hand, he held his .40-caliber automatic. As the pilot's eyes widened, Maleceia shot him twice in the chest, then once more as he fell.

Maleceia stared at the dead man a moment, then shrugged. He turned to his second in command, Colonel Jomo Kariuki.

"Colonel, get this trash out of my office and clean up my carpet. I hate a bloodstained rug."

15

Wednesday, July 21

0014 hours
USS *Monroe*, CVN 81
Off Nairobi, Kenya

Lieutenant Blake Murdock watched as the Navy doctor finished patching up Red Nicholson's left arm. There were three slices in his upper arm where they figured 9mm rounds had ripped through a half inch of flesh and gone on their way. The blood was major, the damage minor.

"Why didn't you say you were hit?" Murdock asked his lead scout.

"You'd call off the war for a few scratches?" Red asked.

The doctor shook his head. "You damn SEALs don't say die unless you've at least got an arm blown off. What is it with you guys?"

"Too damn stupid to know any better, Doc," Nicholson said. "L-T, we started planning for the assault on the *Roy Turner* yet?"

"About ready to."

"This man is confined to his bed for at least three days," the doctor said.

Red laughed.

"Thanks, Doc," Murdock said. "We'll take that under advisement. If this guy can walk, I need him. His left arm never does much anyway. You should see him fire an MP-5 without the suppressor with one hand. He's good. Thanks, Commander. Appreciate your concern."

Red sat up and slid to the floor.

Murdock tossed him a clean desert cammie shirt, and the two walked out of sick bay and up to their SEAL gathering spot.

"How's Ronson?" Red asked.

"Patched and hurting, but no way he'll stay behind. Magic Brown says he's healed up already, but he won't let anybody look at his leg. They're just three crazy sonso-bitches." He grinned as he said it, and Red grinned too.

In the SEAL assembly area, half the guys had sacked out waiting for Murdock. When he and Red came in, there was a small cheer. That woke up the rest of them.

Murdock glanced around at the fifteen men. "You guys look terrible, like you need a late-night supper. You don't even have to wash your hands. We have a man to lead you to the mess. Then I'd suggest a quick shower and about eight hours of sack time. We have no data on the next job, liberating the *Roy Turner*. Now get out of here. I'll let you know when we get together again. Later today sometime. Meanwhile, I've got to have a small chat with Don Stroh. I'll see if he's been talking with our President lately. Now get out of here."

He sat in one of the chairs next to the long table, and looked over at DeWitt.

"Two down, two to go, Two-IC. How's your squad?"

"Fine. You've got the casualties. Can Red do it?"

"Oh, yes, not all that serious. Lots of blood, though. They stuffed a pint in him while we were down there."

"Stroh?"

"Yep, if we can find his digs. Let's go look."

Don Stroh was in the stateroom of a commander he'd bumped. He'd been reading some printouts when the pair knocked on his door. It had taken two guides to help them find the spot. Murdock was sure he couldn't go there by himself again. A carrier was just too fucking big.

"Well done, men," Stroh said, "We're listing the forty-six missing personnel from the *Roy Turner* as either KIA or MIA. We have witnesses who saw the Kenyans murder our badly wounded on the ship. However, there may be as many as ten men who were not on board the *Turner* when the attack came. A number of men were on liberty that evening. We don't know how many of them got on board before the attack."

"So we could have over forty KIAs," Murdock said. "Bastards."

"We're debriefing the *Turner*'s officers now. They figure there might have been a dozen of the attackers killed. Probably ten or twelve of our men got weapons out of the armory and used them."

"Fine, what's next?" DeWitt asked. Then he yawned.

"Next, gentlemen, is a stiff shot of bourbon and a 'well done.'" He took a bottle from a desk drawer and poured three shots in drinking glasses.

"I really shouldn't," Murdock said, and tossed it down. DeWitt matched his CO. "Damn, it's Coke," Murdock said.

"Yeah, Navy regs. Well, we've got a go from the President on the capture of the *Turner*. The wording says at our earliest convenience. When would you gentlemen say that would be?"

"First dark tomorrow, or today, I guess that is," Murdock said. "About eighteen hours from now."

DeWitt nodded. "Yeah, time to rest up some, get plans made, and round up the special gear we're going to need."

"Like what?" Stroh asked.

"Tell you when we figure it out," Murdock said.

Stroh yawned. "That's good with me. Now get yourselves some sack time so you'll be awake by tonight. You've got a whole damn task force waiting for your command." He grinned. "Christ, I love this. I was a corporal in the Army. I love giving orders to these officers. One thing a full admiral doesn't like, and that's getting his orders passed up from you guys, a pair of chickenshit lieutenants."

Murdock heard him and tried to laugh, but it never quite came out. "Tell him things are tough all over. Anytime he wants to trade jobs and rank, let me know."

The two SEALs waved at Don Stroh, who outranked everyone on board including the admiral, and headed for the officers' dirty mess where there would be steak to order or anything else they wanted.

"Food, then the sack," DeWitt said.

Murdock looked at him. "How's that broken arm holding up?"

"Fine. How's your shrapnel ass doing?"

They both laughed. The jabs referred to their wounds during their Firestorm mission. Murdock pushed open the dirty mess door and hurried inside. Food would be good, sleep even better.

Wednesday, July 21

0346 hours
Dockside *Roy Turner*
Mombasa, Kenya

The three U.S. Navy sailors worked up to the mid deck and explored cautiously. They knew the ship like a private playground. They were amazed that there were no more guards in all of the dozens of long companionways and decks.

"Officer country," Vuylsteke whispered. They crept that way expecting a guard. No one was there.

Each of the three had a firearm now, and each a knife pushed in a belt loop. Tretter tried the door to one of the "jungles," rooms for four officers of lower rank. The door was not locked. He edged it inward an inch to look around. A night-light illuminated the area. Four men slept in the bunks. Gear and weapons had been laid within reach.

Perez took a look, then dropped to the floor and slid into the room. He found a bag of grenades, two pistols and magazines, and a silenced stubby little submachine gun and two magazines almost a foot long. He grabbed all of them and wormed his way toward the door while still on the floor.

He was two feet from the door when one of the Kenyans in the lower bunk sat up, said something in Swahili, then fell back and kept on sleeping. Perez had the submachine gun aimed at him in an instant, then lowered it, and worked his way out of the room.

"Yeah, some firepower," Perez said slinging the submachine-gun carry-strap over his shoulder. The huge magazine had to hold sixty rounds, he decided.

They slipped away from the spot, and continued on to the officers' mess. There were no cooks on duty. The lights were all on. They found what they wanted, and pushed it all into a gunny sack that had held potatoes. They took a half-dozen loaves of bread that had been unfrozen, half a cured ham, six bags of potato chips, jars of jam, silverware, apples, oranges, and a case of Coca-Cola.

They all grinned. They had really struck a blow against the enemy.

Ten minutes later, they were in the bilges in aux two. They ate until they couldn't face another sandwich, then turned out their flashlights and went to sleep.

It was morning when they awoke. The only way they could tell was by their wristwatches. They said it was after 0800.

"Could be some company soon," Vuylsteke said. "I've been listening, but I can't hear a damned thing. We're so far down here we won't hear their outrage at two of their men missing and that guy's fancy sub-gun and the grenades gone. Damn, I'd like to see what they do."

The answer came quickly.

They heard the firing from above through the doors, compartments, and decks. It gradually came closer. They identified the stuttering of sub guns, and the flat crack of the AK-47, which was hard not to recognize if a person had heard it before.

"Now we know what they do when they get mad," Perez said. "Hell, it ain't their ship. What do they care if they shoot up the place."

A moment later, one of the watertight doors above them came open. It was thirty feet forward. The blasting of a submachine gun came as a surprise, and made all three men duck and put their hands over their heads where they lay.

The gun chattered six rounds, then six more, then the door clanged shut.

"Looks like they've had their say," Tretter snorted. "Just

wait until tonight when we start lobbing these fucking
grenades into their living quarters. We could come close to
wiping them out if we really try."

Vuylsteke nodded. He was senior here and he still had
some responsibility. Hell, he was the commander, the
Captain of the *Roy Turner,* since he was the highest-rated
man on board.

"Yeah, tonight after things quiet down a little, we're
going to try real hard to cut down the odds," Vuylsteke said.

On the quarterdeck of the *Roy Turner,* Lieutenant Elijah
Koinange stared at the body of his top enlisted man and
scowled. Who had done this? One guard missing, and now
the sergeant stabbed to death. Were there raiders on board?
Had they stolen anything? How had they gotten on and off?
Or were they still on board?

Koinange shivered when he thought about making a radio
report to the general. What could he say? No, better to take
care of the matter himself. He would make a complete
search of the ship starting on the top deck and working
down. He knew little of ships, but he learned quickly. He
could ask a Navy friend to come help.

He shook his head. That Navy friend was on a break-
away ship that had put to sea an hour before the coup. No
help there.

Koinange had twenty-two men left. The colonel, or rather
the general, had said that would be plenty of men to guard
the ship. The general had been confident that the Americans
would make no move against the ship while he had all of the
hostages.

First the search. Yes, a search. He would order his men to
fire at anything that moved or made a noise. That had to
work. If they found nothing, he would have half the men on
guard at night. Yes, that would be a help. Surely they would
find any of the Americans who had hidden aboard when the
capture was made. Surely they would.

Wednesday, July 21

0926 hours
USS *Monroe*, CVN 81
Off Nairobi, Kenya

The sixteen SEALs of the Third Platoon sat and stood around the big table in their assembly area. Several desert cammie shirts had been unbuttoned and sleeves rolled up in the warm room. The air conditioner kept blasting away, but it was no match for the sullen heat of the near-equatorial spring.

"Hell, yes, we could go in with three hundred Marines from the amphib and smother the place, but we don't need them," Magic Brown said. "How many of you been on a frigate before?"

Every hand but one went up.

"So, we know something about the craft. Them shit-kickers on board are Army dudes, for gawd's sake."

"Yeah, Magic, but they been there for three-four days now," Bishop said. "They ain't stupid. They must know somebody will be calling."

"That's why I say a quick hit with grappling hooks on both ends of the ship and the pier just after dark, and we've got the surprise element going for us. We could have half the bastards dead before they knew we were there."

"Use the silencers on everything including the Mark 23 pistols?" DeWitt asked.

"Damn right," Magic said. "We won't even need the sniper rifles or the MGs. Leave them on the ship. All of us with silenced weapons, we go in and do them."

Murdock stood. "We've heard most of the arguments by now. I agree, we don't need the Marines off that amphib. We need to go in silently. The ship is about a klick, maybe a klick and a half from that inlet we were in yesterday. How do we get there?"

"Not the damned air cushions," Fernandez said. "Too fucking noisy."

"Any Special Boat Squadron runners on this task force?"

Jaybird Sterling asked. "We could use two of those new ten-meter RIBs. They do forty knots, and could get us in fast to within a klick. Then we swim in from there for a silent attack."

"We'll find out about the RIBs, Jaybird," Murdock said.

"I still like the IBSs," Nicholson said. "Hell, we can get eighteen knots out of them moving in, then cut it to five, and be on top of the damn Kenyan motherfuckers before they know what hit them."

"We brought four IBSs, so we still have two," DeWitt said.

Don Stroh came into the room, and everyone fell quiet.

"Hey, don't let me stop you. As you were, as you Navy guys say. I'm slumming."

Ed DeWitt went over to him and they talked a minute. Then Don left the room.

"He's going to check on the RIBs," DeWitt said. "He'll shake them loose if anyone has any. Twenty warships out here, should be some of them somewhere."

Murdock resumed the discussion. "Okay, so we're on-site. We stick with the silenced weapons?"

Most of the men nodded.

"Damn right," Ronson said.

Murdock squinted a moment at some notes on the table. "The ship is tied up, so we don't need to worry about the bridge, the engine room, or the main control room. We just have to root out the fucking rangers. How?"

"We start at the top and work down to the weather deck; then we take them one deck at a time," Ken Ching said. "Most of the bastards are going to be holed up in officer country, and the officers' mess eating their brains out."

"I'd Roger that," DeWitt said. "We can go to the quarterdeck, and spread both ways fore and aft. Then we use our Motorolas, and when that deck is clear we move down one. We can clear the coops and the missile storage areas quickly. Any idea how many men will be there?"

"Two dozen, my guess," Ron Holt said.

"They should have twice that many," Doc Ellsworth said. "This is the only U.S. property they still control."

"What about the embassy?" Ted Yates asked.

"I mean anything that's worth ransoming," Doc said.

A half hour later, Don Stroh came in grinning. "Hey, you've got your choice. The amphib has three of the RIBs if you want them."

"Let's use the damned IBSs," Ricochet Lampedusa said. "Hell, we know them, we can get eighteen knots for four klicks, and not make any more noise than some of the small diesel fishing boats that must be working this area. Then we get close, we go down to five knots and slip up on them without a mother-licking sound."

"You lick what you want to, Lampedusa," somebody called, and they all laughed.

"Okay," Murdock said. "We'll go with the IBSs and all silenced weapons. This is all house-to-house killing fields, so the MP-5's will be handy. We can get plenty more from supply, I checked on that. Double ammo, no rebreathers, cammies, so no wet suits."

Don Stroh went out the door, and returned a minute later with a full commander who carried a briefcase and a sheaf of papers.

"Commander Pollard, glad you could come," Murdock said. "Men, meet Commander Pollard, CO of the USS *Colgan*. We've got a two-hour drill on a frigate, how to get around in it. The tough spots to defend, where most of the enemy probably will be, and what to try not to destroy if you don't have to."

The commander rolled out drawings of the ship with overlays that showed in detail the areas of access, and how to get from one part of the frigate to another. The SEALs crowded around and started memorizing everything they could about the layout of a U.S. Navy frigate.

At the end of the two hours, every SEAL in the room knew a lot more about how he would attack the *Roy Turner*.

The commander rolled up his displays and held up his hand.

"Men, I wish you luck, and keep the damned machine operable. As soon as you have the vessel secure, a skeleton crew from my frigate will be boarding the *Turner* to sail her out to sea. Be careful, but be thorough. Find all of those murdering bastards. I don't want to lose any of my crewmen."

16

Wednesday, July 21

General Umar Maleceia paced his office, blowing one blast of cigar smoke after another into the already too-warm room.

"How could they do it? I sent two hundred men in there to put down that raid on the prison, and all hundred and sixty prisoners still got away? You're telling me that they all escaped and got on U.S. Navy hovercraft and charged out to sea? The one hundred and sixty hostages I had in the prison all got away?"

"Yes, my general. There were the jets strafing the prison, and then they had direct hits on our trucks that brought in the men. The men couldn't fight back against hundreds of rounds of twenty-millimeter cannon fire. I'm sorry, my general."

"You're sorry? Hell, we lose this fight and you'll be hanged, you know that, don't you?"

The colonel nodded.

"So, what do we have left? The ship, the stinking little frigate we captured at dockside. How many men we have guarding it?"

"There are twenty-four men under Lieutenant Elijah Koinange. He's a fine officer."

"Have you heard from him today?"

"No, sir."

"Didn't you give him one of our new radios?"

"Yes, sir. I'll get in contact with him at once."

"If the bastards rescued the crew from the prison, sure as hell they'll try for the ship too."

Colonel Kariuki saluted and hurried out the door.

General Maleceia continued to pace. He'd had it in his grasp. He'd had the embassy and forty hostages. Then he'd had the ship and a hundred and sixty hostages. What the hell went wrong? He shook his head, and took a long pull from the glass of bourbon on his desk. Too many things had gone wrong.

There was still time. He would hold the U.S. Navy ship. Send five hundred of his best rangers to pitch camp on the docks with all of their heavy weapons. Yes, that would do it. He looked at the list of the units he had in Mombasa. Not a lot.

He had sent his Fifth Infantry to the prison. A late report showed that they had suffered nearly fifty percent casualties, including more than seventy percent of the officers. That unit was out of service.

The Second Infantry was fifty miles north of Mombasa in a blocking position. Two hundred men, two tanks, and 81mm mortars. Yes. He'd get them moving almost at once.

Colonel Kariuki came rushing into the room, then slowed. He held up a piece of paper.

"General, it seems there have been some attacks on our guards left on the American ship. Two men were killed last night, and some arms and grenades were stolen. Lieutenant Koinange has no explanation other than that there must be some American sailors hiding on the ship and attacking during the night."

General Maleceia threw his drink across the room. The glass shattered on the far wall.

"Idiots! Why am I surrounded by idiots? He was told to search the ship and make sure there was no one hiding. Idiot. Have that lieutenant relieved and broken to a corporal with a note on his personnel file that he is never to be promoted any higher.

"Then, send an order to the Second Infantry posted fifty miles north of Mombasa to de-camp and proceed today to the dock beside the American ship. They are to get there before dark, and let their supplies and equipment follow. I want them in place before dark and ready to fight.

"If the Americans try to retake their ship, they will find a new fighting spirit facing them. Go now, Colonel. I'm making it your responsibility to get those troops there on time if you have to carry them on your back."

Colonel Kariuki let a frown tinge his face. "But General, sir. We have less than five hours until full darkness. It will be impossible for any but a few truckloads of the troops to be in place by . . ."

General Maleceia turned, and stared hard at his second in command. The colonel stopped talking, took a deep breath, then ran out of the office.

For the first time in two days, General Umar Maleceia smiled.

1425 hours
Mackinnon Road
Kenya

Major Meru Mudodo looked at the dispatch his radioman had just brought him:

```
MOVE YOUR UNIT AT ONCE TO THE
DOCKS AT MOMBASA NEXT TO CAP-
TURED US NAVY VESSEL. YOU MUST
BE IN PLACE BEFORE DARK TODAY.
USE TRANSPORT. MOVE NOW.
```

He called in his second in command, who read it.

"A joke, sir."

"No joke, not with Colonel Kariuki's name on it. Get the troops alerted now. We move out in fifteen minutes. How many trucks do we have?"

"Six big ones, maybe five smaller that will run. Sir, it's over fifty miles to Mombasa and at this time of day, the roads will be crowded, and it's market day, and—"

"We use sirens and gunfire and move everyone any way we can. We must be on that dock before dark and ready to fight. Issue ammunition to squad leaders. They are to issue it to the men ten miles outside of Mombasa. Move, now, Captain, move."

They didn't leave camp in fifteen minutes. Two of the big trucks wouldn't start. Mechanics worked on them, and they were ordered to make them start and bring their loads of men as quickly as possible.

That left four heavy trucks, each jammed with twenty men. Four of the personnel carriers were working, and could each carry ten men. Three utility rigs held four men each.

It was nearly two hours before the convoy pulled onto the road. Major Mudodo led them. He punched his utility rig up to forty miles an hour, but found the big trucks couldn't keep up with him. He slowed to thirty miles an hour and established that, then gradually crept up to thirty-five. At that rate they would make the fifty miles in two hours. It was market day. The road was jammed.

That would make it 1815, just to get to the outskirts of Mombasa. If he remembered right, he knew the way to the docks, but Mombasa was a big city, the traffic that time of day would be terrible, and they would have only an hour left then to darkness. If they made it to the docks by 1900, it would be a miracle. That was the same time for sunset that day.

He crept the speed up to forty miles an hour, but the convoy fell behind. Captain Mudodo swore, and told the driver to ease off to thirty again.

Long before they came to Mombasa itself, the road was jammed with market day people going home. His driver was constantly on the horn, and twice the captain had fired a burst from his Uzi submachine gun into the sky to move people aside.

The sun went down a half hour before they came to the Kipevu Causeway to get onto Mombasa Island. They still had three kilometers to travel down the harbor frontage road to Pier 12. Captain Mudodo wondered how long his military career would last. He had gone over to General Maleceia reluctantly, but at the time it seemed the best thing to do.

Now he was questioning it. He had 132 men with what ammunition they could carry and some in reserve, but not much. If it came to a firefight, he couldn't hold out for long. He prayed that 132 men standing guard over the ship would be enough.

1840 hours
USS *Monroe*, CVN 81
Off Mombasa, Kenya

Lieutenant Blake Murdock had made a final inspection of his men. Ed DeWitt had done the same. Each SEAL had a silenced weapon, and his silenced Mark 23 pistol. They wore their darker jungle cammies, and had camouflage paint in various shades on their faces, especially their ears and noses, which could catch light easily. This was billed as a dry operation, so they didn't have their rebreathers or wet suits.

Murdock had everyone in the two IBSs by his Time of Departure, and now the fifteen-foot-long Zodiac-type rubber boats slashed through calm seas toward the coast. The *Monroe* had edged to within four miles of the shore, but would come no closer. At eighteen knots, the IBSs could cover the distance to the Mombasa bay in twelve to fifteen minutes.

"Should be dark right about 1900," Murdock told Jaybird.

"That gives us the run up to the ship in the dark, so we should be invisible," Jaybird said. "Hope that Kenyan Navy patrol boat isn't snooping around."

"We've got the SATCOM, Holt?"

"Right, L-T, up and running."

"We've got two Hornet FA-18's for air cover if we need them. Rather do this quietly, but you never can tell."

The whispers stopped. A brisk wind gave them a small chop to the ocean now, but it didn't slow them down. It meant they held on to the handholds a little tighter.

"Remember, the rail is only twenty to twenty-four feet off the water, depending on what part of the ship we hit," Murdock said. "We have the blind spot on the port side from amidships aft for twenty feet.

"Nobody on the bridge or the flight deck on the fantail can see us. But then I don't expect these Army guys to have a Navy-type watch."

Soon they passed the little town called Likoni on the left-hand side of the channel. It looked about the same. They were quiet now, and darkness was complete. They throttled back to twelve knots to make less noise, and less of a wake in case anyone watched for them.

At twelve knots, it would take a little longer, but their approach had to be quiet. They figured about three and a half klicks to the pier where the *Roy Turner* was berthed. Another twelve to fifteen minutes, maybe five more than that.

The second IBS trailed Murdock's boat by twenty yards. Ed DeWitt was ready with his squad. They would go up the stern onto the chopper flight deck and secure it, then work forward.

Silence was the key. Even the grapple hooks they would throw over the rails had been wrapped with rope to cushion the sound when they hit metal.

The mission looked to be on schedule and on track to Murdock. Another ten minutes and they would be there.

Then Murdock's boat engine went dead.

Ken Ching swore and bent over the thirty-five-hp outboard trying to get it started. DeWitt idled his boat up beside them.

Ken Ching swore again. He tried ten times. It wouldn't start. Murdock had been checking his watch. He waved to DeWitt. The other boat came up and bumped them. The men held the two craft together.

"Hey, sailor, give a guy a tow?" Murdock asked.

"Sure, if that means I have salvage rights, law of the sea."

"We're in port."

"Oh."

A minute later DeWitt's boat growled along on full throttle towing the second IBS. They were making about five knots.

"Makes us thirty minutes late getting on-site," Jaybird said.

Murdock nodded. "If they don't know we're coming, thirty minutes don't mean squat. Let's see how it plays."

17

Wednesday, July 21

1920 hours
Dockside *Roy Turner*
Mombasa, Kenya

Gunner's Mate First Class Pete Vuylsteke eased up and looked down the passageway. Nobody. It was dark outside. They hadn't heard anyone in their section of the *Turner* for an hour. Probably gorging themselves on the chief's mess stores.

He lifted up from the ladder and ran across the passage that led to the quarterdeck and into the aft section of the ship. He heard Perez and Tretter right behind him. They went down a companionway, up two more ladders, and came out where he wanted to be.

He flattened out on the broad deck aft of the stack on the superstructure. They were in the open on the top of the ship, and with a minimum of movement they could cover either side of the frigate.

They had brought their weapons. None of them were silenced, and if they started shooting, they had to be able to defend themselves until they could get down to the roof of the hangar, where they could take a flying dive into the bay.

"Yeah, let's do it," Perez had said. "I'm getting too fucking tired of sitting in the bilge. My ass hurts. At least we'll be in the open."

They had talked it over all afternoon, and when it had

started getting dark outside, they'd worked up to the top deck. It was so easy, they wondered where all the Kenyans were.

They spotted some of them prowling the weather deck.

"Damn poor place for lookouts," Tretter said.

"What the hell, they're shit-kickers, not sailors," Vuyl-steke said. He grinned. "Hey, you guys know that, by rules of the sea, I am now the Captain and commanding officer of the *Roy Turner*."

Tretter snorted.

Perez laughed. "Be damned, you're the senior man, all right. Okay, Captain, what the hell we doing next?"

Before any of them could answer they heard the growl of a truck with lights off edging onto the pier.

"Oh, shit, reinforcements. Tretter, can you kill the driver with your AK?"

It was a fifty-yard shot at most. Tretter cranked in a round, sighted on the right-hand side of the glinting wind-shield, and fired. The round slammed through the windshield, but missed the driver. Tretter's second round punched through the man's chest, and the truck stalled.

The two shots from the ship brought a yell from a ranger on the deck below near the frigate's torpedo tubes. Vuyl-steke aimed the shotgun at him and fired. The load of double-aught buck didn't spread as much as smaller pellets, and six of the thirteen slugs hit the ranger in the chest and slammed him halfway over the rail, where he hung like a ripped rag doll.

They saw no one else on deck. They had the high ground. The only way anyone could get above them would be to climb the mast.

"We just started the shit hitting the fan," Perez said. "Now the fun begins."

They saw a line of men come out of the shadows where the truck had stalled and walk forward.

"Two more rounds in the radiator to kill the truck," Vuylsteke said. "Then nail some of those troops coming up the pier."

The men in green were out of range of the short guns, but

they wouldn't be long. The three sailors also had the bag of hand grenades. Perez had counted them the night before, twenty-one in all. They could do a lot of damage.

The sailors began taking return fire from the troops on the pier. They edged back so the superstructure would protect them. Tretter moved up now and then to send off a pair of shots into the growing line of men.

"Close enough yet?" Vuylsteke asked.

"Not for the sub-gun, the shotgun, or the grenades. But we can all use our long guns."

"How far can you throw one of them bombs?" Vuylsteke asked.

"I used to play some baseball, outfield. Hell, guess I can get it out there sixty yards."

"Give one a try," Vuylsteke said. "Remember, you'll get a bounce on that concrete."

Perez grinned and pulled the pin from the smooth round M-67 grenade, then lifted up and threw it like a baseball with plenty of body in it. He dropped down at once.

Vuylsteke lifted up to watch the bomb. It went about thirty yards down the pier, bounced another ten yards, and went off while it was still in the air.

"An air burst," Vuylsteke yelped. "Must have cut down half a dozen of them bad guys down there."

"Take a shot," Perez said, tossing two grenades to Vuylsteke. He pitched one, not as far as Perez's had gone, but the troops had moved up ten yards and he saw them scatter when they heard the bomb hit the concrete. It came down before it exploded, and he heard a dozen men yell in pain and confusion.

"Aft," Tretter bellowed.

Perez turned, holding the sub-gun, and hit the trigger. Two green-clad Kenyan rangers had just come past the 76mm gun mount. Perez squeezed the trigger on the little jammer and spewed out ten rounds before he let up. One of the rangers went down, the other dove the other way. Tretter nailed him with a round from the AK-47.

"Get their weapons and ammo," Vuylsteke said.

"Good idea," Perez said, and ran bent over to the two

dead men and brought back their two AK-47's and six magazines of rounds.

"Tretter, keep watch fore and aft. We'll entertain the troops below."

Each one threw a hand grenade, and before it exploded they had the AK-47's up laying down a deadly field of fire at the string of rangers who had stopped moving forward. They were still less than halfway down the side of the frigate.

Murdock and his SEALs were three hundred yards away from the softly lit *Roy Turner* when they heard firing. Jaybird looked at his commander, who held up his hands in an I-don't-know gesture. They kept moving at five knots.

"Hand grenades," Murdock said. "Somebody's got a shooting gallery going up there."

A few minutes later, they heard the flat crack of rifle fire.

"AK-47's, you can bet your bippy," Holt said.

They all huddled low in the black rubber boats. The motors had been muffled down to a quiet rumble. Now the firing onshore blocked out any sound the motors made.

They had worked out the debarking earlier. DeWitt would power them up to the port side of the frigate midships. They would throw up their grappling hooks, and get four men up ropes quickly to the weather dock. Those would cover the other four coming up.

DeWitt would take his powered IBS to the stern, send his men up grapple-hook ropes there, and work forward.

"Who is shooting at who?" Jaybird asked.

Murdock shook his head. "Whoever it is is doing us one hell of a big favor. All eyes will be on the dock, leaving us home free."

They were thirty yards from the ship when two dark-clad men ran out the quarterdeck door. They didn't look into the harbor; rather they looked up at the superstructure and fired shotguns that way.

"Take them," Murdock whispered. Two men with si-lenced M-4A1 carbines rose up and fired three-round bursts almost at the same time. The two Kenyan shotgunners slammed against the bulkhead and dropped. One began to crawl away. Another three-round burst stopped him.

On the aft deck of the superstructure, Vulysteke saw they were running short on hand grenades. They had kept the Kenyan troopers back so they couldn't get on board the *Turner*.

"Check the port side," Vuylsteke told Tretter. Tretter edged across the flat deck, and looked down on the water side.

"Jesus H. Kerist." He rolled back, and couldn't talk for a minute. "Hey, coming on the port side, not twenty yards off, two black rubber boats. One's towing the other. Sure as hell they're SEALs. I've seen them suckers train. They'll be on board in two or three minutes."

"Good, let's beat back these green guys a little more," Vuylsteke said. "Maybe we'll get our asses saved after all without a swim."

They used the AK-47's, with hand grenades thrown in to mix things up. There was no heavy-weapons response. Vuylsteke thought that strange, but they kept up the fire for another three minutes.

Tretter took another look to port.

"Yeah, four of them up ropes, and more down on the fantail. Damn, we got SEALs moving all over."

"Let them know we're here so we don't get shot," Perez said.

Then they heard the soft chuffs of the silenced weapons. A minute later, all three sailors were on the port side watching the SEALs. One looked up at the superstructure.

"Hey, you SEALs," Vuylsteke bellowed. "Look up here."

They waited a minute. The SEALs hosed down three Kenyan rangers who ran out of the quarterdeck door.

"SEALs, damnit, you've got some help up here," Perez screamed. "Three Americans up here."

One of the SEALs swung his weapon upward and looked that way.

"Don't shoot, we're Americans. We're crew on here who were on liberty when she was taken," Tretter brayed.

The SEAL hesitated. "Yeah? Who is Beavis's buddy?" the SEAL asked.

"Butthead, who else?" Vuylsteke yelled. "Now, don't shoot us. There's about two hundred troops out front on the dock. We've been trying to hold them off."

"Stay low and keep the topside free of any rangers," Jaybird Sterling called. "We'll mop up down here." He touched the mike at his throat. "L-T, we've got three friendlies on the top of the superstructure just aft of the stack. Evidently crewmen who got back on board. They say there are about two hundred more troops out front near the pier."

"Roger that. We'll clean up on board. Get two men topside and harass those troops with some fire."

Jaybird motioned to Lampedusa, and they scurried up a steel ladder that clung to the side of the ship below the 76mm gun mount.

Topside they found the three sailors, and kept low to the deck.

"Fucking glad to see you guys," Vuylsteke called.

Jaybird slid to the deck beside him. "Glad we're here. Where are those troops?" Vuylsteke pointed them out. About half of them had rushed into the shadows of the warehouse adjacent to the pier. More crowded around the pier just down from the bow of the ship.

The SEALs and the sailors all had found cover to use to hide behind so they could fire at the few Kenyan rangers who moved gradually down the pier toward the ship.

"Wish we had the MG," Jaybird said. "You guys got rifles?"

"AK-47's courtesy of our Kenyan friends," Tretter said. "We still got a dozen hand grenades." He threw one toward the Kenyans, and they edged back as the bomb went off just out of range.

"Let's discourage them," Jaybird said. He had a carbine for the mission, and unscrewed the silencer. "Better range," he said. Then he began sniping at the men on the pier.

Soon there were five weapons firing at the Kenyan rangers. They looked confused, not sure whether to storm

the boat and leap on board, or stay where they were and fire
back.

Return fire against the ship was light. Vuylsteke decided
they didn't want to risk hitting their own men who were still
on board. Gradually the Kenyan soldiers edged back away
from the ship. More of them ran for the deep shadows in
front of the warehouse.

"Let's give them something to think about," Lampedusa
said. He unhooked a Willy Peter hand grenade from his
harness, pulled the pin, and threw it as far as he could
toward the rangers. The grenade went off with a spectacular
starburst of furiously burning white phosphorus. Half of it
reached the troops spread out on the dock, and they
screamed with pain as the unstoppable phosphorus burned
through cloth, flesh, and equipment. More than a dozen
Kenyan rangers took off, running for the safety of the
warehouse across the pier.

On the weather deck below, Murdock's men hugged the
starboard side of the *Roy Turner*'s superstructure on both
flanks of the quarterdeck door. Red Nicholson crept up,
tossed a grenade into the quarterdeck, and leaned back. The
bomb went off with a roaring splatter of shrapnel; then
Nicholson and Magic Brown charged into the companionway with their MP-5's on auto fire. Magic saw two rangers
on the deck trying to get back to their feet. He triggered a
three-round burst into each of them.

Nicholson saw a man running out the far end of the
companionway, but his rounds reached the area too late.
"Quarterdeck clear," Red said into his mike. The two
SEALs worked down to the crossing companionway and
paused.

Murdock had sent Ross Lincoln aft toward the point
where the hangar was built out solidly to the rail. Lincoln
darted forward and stopped, then moved again. A Kenyan
fired once from behind some fixtures alongside the bulkhead. A searing burst from the Kenyan's AK-47 missed.
Lincoln used his M-4A1 on automatic, washing down the
free area under the fixtures, and heard a scream of pain.

He charged the area, and saw a Kenyan ranger bringing

up his rifle. Lincoln nailed him to the deck with a three-round burst of 9mm rounds into his chest.

On the fantail, DeWitt's squad had the small flight deck in control. Then two weapons fired from the chopper hangar. DeWitt saw one of the big doors rolled half open, ran up the side, and dove through it with his night-vision goggles in place. The total blackness of the inside of the hangar came into a dull green focus.

DeWitt saw the second SH-60B LAMPS chopper tied down. Just behind it someone fired a shotgun, but the pellets slammed out the open door. DeWitt missed his Mossburg shotgun. Instead he carried an MP-5 suppressed, and blasted a six-round burst into the Kenyan hiding there. The man groaned, then spilled to the side as he hit the deck and lay still.

DeWitt rolled to one side and waited. Three rounds from an automatic rifle splattered the spot where he had been moments before. He saw the shooter behind some boxes on the far side of the hangar. He returned fire with two six-round bursts and waited. A moment later he heard a gush of air; then a body hit the floor and a weapon clattered on the non-slip hangar deck.

DeWitt looked around. In the soft green glow he made sure that there were no more men in the hangar.

"Hangar clear," he said into his mike.

Murdock watched the bridge wing. He'd seen movement there before. Now he studied it with the NVGs. Yes. A man lay on the deck with a weapon. He lifted his silenced MP-5 and drilled the area with a half-dozen rounds, then three more. The man lying there bent in half as if in pain, then flopped on the deck and didn't move.

"Companionway crossing the quarterdeck," Nicholson said. "Do we clear it?"

"Hold," Murdock said. "Let's get the topside clear before we move there. Jaybird, can you get to the bridge?"

The Motorola brought the answer. "Think so, L-T. These fuckers on the dock don't look real interested in boarding and getting killed. We've got five guns up here discouraging them. My guess is no leadership."

"Good. Move to the bridge, leave one SEAL with the sailors. Keep up the fire on the dock."

Jaybird crawled forward under the radar search antennas on the tall masts, and then checked the bridge wing. No activity there. He saw one body that didn't move. He listened. Over the gunfire he could hear no one inside the bridge. He held the MP-5 ready as he stepped over a rail and worked closer to the bridge wing. Satisfied that he could hear no firing or movement from the bridge, he leaped onto the wing and covered the bridge interior. No one was there. He went to the far side and checked. No Kenyans.

"Bridge clear," he said to the mike.

On top of the superstructure midships, Vuylsteke watched the pier. Something had changed out there. He couldn't tell what. He edged further behind his protection. A moment later, he heard running steps, and someone pounded down the weather deck to the rail up near the bridge. A Kenyan with no weapon. He charged the rail, jumped over, and landed two feet below on the concrete dock. He lost his balance and went down. Before he could jump up, two slugs from the crewmen's AK-47's jolted into him and he screamed and tried to crawl toward the warehouse. He made it five yards, then fell on his face and didn't move.

Vuylsteke motioned to the SEAL beside him. "What's happening out front? Almost looks like they are getting organized."

Joe "Ricochet" Lampedusa had seen the activity too. He keyed his mike. "L-T, something is going on out there on the dock. You can't see it yet. I'd say they're getting ready to assault us. If they do, we could use a few more shooters over on the starboard side."

"That's a Roger. If it happens, let me know. Is the topside clear yet? What kind of an onboard Kenyan body count do we have?"

The men keyed in with the number they had done. When Murdock figured the total, he came up with twelve. There had to be more than that on board—unless some of them deserted the ship when the shooting started.

"Bastards are coming," Jaybird said on the Motorola.

"Everyone who can, get starboard and return fire," Murdock said.

Jaybird watched them. There was a line of green-uniformed Kenyans that stretched almost the length of the ship. They came out of the darkness of the long warehouse firing.

Nineteen weapons answered their attack. Six hand grenades sailed into the marching men when they came close enough. The deadly fire of the three sailors and the sixteen SEALs slowed the march, and then pushed the Kenyans back. Seconds later they broke and ran for the darkness they had left.

"Anyone hit?" the Motorola asked. After a pause, Murdock continued. "They'll be back. DeWitt, get two more of your men on the top of the superstructure. The high ground."

"Roger that."

The three sailors slammed in fresh magazines. They had one full one left each, then no more. The SEALs checked their magazines. The men had taken off the suppressors from their carbines. No need for them now, and the added velocity and range would be useful.

"Here they come," Jaybird said.

The line of Kenyan rangers was considerably shorter this time. Murdock figured there were less than a hundred men. The pier was thirty yards wide here. They came out of the darkness at a trot, then broke into a sprint. One after another they were hit by the nineteen guns now shooting at them from the *Turner*. They still came on.

All of the SEALs had grenades. They threw them when the enemy was ten yards from the ship. The toll was heavy. Twenty grenades exploded within a few strides of the men. Dozens went down screaming in pain.

The sharpshooters picked off more of the men who got through the rain of shrapnel. More grenades fell on the concrete and bounced to give off an airburst that shredded more of the green-uniformed men.

Half-a-dozen Kenyans lived through the barrage and jumped onto the deck. Murdock and two men firing from the quarterdeck door cut them down, and dumped three of them back on the dock.

Two more got on board aft, and fell before they could get to any kind of cover.

A moment later the attack ended. "Chase them with lead," Murdock said in his mike. The men on the *Turner* kept firing as the stragglers and the wounded turned and ran for the safety of the shadows. About half of them made it.

The silence that followed the last shots was eerie. The only sound was a gentle lapping of the water on the ship's hull and against the piling of the dock.

Murdock led a quick search of the ship. He found no hiding Kenyan rangers. Then he met the three crewmen, and had them make a second search.

"You men know where they could be. If you find any Kenyans, Jaybird will give us a call and we'll dig them out. You guys have done plenty tonight helping us."

It took them a half hour to figure how to work it, but at last the SEALs, and their three frigate crewmen got the SH-60B helicopter rolled into the hangar beside the other one and the hangar doors closed.

Murdock got Holt to power up the SATCOM, and he radioed the carrier on the "local call" frequency.

"Rover, this is Inflatable."

The answer came back at once. "Yes, Inflatable. Good to hear from you."

"The party's over and it's time to clean up the place. We're ready here for your arrival. Should be no enemy fire. I say again, there is a negative chance of enemy fire. The flight deck is cleared."

18

Wednesday, July 21

2032 hours
Dockside *Roy Turner*
Mombasa, Kenya

Murdock set up a watch with all of the nineteen men. Each one had protection from the pier area, and each one had a weapon pointed that way to reply to any snipers who had stayed behind to harass them.

Minutes ago they had heard the heavy engines as several trucks behind the stalled one at the end of the pier evidently loaded up and moved out.

For ten minutes, all was quiet. Murdock expected the choppers to be coming at any time. Moments later he heard a clanking and a roaring motor, and frowned. Jaybird looked at Murdock and shook his head.

"Sounds bad, L-T."

Murdock motioned to Holt, who gave him the handset to the radio.

"Rover, this is Inflatable, over."

"Yes, Inflatable. Your birds are airborne. ETA about five minutes."

"May have a problem. You have any air cover up?"

"What kind of a problem?"

"We hear a tank moving up toward the pier. Not sure where it is. A dead six-by truck is blocking one entrance to our site. We can't knock out a tank with our weapons."

"Roger that, Inflatable. We have two Hornets up. They should copy. Wildbees One and Two, do you copy?"

"Affirmative, Rover. We're about three minutes away from the port. Can we have some white flares and some red smoke on the target?"

"That's a roger, Wildcats, soon as we see it. My guess is he'll push the dead truck out of the way and be in our lap. What firepower do these tanks have?"

"Inflatable, they could have our old M-48 Pattons. I think some of them came down here. Kenya was our ally, remember. If it's the M-48, they have a one-oh-five-millimeter long gun and can carry over fifty rounds."

"This is Wildbee One in a flyover of the harbor. I see no flares."

"No target yet, Wildbee, but the sound is coming closer. We'll put a flare over the suspect area."

"Coming around with Wildbee Two. Flare now."

Murdock nodded at Magic Brown, who fired a flare over the far end of the pier. The flare burst with daytime brilliance, and began to float down on its parachute. They could see plainly the stalled truck and the blocked roadway behind it. At almost the same time they spotted the ugly snout of a cannon on a tank as it did a locked-tread turn and rolled directly for the truck.

"Now, Wildbee, we have target. No time for smoke. Do you locate?"

"Have it, but past target. Going around. Wildbee One should be coming."

"Wildbee One. Have target acquisition, at required altitude, locking on. Firing. One Maverick away."

Murdock and the SEALs heard the roar of the solid-fuel rocket as it slammed forward at over Mach 1 and almost immediately exploded directly on the still-visible rolling tank. The detonation of the rocket was followed by a roaring secondary blast that bounced the SEALs backward as some of the ammunition inside the tank went off. Shrapnel and chunks of the tank came out of the sky like huge snowballs—only these could kill a guy.

"Good shooting, Wildbees. The tank is no longer a problem."

"That's a Roger. We'll hang out a while to see if anything more develops."

The SEALs kept under cover in case any of the Kenyan rangers had hung back.

Two minutes later they heard the incoming choppers.

"Inflatable, this is Knight One checking on your situation."

"Knight One, all clear here. Not sure how to get lights on the landing pad switched on."

"Right. We have your position. Coming in now with our own lights."

They saw the bird coming. It was an HH-46D/E Sea Knight. As Murdock remembered, it had no armament. It swung over the ship at two hundred feet, then circled and dropped lower as its landing lights lit up the fantail of the *Turner*. It touched down, and at once the side hatch opened and twenty combat-dressed Marines poured out. Ten surged to the starboard side of the flight deck and went prone with rifles aimed at the dock.

The rest of the Marines rushed through the hangar, out to the starboard side amidships, and all the way to the bridge taking up defensive positions.

Three Navy officers had exited the Sea King as well, and hurried into the hangar. The big chopper took off at once, and two minutes later a second Sea King settled onto the *Turner*'s deck. This time twenty sailors rushed out of the chopper and into the hangar. That bird lifted off the moment the hatch closed.

Before the next chopper could land, Murdock heard fire coming from the dock area. Murdock used the SATCOM, and told the FA-18's to stand by. He also put a hold on the last Sea King chopper. Murdock left the quarterdeck and slid to the weather deck beside a pair of Marines.

"Where's the firing coming from?" Murdock asked.

A Marine sergeant pointed to the bow end of the dock where the ruined truck still lay.

"Up there. Sounds like a fifty. They aren't on target yet."

The Marine held an H&K-21A1 machine gun.

Murdock touched his mike. "Let's get ready with some forty-mike-mike. Throw them up there by the busted truck and tank. Somebody's coming."

Moments later Murdock heard the grenade launchers firing. Two HE rounds went off with a crunch just beyond the ruined and still-burning tank. A WP round exploded back farther.

They could hear the rig coming closer now. Not a tank, maybe a truck or jeep-like rig. Then they saw it in the soft moonlight.

"An armored personnel carrier of some kind," Murdock barked. "Hit it."

The SEAL weapons opened fire. The Marines chimed in with their AR-16's and two machine guns. The first volley of rounds made the rig pause. Then they saw someone swing around the top-mounted machine gun.

Two dozen guns fired at the gunner behind the MG. He took three hits and slammed off the side of the rig. Another man reached up for the gun, but the mass of rounds fired made him pull back. More 40mm grenades exploded near the rig. Then two Willy Peter went off on top and beside the lightly defended carrier. The intensely burning phosphorus exploded both the front tires.

A pair of AK-47's pounded off two bursts each from behind the rig, and were met with a withering volley of small-arms rounds. That was the last activity that came from the Kenyan vehicle.

Murdock waited five minutes. Already he had sensed new sounds on the *Turner*. The main engines must be turning over. Murdock took the mike from Holt, who had been beside him during the firing.

"Knight One, I'd say you have a safe landing zone now. That's a go-ahead to land."

"Inflatable, that's a Roger. ETA is about two minutes."

The big chopper settled gracefully to the steady deck aft, and twenty more sailors rushed from the rig into the hangar deck and to their pre-assigned duties on board the fast frigate. Seconds after the men cleared the Sea King, the hatch door slammed and it took off into the black Kenyan sky.

Murdock and the Marines remained as guards on the starboard side of the *Roy Turner*.

More sounds rumbled in the big ship. More lights came on, and Murdock saw lookouts posted where they were supposed to be.

Murdock settled down to wait. On the carrier, they had told him it could take from five minutes to an hour to get the *Turner* ready to ease away from the dock and start its trip down the channel. It would depend on what condition she was in, what damage had been done by the layover, and if any of the vital components had been shot up during the retaking of the craft.

Thirty minutes after the last chopper landed, Murdock saw sailors casting off the lines that tied the *Roy Turner* to the dock. A second lieutenant with the Marines stationed half of them on both sides around the bow and half of them on the stern.

Murdock touched his throat mike. "Looks like we may have a wrap on this part of our job," Murdock said. "Casualty report."

Doc Ellsworth came on the Motorola. "L-T, we've got one serious I know of. Ted Yates took an AK-47 round in his lower leg. One bone is broken for sure, maybe both of them."

"We have a splint?"

"Not that I know of. He's resting easy. We'll wait for the carrier's corpsmen. He's had a shot of morphine."

"Any others? Speak up, guys. I need to know now."

"I scraped my face on this damn no-skid deck, does that count?" Lincoln asked.

"Not if you can see out of both eyes," Murdock said. "Ronson, Nicholson, and Brown. How are those old wounds?"

They each came on pretending to be not sure what their lieutenant was talking about. In the end they all said they hurt like hell but they would live, and wouldn't be cut out on the next phase of the mission.

"Yeah, we've got to do some high and mighty planning on that one," Murdock said. "Politics is gonna be a factor here soon."

Murdock kept his troops on alert until the frigate moved all the way down the channel and out past the little village on the north shore. In a few minutes, the frigate would come alongside the big carrier, and then the troops could really relax.

2220 hours
RX Military Headquarters
Nairobi, Kenya

General Umar Maleceia had taken off his military jacket and loosened his tie. His shirt showed sweat stains in his armpits and a streak down his chest. He held a long cigar, but hadn't been smoking it. His fury fell on his second in command, Colonel Jomo Kariuki, who stood across the desk from the big commander in chief.

"What the hell you mean, you just heard? You sent that tank and the men out after the ship hours ago."

"The phone lines are not—"

"Phone? Why the hell do we have radios?"

"My general, they are not that reliable. I couldn't get through. I phoned and at last—"

General Maleceia threw a paperweight at the colonel, and hit him in the chest. The colonel backed up rubbing the bruise.

"The tank was destroyed by a missile, the personnel carrier was burned up by white phosphorous grenades," he said. "I have confirmed reports that the U.S. Navy ship left the pier, and then left the port at about 2120."

"Gawd damn!" The general dropped into his large leather swivel chair and leaned back. "I've got nothing left to negotiate with. No trump cards, not a gawddamned thing."

"Sir, we still have our Navy ship and two or three aircraft."

"Sure, send them against the task force out there? Hell, they have a carrier with probably a hundred fighters on the decks, and all sorts of helicopters with missiles, and the missiles from all the covering ships. I've seen them operate. Nothing can get through that screen of missiles, let alone three little ships and a couple of outdated fighters."

"Sir, if I may ask. What is next for us?"

Maleceia picked up an in basket from his desk and threw it at the colonel. He missed. "Next? How the hell do I know? It depends what the Americans do. If they're satisfied with getting their ship back and sail away, we might hang on here yet. If they attack, then the whole thing may collapse."

The telephone rang. Colonel Kariuki leaned over and picked it up. He listened a moment, shook his head, and hung up.

"What? What?"

"I'm afraid some bad news. The TV station and the radio station here in Nairobi have fallen to forces loyal to the President. Our men walked away and refused to fight them."

"Bastards. Cowards. Have them all shot."

"I can't do that, my general. They all went back to the President's side. They took the whole barracks with them. About a thousand men here in Nairobi."

General Maleceia stood and paced the length of the room. He went to the windows and looked out.

"Double the guards around the headquarters. Bring out all of the machine-gun mounted small jeeps we have. Get all of our fifty-calibers out and manned. Make damn sure there is no problem with deserters here. If anyone tries to desert, shoot him on the spot."

Colonel Kariuki saluted the stiffened back of his general, and hurried out of the office to put the new guard orders into effect. It would certainly keep anyone from leaving, and it might keep out a minor attack. Did the President still have any units loyal to him that had tanks? He couldn't remember.

The colonel smiled. If things went from this bad to much worse, he had his own plans. He still had his civilian clothes. He also had the Mercedes stashed in a private area not even the enlisted men knew about. He could be out of the complex, through Nairobi, and into Tanzania in two hours. He had a supply of U.S. dollars and South African rand gold pieces that would last him the rest of his life. Yes, it paid to make plans well in advance.

19

Wednesday, July 21

2140 hours
USS *Monroe,* CVN 81
Fifteen miles off Mombasa, Kenya

Murdock and DeWitt stood beside the hospital bed and watched Ted Yates come out of the general anesthesia. It had been a bad break of both bones. The fibula was shattered. They'd had to do some reconstruction, inserting a rod and some pinning and wiring.

Doc Ellsworth had watched the operation, and he was still showing the sweat. "Damn, but them guys are good. They pasted old Yates back together like he was a rag doll. He'll be almost as good as new."

Murdock nodded. Almost. He'd been through it several times before. There was no chance that Yates would be able to stand up under the strenuous rigors of a SEAL's life. He would be back to the regular Navy for the rest of his hitch, and his career.

"Yates, Ted Yates," Doc called. "Hey, buddy, you're coming out of that wild dream. How was it in there?"

Yates tried a grin. He blinked, and rubbed his eyes. His hands were still in plastic gloves. They hadn't taken time to clean him up before they operated.

"Doc, you bitch. You didn't tell me it was going to hurt. Still hurts like a fucking volcano."

"You had some shots, buddy. Should knock out the pain in a few minutes. Maybe knock you out too."

"So why all the fuss over a broken leg?" Yates asked.

Doc looked at Murdock.

"Yates, it was worse than just a break. The medics say one of the bones was shattered. They had to pull in some reserves to paste you back together."

"Reserves? You mean some pins and wires and things?"

"Yeah, Yates," Doc said. "And a short length of rod. That bone was just in little bitty pieces in there."

Yates frowned at them, then shook his head as a stab of pain drilled through him. He blinked, and looked at Murdock. "L-T, this ain't gonna slow me down being a SEAL, is it?" He blinked again and shut his eyes. He lifted his hand, and then the medications took over as he drifted into sleep.

"You got off the hook on that one, L-T. Course he's got to be told sooner or later."

The three SEALs left the room, and worked their way with some help back to their assembly room. They had cleaned up a little, and Doc went to the EM mess for a late-night supper. He had a steak dinner with all the extras.

Murdock and DeWitt hit their quarters, had showers, and then went to the dirty mess and got their suppers to order.

"We got lucky on that one," DeWitt said. "If those Hornets hadn't been babysitting us, we'd be mincemeat by now in Mombasa harbor. Those one-oh-fives would have riddled the ship and blown us into the bay in tiny little pieces."

"Yeah, thank God for the aviators."

After they had eaten, and were on the way back to their quarters, DeWitt asked the next vital question.

"Now, do we go in and root out General Maleceia like we first planned?"

"That's up to Washington. That's the way we left it in our planning with Don Stroh. He's got the ball now. We lick our wounds, and get ready to go in if he calls."

"Mean we might get a day or two to rest up?"

"If the politicians have to decide it, we might have a whole week. We'll need it to get ourselves into fighting trim again."

Murdock made sure his men had been fed, had showers, and had good bunks; then he crashed in his quarters.

The next morning, Don Stroh knocked on his door at 0700.

Murdock let him in while wringing the sleep out of his brain.

"Hey, thought you'd been up for hours. We may have a small problem."

Murdock took the offered cup of coffee, and sat down sipping at the life-giving fluid.

"Small problem?"

Stroh leaned against the door. "Well, maybe not all that small. You remember we left the ending open here. We said when we got the ship and all the people back, we'd worry about what to do about Colonel, now General, Maleceia."

"You said it was a political, not a military matter. What did the politicians say?"

"Not a damn word. They haven't even considered it yet. My boss said he talked to the President about it again yesterday, and he got put off."

"So, can we fly back to San Diego?"

"You're officially on hold until the politicos decide. I still say we don't make the same mistake we did in Iraq. We go in and blast the guy into hell so we don't have to come down here and do this job again."

"So when will we know how they think?"

"Maybe a day, maybe a week. Maybe never. Politicians have a weakness for letting the hard decisions slide until everyone forgets about them."

"What's so hard about this one?"

"Our stature in world opinion, or our relations with President Daniel Djonjo, who it seems is gradually retaking control of his country. He's got Mombasa almost totally recaptured. He is working north with a large force of troops that remained loyal or came back to his command. So we, and he, don't know what the hell is happening."

"Why wouldn't he want us to rip up the last of the general and get him out of the President's hair?"

"You got me. Maybe they are both from the same tribe or

something. It's all a mystery to me. I've sent three signals to my boss this morning with the hope that we can get a go/no-go by tonight."

Murdock stretched and reached for his pants. "So I'd better get my men looked over, shaped up, and rested for another go-round. We need to do our basic planning just in case it is a go."

"I'm with you. I don't see how the President can turn us down on this one. We've asked for a go, and he's conferring with some members of Congress and his staff and cabinet. That could be trouble. We'll have to wait and see."

The two had breakfast, then went to the SEAL assembly room. Again Murdock had to have an escort to get him to the right room on the right deck.

The SEALs looked a little tired but in good spirits. Doc Ellsworth reported that he had taken Nicholson, Brown, and Ronson to the medics to have their wounds treated and redressed. All had broken open again, but the medics said they weren't serious, and if the men wanted to stay on duty, it was their call.

Jaybird had them all cleaning their weapons, and he'd already made an invoice of what ammo they had left for each type of weapon. Six of the men had brought back the AK-47's with them.

"A damn souvenir," Miguel Fernandez said. "Hell, ain't every day I get a chance to look down this end of one of them weapons. It's a pretty fine piece."

Murdock filled them in on the chances of taking on General Maleceia. They groaned at the delay.

"Didn't we learn anything in Iraq?" Ron Holt asked. "Jeeze, think them Washington guys would think back and see what we didn't do back there. Time we finished the job here."

Half the men had a comment. Murdock listened, realizing that most of the bitching was along the lines of what he thought.

"At least it gives us a small window to get our breath, check over our weapons, see if we can find anything new we want to use, and maybe even do some training," he said.

That brought a groan from the men.

"Besides, we need to get in some head work on how we'd take on that RX Military Headquarters where the general hangs his hat."

Stroh came forward to the long table and began spreading out satellite photos.

"These were taken during the past twenty-four hours," Stroh said. "About as current as we can get. We also have a man in Nairobi who is trying to pin down exactly where General Maleceia is, where his headquarters is on the complex, and where he spends the most time.

"If we could get a lucky missile targeting him, it would save you guys a hell of a lot of work digging him out of his hole."

The SEALs moved in close, and the planning process began. Murdock hung back and listened. If anyone thought that only officers had the brains to plan an operation, he was missing one hell of a lot of good advice.

Murdock listened to the kicking around of ideas about how to dig out a general from his stronghold. All the while he was planning what he and the men would be doing for the next two days to a week. He was sure it would take Washington that long to make up its mind what to do about General Maleceia.

As had happened often before, his mind flashed back to that last leave he'd had after the China affair. He had gone to Washington D.C., to see his parents. His mother had taken over as usual.

20

Saturday, May 31

Blake Murdock squirmed in the metal chair at the small white-painted table across from his mother, who had that cat-canary expression he'd seen several times before. He glanced at his wristwatch.

"Look, Mom, it's almost one o'clock. She isn't coming. Hey, I've been stood up before. Let's order, eat, and get out of here."

Mrs. Ruth Mae Murdock smiled at her son. "You're getting more and more like your father every year. I swear he's said the same thing a dozen times when someone is a couple of minutes late. She's a busy lady. She probably is running a little behind on her schedule."

Murdock shifted in his chair and took a long breath. He'd rather face down a charging knife-swinging terrorist any day than have a lunch with his mother and one of her blind dates for him.

"Mom, you're sure this is the same girl Dad sent the picture of to me?"

"Yes. Now relax. She's Ardith Manchester, daughter of Senator Manchester. Same girl. Lovely, and brilliant from all I've heard. I've met her a few times. She's a fine young woman."

177

"Sounds like the kiss of death, Mom. Remember Harriet Larret? Now there was a perfectly fine young woman."

His mother laughed softly. "Yes, that was a mistake. How did I know she was two months pregnant at the time? Ardith is different."

She stopped talking, and looked past him. Murdock turned, then stumbled as he stood up quickly, and almost knocked over the metal chair.

Ardith Manchester came toward him moving like a dancer. She was prettier than her picture. Blonde hair like gold swept around her shoulders. She wore a light blue suit that showed just enough of her slim figure to be intriguing. Blue eyes were laughing at him as she came to a stop between him and his mother. Her face had delightful high cheekbones without being obnoxious about it, clean brows, and a smile that dazzled.

"Mrs. Murdock," she said, her voice just a little husky, yet smooth and mellow. "Sorry I'm late. That committee hearing just never ended." She turned, and looked at Murdock.

"So, from what your father tells me, you must be the famous Navy guy Blake. Right?"

"Yes, ma'am. I'm not famous, but I am Navy. Here, a chair." He was sweating, flustered, unsure of himself, acting like a sailor on his first date. He held the chair, and edged it into the table, then sat down.

"So good to see you again, Ardith," Mrs. Murdock said. "Blake here was sure you wouldn't arrive."

She looked at him, and lifted her brows. "Men are always in a rush, except when it comes to committee meetings."

"A Senate committee meeting on Saturday?" Blake asked.

"Appropriations. They are having problems. Big push. But no more of that. Lieutenant Murdock, I understand you just love the Navy."

He at last found his real voice. "Yes, absolutely. Mother tells me you're a lawyer, and about to be snapped up by some cabinet member as an under secretary."

She smiled. "I wouldn't know about that. I just try to do my job the best way I can. What do you do in the Navy?"

Murdock had a stock answer for that one with any civilian. "I have a friend who is with the FBI. When anyone asks him what he does with the bureau, he says he'd be glad to tell them, but then he'd have to kill them."

She laughed, and he liked the sound of it, the way it made her face light up. "I see. So it's secret stuff. Yes, I can understand that. It must be a wonderful job that keeps you in the Navy. I know your father wants to get you into politics. Your father could give you a big push up the ladder."

"Politics isn't really of much interest to me. You make the laws, I'll help the Navy keep us safe."

"Now there is a really great line. I'll remember that."

Mrs. Murdock spoke up. "Oh, goodness sakes, I nearly forgot. I have a hair appointment. If I miss it I may never get another time with Rene. You know how touchy he is. You have to pay for it if you miss, so I might as well hurry over there."

She turned to her son. "Blake, dear. I do hope you don't mind my leaving you this way. I thought I'd have time. I really did. You'll excuse me, won't you, Ardith?"

"Yes, of course. I've never met this man before, but he does look civilized, and we're in a public place. I don't think he'll use any of those vicious military weapons on me. You run along and don't disappoint Rene."

Mrs. Murdock stood, and Blake hurried to his feet. His mother leaned in for a kiss on the cheek from him. Then she walked away through the tables. Blake sat down.

"Ardith, forgive my mother. She probably doesn't have a hair appointment at all. She's one of the all-time persistent matchmakers."

Ardith watched him from soft blue eyes. She smiled. "I hope you don't mind too much my being dumped on you this way."

He laughed. "Not at all. Usually I don't have any trouble meeting pretty girls, but my mother . . ."

"I understand you're here on leave after your last deployment."

"Yes. I have two weeks, so I thought I'd see the folks again. I'm stationed out in California."

"Your father told me. Coronado, to be exact. Isn't that where there's a Navy Special Warfare Detachment?"

"Right. Most people don't know that."

"The senator likes to keep up on the military. He was an Army pilot back a few years."

"Coronado is a real Navy town. It has North Island Naval Air Station and a batch of other Navy facilities. Nice little place, about thirty thousand people, and no room to get any larger."

"You live there?"

"I have an apartment off base."

A waiter hovered, and they took menus and ordered.

They ate, but Murdock didn't remember what it was. They tarried over a second coffee, and he found himself relaxed, and enjoying himself. This was a remarkable woman.

"How did you get so smart?" he asked.

Ardith looked up at him with curiosity, then glanced away.

"Oh, dear. I feel like a first-year law student sitting in on her first real murder case. Not exactly embarrassed. More than a little surprised, and pleased, and mostly glad that you didn't cut and run as soon as the dessert was over. I'm not all that smart. I try to pick my spots, I try to know as much about a subject or a person as I can before I meet them, and I do have a retentive mind. My memory doesn't often fail me. My speech is over."

Murdock realized he was smiling. "So you researched me when Mom set up this little meeting, and you came anyway."

Blue eyes looked down at the table. "Yes, I know something about you. I've known your father for several years. Frankly, I was curious to meet you. Oh, I did like your picture."

"Picture?"

"Your mother sent me one about a month ago."

Murdock laughed with enthusiasm. "Yes, I bet she did.

My dad sent me your picture through a top-secret fax machine when I was in the China Sea."

They both laughed.

He caught the waiter's attention and asked for the check.

"It's already been taken care of, sir. The lady who had been at your table."

"Mom strikes again," Murdock said. He stood, and helped Ardith from her chair. She put her hand on his arm as they walked out of the restaurant. Her hand felt good, and it seem natural for it to be there.

That afternoon they walked Washington like two tourists. They both had seen it all many times before, but somehow this was different. Murdock couldn't remember when he had enjoyed himself so much.

There were three more stops for coffee at those little coffee bars that had cropped up. They talked.

"Hey, you know that I just realized?" Murdock said. "We've been jabbering away, and what we're each doing is laying out our life's story for each other. This is first-date kind of talk, do you realize that?"

She smiled, and Murdock melted a little more.

"I figured that out about five minutes ago," she said. "So much for my quick study. I don't want anything to be quick when I'm with you, Lieutenant Murdock."

He reached across and took her hand. "What in the world is happening here, Miss Manchester?"

"I'm not sure I want to evaluate it right now, Lieutenant Murdock."

He looked into her blue eyes, and she stared back at him. Her hand gripped his harder, and then relaxed.

"Are you involved with anyone?" he asked.

"No. I date now and then, but I've been too busy, too rushed to get my career moving. Law school was a terror, then the bar exam and a year in a Portland law firm, and then a bid to work here in the center of the whole universe."

She paused. "You almost got married once."

"Yes. I was totally mystified, and thrilled, and desperately in love with that lady. I still miss her."

"That's good. You should never forget her."

"You must know the whole story."

"Your mother told me when I asked."

"Any close calls for you and matrimony?"

"Not really. One guy thought it would be a good idea, but that was our last year of law school, and the studies just washed us away from each other."

"Sounds like confession time," Murdock said.

"Almost. I know what work you do."

"If you're not cleared, I may have to kill you," he said.

She smiled. "You're not that top-secret. Just hush-hush. Your father told me. He worries about you. How is that shrapnel wound, all healed up?"

He laughed. "You heard about that too? My major embarrassment. My men called me old Iron Ass. I'm going to have to have a long talk with my parents. Yes, yes, all healed. Not more than a pound or two of Chinese shrapnel still in my hindside."

Ardith sobered, frowned slightly, and put both her hands over his.

"You like the work you're doing with the Navy?"

He watched her closely. Was she curious, concerned, or was it something more? "Yes. I'm doing a job that needs to be done. Not a lot of people around who can do what me and my men do. For that reason, there is a great satisfaction in it."

"But it's so dangerous. Not just once, but several times, you've been in great danger."

He grinned. This was more familiar ground. "Hey, it's dangerous in this town just walking across the street. Or you could have your car hijacked and be shot dead at any intersection. Danger is where you find it. When we go into action, we are remarkably well prepared and ready for any danger we get into."

Ardith sipped her coffee and nodded slowly. "Yes, that's about what your father told me you'd say."

They sat there working on their coffee and watching each other. For a time they didn't say a word.

"We could go somewhere and get out of the weather," Ardith said.

"Like shopping or a movie?"

She shook her head. "No, I was thinking about my place. I'm not a bad cook. How about really doing something dangerous and taking a try at one of my home-cooked dinners?"

"Oh, yes, fine idea," Murdock said.

Ardith Manchester, daughter of the senior Oregon senator, smiled and said, "Good."

A half hour later, Ardith led him into the fourth-floor apartment in one of the better sections of Arlington just across the Potomac River from Washington, D.C. It had two bedrooms, a big bathroom, a working kitchen, a living room, and a den.

"I used to have a roommate, but last year we both could afford to have our own places, so she moved to an apartment of her own."

She dropped her coat on the sofa and went to the kitchen. He put down his coat and followed.

Ardith turned. "So, will it be coq au vin, spaghetti and meatballs, or steak and country vegetables?"

"No TV frozen dinners?"

"I save them for company I don't like."

"I'm partial to a good steak."

"I just happen to have some T-bones I've been saving. Don't worry, I love to cook, really. I usually don't have much time. I'm going to call my father and tell him I'm taking the next week off." She watched him closely. "I hear you have a two-week leave."

"True."

"I hope you'll be spending the first week here in the D.C. area."

Murdock smiled, and couldn't help but chuckle. "That's what I had in mind. Unless you'd rather I be somewhere else."

She reached up, kissed him quickly on the lips, and pulled back. "No, I want you right here. Now, go do some man thing while I cook."

The dinner was a mouth-watering success. He had watched, and helped some with the preparation. Ardith brought out the tall candles, and turned down the lights, and had just the right red wine.

"If you ever need a job as a cook, I know where there's an opening. It's in Coronado. . . ."

Ardith grinned, and passed him a special ice cream dessert topped with whipped cream and a red maraschino cherry. Beside the dish were two soda crackers.

"The crackers, in case you aren't from mid-America, are to create a delicious contrast with the sweetness of the ice cream. Try it, it's really interesting. I learned this from a little old lady in Shelby, Nebraska."

Later they started a blaze in the fireplace, and sat on the sofa watching it.

"I love watching a fire," Ardith said. "It's like discovering a small bit of the universe. Like a star going supernova, blazing up in a blinding brilliance, and then fading, and dying out to a huge ash somewhere out there in the universe where nobody can see it anymore. Look at that small stick. It blazes up, then glows red for a moment, then it's nothing but a falling line of ashes."

"A philosopher too," Murdock said.

He pulled her closer and kissed her gently on the lips. She eased away and looked at him, then returned the kiss, hard and insistent and with an urgent need.

They eased to the side until she lay on the couch and he was half on top of her. Ardith smiled, and traced one of his eyebrows with her finger.

"Hey, nice. Now please kiss me again."

The next morning, which was Sunday, Murdock made eggs ranchero for them for breakfast, and they figured out what they would do that day, which was a bit warmer than usual.

On Tuesday they called on Representative Charles Fitzhugh Murdock in the House Office Building. The congressman was in the middle of a floor fight before a roll call vote on a money bill he had been working on for two months.

He had the phone on a shoulder mount, and was working hard.

"Yes, Gunderson, I know you represent some of the

people who will be affected, and that's why I say you should support the bill. It will bring stability to the area, it will mean better markets for the farmers, and more availability of raw materials for those producers in your area who need them. It's a win-win situation. Can I count on your vote at four o'clock?" The congressman paused, and waved at his son and Ardith.

"Good, Gunderson, you bet I owe you one for this. I'm a man who always pays my debts. Yes, you can put one of those damned red three-by-five cards up on your tote board. I never forget a friend or a favor. See you at four." He hung up, and turned to Blake and Ardith.

"Well, well, well. I see that picture I sent you did some good."

Blake shook his head. "It was really a bad picture, didn't do this lady justice at all." They sat down in the chairs near the desk.

"Looks like you're hard at work in the trenches, Dad."

"Roll call vote coming up on Bill 4439. I want that sucker. Working my tail off. You two want to make some calls for me?"

"Afraid I'm not all that good on a phone, Dad. Just wanted to be sure you and Mom are still on for that dinner tonight on me. I've got reservations and the whole thing."

"We'll be there. Let you know how the vote comes out." His phone buzzed, and he picked it up.

"Stan, good to hear from you. Now, about that bill I've been working so hard on."

Murdock and Ardith stood and went to the outer office.

"Is it always this way?" Murdock asked the assistant at the front desk.

"This is an easy day," she said. "He said he was glad you dropped in."

That afternoon they checked in at Senator Manchester's office and met the Oregonian. He was small and gray, older than Murdock had guessed, but with a lean, hungry appearance that told you he got things done, and done the right way. Senator Manchester was warm and gracious, and Murdock liked him at once. They made a date for dinner three days hence, and then Murdock and Ardith went back to her Virginia apartment.

The two weeks slammed past so quickly that Murdock couldn't believe it. He had a last dinner with his parents and Ardith at his parents' home, and a long good-bye with Ardith that night. The next morning he hitchhiked a ride on a MATTs plane out of Andrews Air Force Base outside Washington, and set down in San Francisco.

He realized that he hadn't thought about his SEALs more than twice during the whole leave. Ardith was more than he had expected. He wondered just where they were going. They had left it open-ended. He knew she hated what he was doing, from the standpoint of danger if nothing else. He'd half convinced her that it wasn't all that dangerous, but he wasn't sure that she would accept that for long.

At last she had looked down at him and kissed him softly. "Look, I know what you do, and I'll freeze up with terror every time something happens in the world and I know you're going to be there. I'll endure it. I'll hate it. I'll put up with it to be with you. But one of these days I hope that you'll decide that you've done enough for your country in the Navy, and that it's time for you to serve in some other way, or to get out of government service and go in a different direction. That's what I'll be hoping."

He had gone over it a dozen times as he flew to San Francisco. Now he was waiting for a Navy plane to take off for North Island. He'd be home in a few hours. For the first time in two weeks he wondered how DeWitt was doing in the training sessions he had laid out for the platoon. They'd all deserved some time off. Each man had had his choice of a week's leave or two weeks'. Some of them had no family to go to, and felt a little uncomfortable out there in the civilian world. He knew the feeling.

It would be good to get back to Coronado and back with the SEAL program. He had a platoon to get filled up and trained as sharp as a fine saber. You never knew when a call to action might come.

21

Thursday, July 22

The men had pored over the satellite photos, plotted out the area around the military headquarters, and come up with half-a-dozen different ways to roust the coup leader out of his stronghold.

"The one thing we don't know for sure is just where in that place the general has his headquarters—and if he's there," Don Stroh said.

"We have a few more problems too," he added. "Kenyan President Daniel Djonjo said he had Mombasa under control, but now we hear from him on a SATCOM radio that he was too optimistic. He's turned his force around, and is now concentrating on putting down a battalion of holdouts on the north side of town, off the island. He says he might be delayed there for four or five days before he can rout this bandit band."

"Thought you said you had a spy up in Nairobi trying to find out where our fat general is," Jaybird said.

Stroh grinned. "True. Last thing we heard from him, he was on his way to get inside the military headquarters. He's going in as a soldier, and hopes to fake his way through and pin down the spot we could hit with a few smart bombs."

"So why don't we just do it and worry about it later?" Magic Brown asked.

Stroh laughed. "Yeah, the military mind is working. I told you guys in China that you're in the diplomatic arm of the Navy right now. We can't spit until the politicos say we can. We can piss our pants waiting, but that's about all. There may be another complication.

"President Djonjo isn't happy the way our planes have been bombing his country. He says there must be a better way. We asked him how he would have stopped the tank, and he backtracked on that one. So even if we get a go from our President and his boys, we still have to clear it with President Djonjo."

Murdock stood. "Enough for today. We're all getting punchy. We'll take the afternoon off and rest up. I want our three tough-guy wounded SEALs to get checked out by the medics. Doc, your job is to get them down there. It wouldn't hurt for the rest of you to go see Yates in the hospital. He'd appreciate some visitors. Not all of you at the same time. Spread it out. After chow, we'll get together here at 1900 to go through this again. We might know more by then. Take a hike."

Ed DeWitt and Murdock talked to Stroh after the men left.

"What's the chances of the President's men making a decision on this soon?" DeWitt asked.

"Unlikely. Maybe in another day. Tomorrow sometime is my guess. Time difference is a big factor."

"We'll keep hoping," Murdock said.

1345 hours
RX Military Headquarters
Nairobi, Kenya

Muhammad Maji studied the boundary fence of the large military facility north of Nairobi. He had spent two days watching the place, trying to find a way inside. He had to get in, find out where the general was, get out, and radio the information to the U.S. military offshore. Not a tough job. . . . an impossible one.

He had seen the guards at all three of the gates doubled within the past hour. There were interior guards walking the fences. The only way inside was through the gate in a vehicle. All he had to do was capture an army truck, kill the driver, take his clothes and ID, and drive in through the gate.

Simple.

Yes, and deadly if he failed somewhere down the line.

He moved to a better position along the road that led to the main gate. It would be the busiest. The best chance to get in and out. Now for the vehicle. There were some copies of old American jeeps, rugged little rigs, and most of them held only a driver. How?

He backtracked along the main route to the headquarters. Down a side street he spotted a bar where some lone soldier might stop to have a drink.

As he came closer, he saw it might be what he needed. It was a small drinking spot that had two of the jeep-like Army rigs parked outside. Why not just hot-wire one of the rigs and drive away? No. If he tried that, surely the bumper numbers on the stolen rig would be called in, and he'd never be able to drive out the gate. Besides, he needed a uniform.

He waited a half hour. Then a military man came out and headed for one of the rigs. He was a lieutenant, one with a swagger. Maji came out of the doorway and fell into step beside the officer. He was no larger than Maji.

"What are you doing?" the officer asked.

Maji showed him the .38-caliber snub-nosed revolver that was aimed at his side. "I'm going to borrow your transport. Hope you don't mind."

At the rig Maji had the officer get in and drive. Maji was close beside him. They went down a side street and into a small cluster of brush and woods just outside of the town, but short of the military headquarters.

Maji pushed the revolver into the man's side and fired. The round rammed through a lung and into the officer's heart, killing him instantly.

Five minutes later, Maji had pulled the uniform off the man, donned it himself, hid the body under some brush, and with the officer's credentials and wallet drove toward the main gate. He would simply hold up his ID card the way he had seen many others do. Since he was an officer, he would be given less scrutiny. It seemed to him today that the guards were more concerned with people leaving the complex than entering it.

He came up to the guard post, showed his ID card, and was waved on through before he could stop. He shifted the stick drive into second, and drove on into the headquarters. He did a quick tour of the area, driving most of the streets. The building that had the most guards was a three-story affair with no windows and .50-caliber machine guns mounted and manned at each corner.

He stopped two soldiers walking by. They saluted, and he returned the salutes, then spoke to them in Swahili.

"Men, where is the general's office? I have some dispatches for him from Mombasa, but I can't find out where he is."

"Sir, it's there, right in front of you. The only entrance is on the other side. You'll need all sorts of clearances to get in there."

"That I have," Maji said. He nodded at the men, and they scurried away. Maji drove around again. Better to keep moving. How did he know for sure the general was inside? He had to have precise information to send to the men on the American carrier.

He drove to the far side, and saw the doors with six men guarding them and heavy machine guns mounted there as well. He drove down the street that let him see the headquarters, and parked.

For two hours, he watched the big double doors. More than a dozen men came and went, but there was no activity to indicate that the general would be leaving. He always traveled with a three-car caravan with an armored car in front and one in back. Maji had observed that there was only one three-story building on the base. That much would be easy for the jets, but which area inside the block-square building was used by the general?

He started the rig, and turned toward the headquarters. This time he drove all the way around it and found a service entrance on the rear side. He parked half a block away. There were no guards and no machine guns at this door.

With his officer bars he could bluff his way in here. He looked at his stolen credentials. The officer was attached to an air wing flying from just north of the complex.

Good enough. He drove closer to the entrance, then parked and left the rig, pocketing the keys. With remembered military precision, he strode up to the door and reached for the handle before a lackadaisical guard called out.

"Sir, this is a restricted area."

"I know that, soldier. I'm on a special investigating mission to check on security. What's your name?"

The private looked worried, and gave him a name that probably wasn't his. Maji wrote it down in a notebook the officer had carried, nodded at the man, and walked on inside.

He had no idea where he was or where he should go. The center of the building on the ground floor would be the safest. But would Maleceia do it that way? He was a showoff. Wouldn't he want something with some class and some splash?

Ahead he saw a door that was marked "Janitorial Services." Yes, brilliant. They would know exactly where the general's offices were. He moved through the door with the hint of a swagger, and watched as two surprised sergeants looked up.

"Sergeant, who's in charge here?"

"Must be me. The captain is out of the area."

"We've had complaints about the cleanup in the general's quarters and his office. Can I see the schedule of cleaning in those areas and who is responsible for that work?"

"Schedule? No, sir. I mean, we don't use no schedule. We just clean up the general's offices once a night, and then again during the day if he isn't using them. No schedule. We send men up there who we have available."

"Sounds sloppy. We're talking about the same area?"

"Yes, sir. His main office on the third floor front of the building with the big wall of windows, and then his apartment down on floor two with the seven rooms."

Maji scowled for a moment. "Not sure just how I can tell

the colonel about this. I'll use your name since your officer isn't here. Your name again, Sergeant?"

He wrote it down. "That will be all. Carry on." Maji turned and strode out of the room. He'd learned his military behavior as a two-year Army man who had been discharged three years ago. Being a corporal in a rifle company back then was coming in handy.

Did he have enough? He wondered as he got lost once, then found his way out the same rear service door he had come in. No one even noticed when he left the building. Security might be fine in the front, but here it was terrible.

Maji walked to his car. He had everything he needed. When he looked at the jeep he had stolen parked half a block ahead, he saw two military police checking it. They looked around, then got back in their patrol rig and parked behind the jeep. It looked as if they were going to wait and see who came to claim the rig. How could it be reported stolen already? If so, his ID wouldn't be any good to get him out of the camp.

If he tried it, and they caught him, he'd be shot on the spot. He needed another way to get off the base.

Five minutes later, he had strolled down to where he could see the main gate. The double guards were still in place. Few cars or trucks left the base. He saw two come in and only two go out in half an hour. No one had been allowed to walk out through a special gate at one side. Several men who had tried to leave had been turned away. A general lockdown?

How could he get off the base?

He walked around again, then checked the dead man's wallet. It was stuffed with hundred-shilling notes, each worth about two dollars American. Might be worth a try.

At the nearby officers' club, he had a beer and listened to the men talk. He found two who were heading for town. They said they had special passes to get through the gate. The captain excused himself, and went to the men's room. Maji went there a moment later.

In the bathroom they were alone. Maji asked the captain about the pass.

"Yeah, got one. Getting married in the morning. Even the general figured I should go in. Damn fine girl." The captain was half drunk.

Maji chopped him twice in the side of the neck with the hard side of his hand, and the captain went down. Maji dragged the captain into a toilet stall, took the pass and the man's ID card, closed the door, and hurried out.

Five minutes later, he flagged down a truck heading for the front gate and scowled at the driver.

"You heading for town, Corporal?"

"Yes, sir. Special duty."

"I've got to get to town, and my transport broke down. No time to get a new one from the motor pool. I'll ride with you."

At the gate, the driver showed his pass, and the man there waved them through without a second look at the lieutenant in the other seat. Being an officer, even if for a short time, did have its advantages.

Maji dropped off the truck a mile from the base, walked to his car, and dug the SATCOM from the truck. He was in a little-used area behind some warehouses.

He keyed in the right frequency, and adjusted the antenna.

"Rover, this is Quest One."

There was a long silence from the speaker. He checked his dials and sent the same message again. This time the speaker came to life.

"Quest One. Rover here, over."

"Rover. Best bet: three-story building, top floor front. Personal apartment second floor. Security doubly tight on the site."

"That's a roger, Quest One. Take care."

Just as the last word came from the speaker, the flat crack of an AK-47 sounded and Maji looked up in amazement, slammed backwards, and dropped the SATCOM microphone. The single round had jolted into his shoulder, and he clawed for the small revolver in his pants pocket.

The AK-47 fired again, this time on full automatic, and six rounds bored into the Kenyan spy. Two hit the SAT-

COM, smashing it, and both the man and his radio died at
the same instant.

Two Kenyan Special Agents ran up and stared at the man
on the ground.

"You sure he's the one?"

The other man nodded. "Oh, yes, he's the one. Let's see
how much spy pay he has in his wallet. Our captain will be
pleased that we have closed one more leak in our intelligence division."

22

Thursday, July 22

0814 hours
Oval Office
Washington, D.C.

President Wilson Anderson rolled back in his big leather chair, and scanned the four men and one woman facing him around his desk. These were the advisors he had learned he could rely upon. They had individual specialties, but could see the broad picture better than anyone else in D.C. He watched each one intently.

Phillips served as National Security Advisor. Phillips was rock-solid in international affairs. He stood only five feet six inches tall. However, he had a surgical mind that bored into the heart of a problem and dissected it with unerring skill.

Lambert J. Waldpole was his CIA director. Steady, a man who'd moved up through the ranks. He was a former field agent who had done his share of hand-to-hand killing in Europe during the Cold War. He was a top administrator who could evaluate the hell out of a situation even if he hated it. He stood six four, and carried 210 pounds like a small tight end.

Mabel Thorndyke, the only woman in his cabinet, was the first woman Secretary of State. She was a brilliant foreign affairs strategist, a longtime diplomat who could negotiate with the best, and win. She had an unerring antenna for the downstream results of actions taken today. She was an inch shorter than Phillips, and a calming influence when things heated up.

Greg Sweibel was his Chief of Staff, and carried more weight than some of the others at the table. Some called him the First Vice President, and the un-elected Vice President. He was neat, a fashion-plate dresser, single, at the peak of his career after twenty years in rough-and-tumble national politics. He had a keen eye for the immediate effects of decisions.

Hart Kilburn was the Secretary of Defense. A career soldier, he had come up fast, and held pivotal roles in the Gulf War. From there he had retired and turned down a bid for the presidency, preferring to work out of the spotlight until his appointment to Defense. He was a tactician who understood war, force, showing the flag, and how much pressure a task force of Navy ships and planes can bring to bear on a situation.

President Anderson turned to Kilburn. "Hart, just what's the situation now in Kenya?"

"Getting better. The Navy SEALs rescued our diplomats and staff there after the embassy was overrun by the rebels. Then they broke the one hundred sixty men out of that prison, and got them on hovercraft and then to the ships offshore. Now I hear they have liberated the frigate that had been captured.

"My Naval commander in the area tells me that President Djonjo is gradually regaining control. He now has over fifty percent of the Army and Navy back under his control. He's cleaning out a pocket of resistance in Mombasa. Then he will control that vital port on the southern coast.

"He hasn't said anything about wanting help in eliminating General Maleceia."

"Mr. President," Waldpole said. "My CIA man with the fleet down there reported about an hour ago that President Djonjo was vitally interested in getting help to knock out Maleceia once and for all so they could bury him. Maleceia's holed up now in his headquarters north of Nairobi."

George Sweibel turned to Waldpole. "Yes, but didn't he

say that he was not too happy with the bombing and strafing runs by U.S. fighters?"

"Yes, George, he said that," Waldpole replied. "However, he also said it was vital to knock out Maleceia so he would never upset peaceful democracy in Kenya again."

"He wants us to kill Maleceia?" President Anderson asked.

"That's the general idea, without having to use the word," Mrs. Thorndyke said. "He put it about as strongly as a politician can. Yes, he wants us to blast this colonel-general right into Hell."

The President looked at Jared Phillips, who had been drawing a large black man on his pad. "Jared, what do you think?"

"I'd guess that the President down there would love to get somebody, namely us, to blast General Maleceia into the nether regions so he would never have to worry about him again. From the point of view of worldwide opinion, it might not be the best move for us." He held up his hand as several others started to speak.

"Just a minute, let me finish. Yes, we are regarded as world's enforcers. We went into Kenya for legitimate diplomatic and hostage-rescue reasons. For this the world is with us. Once we go a step further and try to wipe out the man responsible for the U.S. embarrassment, then most of the nations will say we're stepping over the line and getting involved in the internal affairs of Kenya."

The men in the room looked at Mabel Thorndyke. She nodded and studied her notepad, and then her head came up, her eyes hard, her jaw slightly set.

"Gentlemen, this one is tricky as all hell. If we do what we want to do, go in with a dozen planes and bomb that headquarters of Maleceia into kindling, we accomplish a good for Kenya, and maybe ourselves down the line. We also get a black eye in world public opinion. However a good steak soon reduces a black eye to a distorted memory. I'm not sure yet which way to go."

"Do I have to remind you about Saddam Hussein?" Kilburn asked. "We had him by the *cojones* as Mrs.

Thorndyke might say, and we let him get away. No, we *invited him to keep on living*. He's caused us trouble ever since. There's a good chance that he'll go on messing with us for as long as he stays in power. Now this self-made general in Kenya is not as big a threat. By that I mean he controls no oil. However, he will continue to irritate us, and to cause all sorts of hell in Kenya, if we don't go in and take him out right now with a good bombing program on his HQ, and then send troops or the SEALs in to make sure that he's blasted straight into Hell."

President Anderson held up both hands. "Okay, time out. I want all of you to go to your benches and think this through a little more. We've had input from everyone. Let's see what we can work out as a practical approach that will benefit us currently and that will be best for us downstream in Kenya and in the world." He grinned. "Hey, if this job was easy, I wouldn't need you folks."

The five filed out, and went to the nearby conference room, where they found fresh coffee, rolls, and bottles of cold water.

"Now we get down to work," Zweibel, the Chief of Staff, said.

In his office, the President looked over his calender, canceled three appointments, and paced the room. By the time his advisors returned two hours later, he had a rough idea of what he wanted to do. He'd see if the suggestions of his cabinet people coincided.

Zweibel led the people in, and kept standing when the others sat down.

"Mr. President, we have worked out what we think is the best move for the United States. First we route our response to the President of Kenya through State. This will give it a more rounded and subtle approach.

"Second, we think Mrs. Thorndyke herself should send the message and then phone President Djonjo.

"Here's our suggestion. We should indicate to President Djonjo that it is his best interests to wipe out General Maleceia so he will not be a troublemaker in years to come. We suggest this be done with smart bombs or ship-launched missiles targeting the complex where the general has his offices.

"Mrs. Thorndyke received a message relayed from an operative in Nairobi who has penetrated the military complex and who reports that the general's main offices are on the top floor of the only three-story building in the complex. It has a window wall on one side, and is on the outside of the building. He also has an apartment on the second floor.

"Secretary Kilburn suggests that the Navy be assigned to do the bombing of the HQ, and that the SEALs already on-site off Mombasa be used to go in and make sure that Maleceia is dead in the ruins. If for any reason he escapes, it would be up to the SEALs to track him down and dispatch him."

The President leaned back in his chair, and peaked his fingers as his Chief of Staff sat down. He looked at each of them.

"Say you all?"

The heads nodded.

"That's about the scenario I'd come up with. I don't think we can rely on the ship-to-shore missiles to do the job here. We need pinpoint precision bombing. This can be done with computerized targeting, as I understand." He looked at the Secretary of Defense.

"That's right, Mr. President. The complex has already been mapped in flyovers, and is all in the shipboard plotting computers."

"I hadn't thought about the SEALs moving in," the President said. "They are as efficient on land as they are in the water?"

Kilburn nodded. "The acronym stands for Sea, Air, and Land, Mr. President. I followed them one day from the ocean into the beach and inland for five miles. They are awesome with their tactics, their discipline, and their firepower. They are undoubtedly the best and the deadliest special forces organization in the world."

"All right. Mabel, it's your move. Make that call to President Djonjo, and let's get this moving. Eight hours. The time in Kenya right now should be about 8 P.M. Maybe a dawn attack could be worked by the Navy. Secretary Kilburn, see how they want to play that part of it.

"Mabel, and gentlemen, I think we have a solution that will be effective now and work for us in the future."

23

Thursday, July 22

2140 hours
USS *Monroe*, CVN 81
Off Mombasa, Kenya

"Damn right I want to take the fifty," Magic Brown said. "Look, the medics gave me an okay. I did moves and exercises for them and the wound didn't break open. I got a go. I want the fucking fifty in case we need to slow down some armored cars or trucks. Can't tell what we'll wind up working against up there."

"Okay," Lieutenant Blake Murdock said, grinning. "You have to carry the bitch, not me. Now, any other ideas about how, what, and where? If we go, I'd say it could be either day or night. They might want to hit his HQ during the daytime with the hopes that he'll be inside. A good five-hundred-pounder right through that plate-glass wall up there on the third floor would be great shooting."

Don Stroh had given them the word from the company spy in Nairobi a few minutes earlier about where the general would be hanging his hat.

"So we've got fifteen men," Jaybird said. "How many of the bad guys will be on that base?"

"No idea. Our spy didn't find out that kind of information. At one time I heard the general had five thousand men up there in Nairobi, but the way whole companies have been deserting, I'm sure he doesn't have anything like that left."

"Still should be worthwhile odds," Jaybird said. "I hate it when we got to go up against somebody one on one."

The SEALs hooted him down.

"To business," Murdock said. "We need to finalize our plans, so Don can get them up to the XO as soon as possible, so he can coordinate the rest of it. We're assuming that the President will give the flyboys a go on dropping some eggs on this place. Then we go in and mop up. If for any reason the general survives and tries to run, we run with him, only faster, quicker, and with better marksmanship. If we have to, we run him to ground and chew him up and spit him out for fertilizer."

"We still going in by chopper?" Ching asked.

"Best way this time. No real need to do a parachute drop. Those old Seahawks can dump us out there in about two hours. The carrier will move up toward Formosa Bay, which is about twenty miles closer to Nairobi than Mombasa. The bird cuts back for the ship and we go do our thing."

"Double ammo?" Al Adams asked.

"Yes, except for the fifty," Murdock said. "Not even Magic can pack that much and still fight. We'll go with our jungle cammies—could give us better cover—and the rest of our standard equipment. Bishop, we found a replacement SATCOM box that you get to pack along. It came in damn handy last time."

"With that bird sweeping in, they gonna damn well know that trouble has arrived," Ross Lincoln said.

"That's why the Seahawk will swing around on the opposite side of the base and work its machine gun on the far gate to give us a diversion," Murdock said. "We hope most of the bad guys will rush over on that side. We don't know for sure, but the aerials look like there's some woods to cover our landing about a quarter of a mile from the fence."

"We all using our weapons of choice?" Jaybird asked.

"Almost. As long as we keep the balance we need. You take your MP-5 along, but you can smuggle in that shotgun you like if you want to. You've got to carry it."

They went over the satellite photos again. They would

come in from the back side of the place, with the main entrance in the front and side gates to the left and right. There was no rear gate. The land looked comparatively flat, and evidently had been cleared of all brush and trees for about a hundred yards.

"Lot of real estate to cover if they've got machine guns trained on that open space," Ed DeWitt said. "If we get a go, why don't we go in on the chopper an hour before daylight. We get down, move up to the fence in the dark, cut our holes and get inside quietly to some kind of cover, and wait for the bombers to come over at dawn."

Murdock nodded. "Damned fine. Stroh, what about that?"

"Should be no problem. You'll be going in far in advance of the takeoff of the bomber-fighters anyway. I'd guess they'll use the F-18 Hornet. She'll pack almost eight tons of bombs, and they have the twenty-millimeter Vulcan cannon as well."

"The eighteen," Murdock said. "Yes, probably what they'll use. Just so they blow that top-story front into the basement. Anything else anybody is wondering about?" Murdock asked.

Somebody came to the door and asked for Don Stroh. He went out quickly.

"Something cooking with the go-ahead?" Magic Brown asked.

"Hope so," Murdock said. "Now, if we run into a heavy force along this rear perimeter, what is our alternate course?"

They went on working, planning, trying to come up with a solution for every problem they could think of.

"What if the bombs miss the three-story building and we're already inside the fence waiting to assault it?" Horse Ronson asked.

"We go right ahead and assault it," DeWitt said. "We get inside, clear rooms, move to the top floor, take out everybody up there we can see, and make sure that one of them is a big fat tall son-of-a-bitching general."

The men laughed.

"No chance these Navy aviators are going to miss a big target like that," Murdock said. "They have smart bombs too, computer-guided bombs that are supposed to be able to hit dead center in a three-foot circle."

They were still working an hour later when Don Stroh came into the room. Everyone stopped talking, and watched him as he went to the front.

"Anybody here want to go on a short trip to Nairobi? We just got a firm go-ahead from the President." The SEALs cheered, and he shushed them. "The President said that his council had decided to make the hit. The Secretary of State has already phoned President Djonjo of Kenya, and he's given us permission for one more air raid on his country. After this we can't use any more air attacks."

"So it's a go," Murdock said. "What about the timing?"

"Told the XO about your idea of a night drop for you guys just before the bomb run. He liked the idea. No problem for the bird. They made the run before in the Seahawks. He worked out a schedule. Two hours for the flight. The *Monroe* is moving up to that bay to cut down the flight time. Sunup here tomorrow is supposed to be about 0530. We get you out of here at 0200, gives you over an hour after you arrive to move up, get inside the fence, and find some cover. Enough time?"

"Should work," DeWitt said. "We get a diversion with the bird's machine guns on the front gate?"

"You got it. As soon as he dumps you, he goes strafing. This bird will bring M-60 7.62-millimeter machine guns in both cabin doors."

"Little buddy, you just got yourself a deal," Murdock said. "Now we can get the final touches to our plans. We're going to need some more ammunition and forty-millimeter grenades and some WP. We better get some M-67 fraggers too. Jaybird, make a list. See if all the men have all the ammo they need. Then get a guide and find the armory or the arms locker or whatever they have on this ship. Looks like we're about ready to go catch ourselves a general."

By 2300, the SEALs were outfitted and ready to go. They had all the ammo they could carry, but they didn't have to worry about sinking in the ocean. The ammo load would lighten quickly as they moved up to the HQ building. Murdock arranged a 0100 supper for the SEALs.

Before he ate, Murdock and DeWitt talked to Don Stroh, their CIA mother hen.

"The XO tells me they will send six F/A-18 Hornets up to do the job," Stroh said. "That's over forty-five tons of bombs. XO said he'd also have one Hornet go in early to tail you and the Seahawk into Nairobi the last fifty miles or so in case they pick you up on radar and come after the chopper. We're not sure what kind of air power or radar the general still has up there."

Murdock and DeWitt took one more trip to sick bay and talked with Ted Yates. He yelled as soon as he saw them.

"Hear you guys are going out early in the morning. Damnit, wish to hell I was going with you. Why did this have to happen to me? Probably wash me right out of the SEALs."

They talked him down a little.

"Hey, you were in three of the phases already," Murdock said. "Worth at least a Purple Heart. Maybe your leg won't heal up well enough. We don't know that. I heard about a Marine who was in their advance recon outfit. Most elite bunch the Marines have. He lost one leg below the knee on a practice parachute jump when the wind blew him into some power lines. He healed up, got an artificial leg, and qualified again with his unit. He'd come home from a ten-mile hike and pour blood out of the place his stub leg connected with the leather of the metal leg. Now there was one tough Marine."

"Yeah, but he didn't have to do the SEAL tests. Damnit. I'm mad as hell, L-T. You see what you can do for me when we get back. If I wash out of SEALs on a physical, maybe you can wrangle me a quarterdeck job back at the grinder. Can you do that, L-T?"

Murdock took a breath so he could talk normally. The kid was so much a SEAL. "Yes, Yates, I promise you we'll take the best care of you, and try to get that leg to SEAL fitness. If it doesn't work, I'll see about a quarterdeck deal for you.

Now, get some rest. Let that leg heal itself up the best it can."

2000 hours
RX Military Headquarters
Nairobi, Kenya

Colonel Jomo Kariuki had taken great care to cover his tracks. Now he stepped into a double-locked section of a little-used warehouse and turned on the lights. Yes!

There sat his Mercedes Benz, a two-year-old sedan with civilian plates. It was gassed, had a week's worth of survival food and water, fifty gallons of extra fuel, and three light weapons including an Uzi and six full magazines. He was ready. He quickly changed into his civilian clothes and opened the rear door.

At the east gate, the guard sergeant was curious. He'd never seen the colonel before, so he couldn't identify him. Kariuki had put on horn-rimmed glasses and a heavy mustache, and now had a sporty billed cap on to help conceal exactly who he was.

"Could I see your papers, please," the sergeant asked. The colonel gave him prepared identification papers showing him to be a civilian supplier of large amounts of fresh fruits and vegetables for the base.

"Is there any problem?" the colonel asked.

"No, I've heard of your company. We've been told not to let any military personnel off base this late. I guess that doesn't include you. Looks like you're heading out for a trip."

"Not really. I always carry some provisions in case I get stalled on my way out to the farms. Is there anything else?"

The guard hesitated. Colonel Kariuki knew the procedure. He'd just never had to participate before. Now he took a five-hundred-shilling note from his pocket and let the sergeant watch him fold it four times. Then he held it out, and shook hands with the sergeant. The money vanished at the same time into the sergeant's palm.

"Yes, sir. That will be all. Have a good trip."

Colonel Kariuki eased the Italian-made Bernardeli auto-

matic back under the sweater that lay on the seat beside him.
The little .22 was quiet and deadly. It was his favorite
handgun.

He was out.

It took him less than a half hour to power through the
fringes of Nairobi and then swing out on the north road. He
hit Narvasha, and later Nakuru, with no problems. By now
he has his military cap on and his military identification in
place in case anyone questioned him. Shortly past Nakuru
he came to a military roadblock. He pulled into a short line
of cars and farm wagons, and waited.

A captain came up and saw the military cap, and then
looked at the ID, which the colonel held up and displayed.

"What is the problem here, Captain?"

"No problem, Colonel. Just making a regular citizen
check and watching for renegades. With the change in
military leadership, some troops took to the hills, and we're
watching for them."

"Well done, Captain."

"Begging your pardon, Colonel, but this is a fine car. Is it
a part of the new regime's . . . er . . . compensation?"

"No, Captain, it's my personal car. I saved for ten years to
buy it. Now, if there's nothing else?"

"Of course, Colonel. Please proceed around these wagons. The road is clear now all the way to the lake. I'd guess
that's where you're going on your vacation."

"Precisely, Captain, and I'm a bit behind schedule. Thank
you." He drove around the wagons and honked at the bar
across the road, and it was lifted. He breathed easier as there
was no pursuit.

Now all he had left was a straight run west to Kisumu and
the small port on the bay of the great Lake Victoria that
bordered on three nations. He'd get a boat large enough to
carry the car, and go south to Mwanza in Tanzania, and then
to a small town he knew of that would welcome him and his
South African gold with greatest of pleasure. Eventually he
might go on to the coastal capital of Dar es Salaam.

He smiled. Yes, he had timed it about right. The Maleceia
coup could not last more than two more days at the most. He

had taken off just in time, and with everything he had profited from the short-running coup and his former office in the government.

The road here was two lanes of blacktop with numerous chuckholes and narrow places. He saw them, but didn't understand until too late. The narrowed road was crossed with three lines of glinting metal triangular spikes. Two prongs of each one lay on the pavement, but no matter how they fell, one sharp three-inch spike always stuck upward waiting for a tire.

He hit the brakes, but he was too late to swing into the gravel at the side of the road and go around the tire-killers. Two tires on the passenger side missed the spikes, but the other two tires picked them up and blew out in an instant. He fought the wheel to keep the big car heading down the roadway.

He lost the fight, and it angled across the road to the left as the left front tire spun off the rim and the metal ground along the blacktop leaving a deep gash and throwing the car to the left.

By the time he got the Mercedes stopped, it had two wheels in the shallow ditch, and everything so carefully packed inside had erupted forward in a cascading jumble.

He grabbed the pistol and pushed the door open. Some damn road bandits. He dropped the pistol and pulled the Uzi out from under the sea, then looked around. Half-a-dozen men showed themselves in the moonlight from behind trees, then stepped back out of sight. The first round shattered the windshield, and he dove to the floor. When he came up, he triggered a six-round burst out the door, and caught a young man peering inside.

The bandit slammed backward screaming as he died with three rounds in his neck and chest.

A dozen more rounds hit the car.

Colonel Kariuki fired out the open car door again, then too late realized it was a two-front war. A round jolted through the passenger's side window, shattering it. The second round dug into his back just below his lungs, and missed his spine by inches. He bellowed in pain, and tried to swing the Uzi around.

A huge man dove into the car and wrestled the weapon away from him, then dragged him out to the dirt beside the ditch.

Four men leaped into the car and shrilled in delight. They had found the food. Two more bottles of whiskey, and already one was open and being sampled.

Colonel Kariuki turned over to watch the carnage of his carefully laid plans. Maybe all was not lost.

"Who is your leader?" he asked loudly. His body gushed with pain, but he could not let them know he was hurting.

"Who is your leader?" he bellowed this time.

A small man with a full beard and nearly white hair came out of the car carrying his pistol and nodded.

"I am Kinadi, the leader of this squad of patriot soldiers. Who are you?"

"I am Colonel Jomo Kariuki, the second in command of the New Republican Army of Kenya. I sit at the right hand of our leader, General Umar Maleceia."

The man in front of him wore no uniform. He had the white shirt and dark pants of the peasant farmer of the hills. The man laughed, fired the pistol three times in the air, and laughed again.

"Maleceia is a syphilitic idiot. I knew him before he went into the Army. He's a stupid lout with more guts than brains. I was his sergeant his first time in the Army. If you run with him, I should shoot you now."

"I left him. His regime is falling apart. I was on my way to Tanzania."

"Doubt if you'll get much farther."

"Can we speak in private?" the colonel asked. He lowered his voice so only the leader could hear. "It could be well worth your time."

Kinadi motioned three of his men away. He kept the pistol aimed at the Army man. "So, talk."

"At this point I can do you a lot of good. I can make you a quite wealthy man. None of your group needs to know. Let them have the food and the weapons, and you stay here with me. We will change the two tires. I have two spares. Then we will drive to the nearest village, where I will present you with more than a hundred thousand shillings."

"You have money hidden in the car," the robber said. "Why don't I just kill you and take all of the money you have?"

"Because then you'll have to split it evenly with six or eight men, and you'll wind up with a pittance. This way you'll have more cash than you have ever seen in your lifetime."

"True. But if you will give me a hundred thousand, you must have three times that much. Why don't I want to take it all?"

"You'll have to share it with your band. No one will get much. There may be some fights, some killings, jealousies. It happens in the best groups of mere men."

"You have a good point, Colonel. By the way, this is a fine little pistol, a twenty-two caliber I believe." He turned and shot the colonel in the right leg.

"Bastard!" Colonel Kariuki brayed in pain and fury. He beat down the waves of agony. "Why did you shoot me? We were negotiating. I can make you rich."

The bandit leader nodded. "True, Colonel. All true." Then he shot the colonel in the left knee.

Colonel Kariuki screamed until he passed out.

"Tear the car apart," Kinadi ordered. "But don't damage it. Take everything out that will move, the goods, the seats, everything. There may be a surprise in there somewhere."

There was.

The men had taken out the front seats, and then lifted the rear seat to pull it out. A pair of furious Hinds montane vipers struck out repeatedly, shooting venom into two of the men, who wailed and reeled back, sucking at the fang marks to pull the poison from their systems.

Two other men clubbed the vipers to death and carried them deep into the brush.

Colonel Kariuki came to consciousness with the shock of the water that hit him in the face.

"What? Oh, God. Why . . . why are you shooting me? I offered half of the money to you."

"Where is the money hidden, my colonel?" the leader asked.

"What money?"

The leader shot him in the left shoulder with the snarling little .22-caliber. Colonel Kariuki jolted backward, but didn't fall over this time. The pain billowed around him. He felt as if he were in a giant metal barrel and someone kept banging it with a steel hammer.

"Where is the money, old man?"

"Money. If I tell you, will you let me go with my car?"

"Sure, sure we will. Why not? What good are you to us without your money?"

"Good. It's a deal, a bargain. See, good men can come to reasonable arrangements. The money's in a compartment under the rear seat. It looks like the gas tank, but it comes right out and is hinged. Take it out carefully so you don't rupture the real gas tank directly below it."

The leader motioned, and three men cautiously looked in where the rear seat had been. One more snake darted out, but was clubbed before it could strike.

One of the men yelped, and tugged, and the metal box came loose and moved forward. They lugged it out carefully.

"Damn heavy," one of the men said.

The metal box was eight inches deep, two feet wide, and nearly three feet long. They brought it out and put it on the ground beside the leader. He called the men over, and then counted them.

"Is everyone here? I want no mistakes if this is valuable and we split it. Seven of us, right? Including the two snakebit ones who are still alive." He laughed. "Don't worry, the little viper is vicious, but not all that deadly."

He reached down, undid a hasp at each end, and lifted up the hinged top.

The men gasped. In the moonlight they could see that the box was filled with money. One section had banded stacks of hundred-dollar U.S. bills. Another had banded stacks of thousand-shilling notes. Half of the chest was filled with South African gold pieces.

The leader of the band hit Kariuki in a shot-up knee, setting off a series of wailing screams.

"Can the bills be traced? Are the numbers recorded anywhere as stolen? They're all new and in order."

Colonel Kariuki knew then that he would not live out the night. He screamed at them that of course they were stolen.

"Yes, the numbers are with every police in the world. All stolen, and you'll never spend a dollar or a shilling."

The leader laughed at him. "Old man, you wouldn't have kept them if they had been recorded. What did you do before you were a colonel with the killers down in Nairobi?"

The colonel didn't answer.

The leader hit him again in a wounded knee, and Kariuki bleated in surging waves of pain that made him nauseous. When he could talk again, he realized he was still alive. Maybe he could still get through this and get away.

"Before I went with the Army, I was the Minister of Finance and Administrator of Foreign Aid. I . . . I helped myself to some of the foreign aid. It was never missed."

"About what I figured." The leader turned away from the Army man. He pointed to three of his men. "You three start dividing it up into seven equal piles. We'll all be rich tonight. But don't damage the mother vehicle. It's mine. The rest of the goods we split equally. Any arguments?"

There were none.

Colonel Kariuki had some hope. He called to the leader.

"Now, Mr. Kinadi, I gave you what you wanted. Will you help me into the village where I can get some medical aid? It's the right thing to do."

The leader looked down at the colonel and asked him to repeat what he had said. When he heard it, Kinadi shrugged and turned away. Then in one swift movement he spun back and shot the colonel three times in the chest. After Kariuki fell to the ground, Kinadi shot him twice in the head to make sure.

24

Friday, July 23

0045 hours
USS _Monroe_, CVN 81
Off Mombasa, Kenya

The SEALs had eaten a big breakfast and loaded up on carbohydrates. In the ready room, they were suiting up and making final checks on their weapons and the quantities of ammunition each man wanted to take over the minimum.

Murdock and DeWitt double-checked each of their men. DeWitt was one SEAL short with Yates still in sick bay. He would make do.

By 0130 they had assembled on the flight deck near where a Seahawk chopper was getting a final preflight check. Five minutes later they boarded the craft, fitting in around the rig's normal supply of weapons minus the heavy Mk 46 torpedoes. They settled in for the rest of the preflight check.

Don Stroh came on board and talked with Murdock.

"Just had late word from the President. He says good luck on this mission. He congratulated your platoon on the great work you've done so far down here, and hopes all goes well today."

Murdock nodded. "We don't expect a lot of trouble. If we run into any, we may call on you for some assistance. I know, the President of Kenya said no more air strikes, but that wouldn't include an evacuation. We're going to have to be lifted out of there at some point. No way we walk three hundred miles to the coast. As we planned it, we'll need to exfiltrate with a Seahawk. Two hours for the big birds to get there when we need them. We'll remember that. Better remind the XO to have one of these Seahawks standing by for the next few hours, or maybe days, until we call."

The two shook hands, and Stroh left the chopper seconds before one of the crewmen closed the hatch.

Ten minutes into the flight from the carrier, Murdock looked around at his fourteen men. Half of them were sleeping. He grinned. Not at all uptight. Most of them had been this route before. Just another day at the office. This one could be a damn dangerous office. He checked his watch.

This mission seemed to be a simple one. Go in, determine for sure that the big general had been killed in the bombing, get out, and call for a pickup. It would be a two-hour delay between the call and the bird arriving on site, but they should be able to sustain that with no problem.

It all depended on a lot of things.

How many troops were still in the headquarters?

Were they still in a fighting mood?

How close to collapse was the new regime?

He pushed the questions out of his mind, and tried to relax. No telling which way this one would go. The bombs might get the general and his top staff, and they might not. The powers that be had decided that sunup was too early to expect the big man to be in his office. So they'd slated the bombing at 0800. He should be there by that time.

Which meant the SEALs had to remain hidden for two hours more before the raid.

So they would do it. They were SEALs.

Murdock felt the hand on his shoulder, and came awake. He must have dozed. The chopper crewman shook his shoulder again.

"Lieutenant, we're five minutes from our LZ. Figured you'd want to know." The crewman grinned.

Murdock lifted up in his seat. "Okay, SEALs, up and at

'em. Time to rock and roll. LZ coming up in about five minutes. Time to lock and load. Everybody conscious?"

He heard a chorus of grunts and groans.

"The ones who ain't conscious ain't talking," Jaybird cracked.

Murdock checked out the small window. They were still high over the land, but they were dropping quickly. A crewman came in, unlatched the big hatch door, and pushed it open.

"Stay clear," he said. Murdock was first man next to the hatch. He could see the ground rushing up at them now. They leveled out about fifty feet and slanted over the terrain. Ahead in the darkness he saw a clump of what might be trees. The Seahawk pivoted around them, came in behind them, and settled slowly to the ground. The second they hit ground, the crewman slapped Murdock on the shoulder, and he jumped to the ground and zigzagged toward the dark mass of trees thirty yards away.

Fourteen SEALs followed him in rapid order. The noisy chopper behind them took off at once. The men hit the fringe of the trees in a line staying five meters apart. Murdock waved at Red Nicholson, who sprinted into the trees silently. He was gone two minutes by Murdock's watch. Then he came back nodding, and the SEALs moved into the trees.

Murdock's watch showed it to be 0407. On time, with time to spare. The men remained quiet. Nicholson vanished again toward the front of the trees.

That was when they heard firing from somewhere in front of them. It was the solid rattle of the Seahawk's 7.62 machine guns hammering away at what Murdock figured must be the front gate.

"Should pull any suspicion from the chopper's sound here," Murdock whispered to Holt, who was two meters away. They heard small-arms fire, but not much of it, evidently coming from defenders at the front gate. Then the machine gun made another series of strafings before the night turned quiet.

Without a sound, Red Nicholson slid in beside Murdock.

"L-T, we've got about a hundred fifty yards of open space beyond the trees to the fence. I didn't see any guard towers or guard posts. One guard did a lackadaisical walk of a post inside the fence, but he didn't show up again. Either a damn big post or he's goofing off somewhere.

"Fence looks easy enough for our wire cutters. Inside the fence maybe twenty yards is a big pile of trashed lumber. Looks like a bulldozer smashed a building and they dumped the remains there. It's ten, twelve feet high and thirty yards long. Should be enough for us to hide behind until we make our move."

"Maybe an hour or so to dawn," Murdock said. "Take Lincoln with you, and two wire cutters, and make us a door. Send Lincoln back when you're ready for us."

Red and Lincoln moved out through the trees and brush without a sound.

Four minutes later, Lincoln came back through the trees and waved at Murdock.

All had on their Motorolas. Murdock whispered into the mike. "Let's move it."

They went in squad formation with the men spaced out ten meters apart. The wire had been cut and tied upward, leaving a four-foot-high opening. Lincoln stayed with the wire to fasten it back in place when everyone had entered.

Murdock stepped behind the pile of wood, plaster, and trash and nodded. Yes. It was jumbled enough that they could fit into holes and crannies. If they didn't move, somebody walking past along the fence probably wouldn't notice them. He found a spot and slid into it, as did the other men.

Lincoln came along a short time later and picked his place.

"Now we wait," Murdock said into his mike.

Holt moved up closer to Murdock and passed an earpiece to him. He had set the frequency to UHF so he could talk to or listen to the tactical aircraft. The sound came through clearly.

"Cover One to Rover."

"This is Rover."

"Cover One. We shadowed the big bird in the last twenty miles. They landed, discharged, and did their thing at the front of the complex. We find no air in the vicinity whatsoever."

"Very well, Cover One. Come home."

"That's a Roger, Rover."

The radio went silent. Murdock handed the plug back to Holt. "Monitor it so we'll know when the bomb runs start."

Holt nodded and eased back from Murdock into his shelter in the wreckage. Murdock checked his watch. It was 0435. Another half hour at least to dawn, then another three hours to attack time for the Hornets.

"We've got some wait time. Guard duty for the man on each end. Rest of you rest easy but watchful."

It grew light gradually, which fooled Murdock for a moment. Then it seemed suddenly to be daylight, with the sun brimming the far eastern sky. The men wormed deeper into the rubble. Some of them pulled boards over them to help the jungle cammies blend in better.

It was just after 0600 when two men on bicycles pedaled along the outside of the fence. They were young, not soldiers. They never even glanced at the pile of rubble. Murdock held his breath when they came to the spot where the SEALs had cut the fence. Neither of them looked at the spot. Instead they shouted to each other, then pedaled hard in a race. Murdock relaxed.

Murdock's legs started to cramp. He moved, and bent them, and tried to get them relaxed. As he did, he checked his watch again. Had it stopped? No, it showed almost 0700. Another hour. The birds should be talking soon. From the deck of the carrier to this spot the Hornets should take about fifteen to eighteen minutes at their jet speed.

Murdock looked to the north, and saw a small military jeep-like vehicle working its way slowly along the outside of the fence. He frowned. He didn't remember any road beyond the fence. The rig came closer and closer until it was less than seventy-five yards from the far end of the trash pile. Then the driver did an abrupt turn and went back the way he had come. The second man in the rig had a pair of binoculars, but didn't seem all that interested in using them.

Murdock gave a small sigh of relief. Time dragged. No one seemed interested in the trash. Red Nicholson had been to both ends of the trash pile checking the area directly ahead. He came back, and talked in whispers with Murdock.

"Looks like the top of the thee-story building is dead ahead, north," Red said. "I figure we have some barracks between here and there, and then a parade ground and maybe some shops and even a motor pool. Can't be sure."

"So we blast right up the street and take out anybody who gets in the way," Murdock said.

"Looks that way, L-T. Course when we get there, it may look different. Situation and terrain."

Murdock grunted.

At 0734, Holt handed Murdock the SATCOM radio ear plug and handset. He listened.

"Dropper One to Rover."

"Yes, Dropper."

"I have five chicks with me heading upstream. We have cover?"

"One Cover on station waiting and watching."

"Roger. We'll stay in touch."

Murdock used his Motorola mike. "The flyboys are on the way. Another ten minutes or so. Let's get awake and ready."

SEALs were good at waiting. It was drilled into them in their training and in operations. There was one optimum time for every attack, every phase of every operation. When it was time to go, the SEALs would go.

Murdock monitored the aircraft as they came closer. The one Hornet on cover duty overhead reported no aerial activity around the small country of Kenya that its radars could pick up. They could scan two hundred miles in every direction.

Then the radio message came that Murdock had been waiting for.

"Dropper One making run. I have one egg away."

Murdock had worked his way to the near end of the trash pile, and now moved up so he could see around it and watch the attack. He didn't see the Hornet fighter-bomber until it had passed overhead. At almost the same time a shattering explosion took place ahead of them. Murdock felt the blast of hot air, and then the sound flashed past them. He spotted smoke and dust from the top of the three-story HQ building less than six hundred yards from them.

Before the dust had settled on the first bomb, a second, and then a third hit the target.

The pilots' chatter came now and then, mostly indicating that they were on final approach. Murdock had no way of knowing how many times the aircraft passed over the target. He knew six planes were in the air. They could have five-hundred- or thousand-pound bombs, probably with delayed fuses to penetrate the building. When the sixth bomb hit, he spoke into his lip mike.

"Let's move out. On me, now. We'll take squad arrowhead formation, Second Squad on my left, and we'll sweep down this street and get into position at any cover we can find about a hundred yards from the target. Go, go, go."

The men ran to get into formation, then the two inverted V's moved down the street at a steady jog. Murdock and Nicholson led the point on the right. They saw no targets. As the bombs kept coming, they heard sirens and some trucks careening around. A dozen men ran out of one building, but when they took fire, they darted back inside, leaving two dead or dying on the street.

Murdock ran the platoon past that building and two more, then came to the parade grounds. The far end of it butted against a street next to the command headquarters.

No cover out there at all. One-story buildings on the right. They were 150 yards from the HQ. Murdock and Red stormed the second building in the group, kicked open the door, and blasted inside. It was some kind of support group. Six men and two women held up their hands.

Magic Brown covered them with his sniper rifle and bellowed. "Down on the floor, all of you. Anyone else in this building?"

One man shook his head. Murdock went to the door, and

had DeWitt take over the next one-story building. He met no resistance either.

The bombs kept falling on the three-story building. Murdock had a view of it out one window. He saw smoke coming from the front of the structure, but couldn't tell if any of it had collapsed yet. Another bomb hit, and he could see part of the corner at the front of the building shake, and then lazily fall away from the rest of the structure.

Murdock had lost track, but figured at least twenty of the big bombs had hit or come close to the structure. Holt touched Murdock's shoulder.

"L-T, that's it. Last bomb is down, the six planes are heading for the carrier. Our one Hornet cover is waiting to see if we need any more support."

"Right. Tell the cover man we'll stay in touch." Murdock spoke into his lip mike. "Okay, let's get outside. We make our move." His squad formed up outside and found De-Witt's ready. They ran for the big building with a fifteen-man front, every man had an open field of fire ahead of him.

DeWitt spat out a dozen rounds from his MP-5 as four soldiers ran across the street a half block down. Two of the men went down. The others didn't wait for them.

Holt caught up with Murdock. "We've got one cover plane circling so he can see what's going on down here. I said we might need him. He's holding his pattern."

Murdock nodded, and they kept going. Small-arms fire chattered at them from the front. The men slanted to the sides of the street returning a steady blast of lead at the flashes.

DeWitt and two of his men took cover behind a pair of cars parked along the street.

"Throw some WP at them," DeWitt said. Quinley and Bishop both fed phosphorous rounds into their grenade launchers under their M-4A1's and fired. The rounds hit just in front of the troops, and sprayed them with the furiously burning white phosphorus. The troops screamed and scattered. The two SEALs lofted two more rounds each, and the firing ahead tapered off.

The SEALs charged forward again. They came even with

the rear of the building, and saw people streaming out of it. Murdock put a six-round burst over their heads, and they stopped moving.

"To the front," Murdock said into his mike. The SEALs sprinted down the street past cars, and surprised soldiers who had no weapons.

They ran into no more opposition as they rounded the jumble that was the front corner of the building. A giant scar showed where it had torn away from the structure. There was no window wall on the third floor. At the front there was no third floor. What was left had collapsed onto the floor below, and that had fallen into the first floor.

A terrified man with cuts on his arms and legs, and bleeding from a gash on his head, ran out a side door and turned toward the SEALs. He evidently didn't see them, and ran right into the big arms of Magic Brown.

Magic held him, and talked softly to him until the blazing fright faded from his eyes.

"You were inside?" Brown asked.

The man nodded.

"On the third floor?"

"Second."

"You know if the general is still inside?"

"Don't know. Five men near me all killed!"

"Sorry. Where's the general?"

"Don't know. Somebody said they saw him inspecting his two tanks. Don't know."

Murdock held the people there, and waited for more survivors. Three more rushed out the side door, and De-Witt's men grabbed them and asked about the general.

All said he hadn't been in the place when the bombs hit. Two of them agreed that this was the morning he was supposed to inspect his last two tanks.

Murdock had heard it. He got Holt's radio. "Cover Bird, you see any tanks in this area?"

"SEALtime. Yeah, two about half a klick west of the target. Seems to be quite a bit of action around them."

"Can you take them out with your twenties, Cover Bird?"

"Doubt it, but I've got two missiles. One is a Maverick-

65. It's a nice little bird that's made for antitank work. Boss thought there might be some need for an AGM shot around here. Packs a real wallop. Want me to make a run on that tank?"

"That's a go, Cover Bird."

"West," Murdock said in his Motorola mike, and the fifteen men turned and ran down a street again in their offensive formation of two side-by-side arrowheads. Nobody tried to stop them.

Three blocks ahead, they came on a string of heavy trucks lined up across the street. Small-arms fire rattled from under, and at each end of, the trucks.

"Take cover," Murdock bellowed. The trucks and fighting men stood between him and where the general probably was. How in hell did he get around this kind of a manned roadblock?

25

Friday, July 23

**0842 hours
RX Military Headquarters
Nairobi, Kenya**

"Magic, front and center," Murdock said into his lip mike. His men had flattened against the sides of buildings, dropped behind cars on the sides of the street, and sprawled behind trees and shrubs. They returned fire on the line of trucks.

Magic Brown sprinted past a car and came to the small truck where Murdock had landed.

"Fifty?" Brown asked. Murdock nodded.

The big black man unfastened a drag bag he had lugged all the way from the grove of trees. He brought out the McMillan M-88 .50-caliber sniper rifle, and shoved a magazine of ten incendiary rounds into the receiver. He flipped out the front bipod, and lay down at the edge of the truck with the big barrel and its muzzle brake showing around the rear tire.

Magic grinned as he sighted in through the Leupold Ultra MK4 16-power scope.

He fired. The round slammed into the gas tank showing as a side step on one big truck. The explosion was immediate as the gasoline vapor in the top of the tank ignited and detonated, engulfing the truck, and the one next to it, in a furiously burning gasoline blaze.

223

Magic worked the bolt, shoving a fresh .50-caliber round into the chamber, and sighted in. He moved down two trucks, and fired again. This time there was no exposed fuel tank. He put the round into the motor compartment. Then he fired three rounds as fast as he could. The last one connected with another fuel tank in the last truck in the line, and it exploded into a huge fireball sending troops scattering.

A driver in one truck at the head of the line tried to drive away. Magic sighted in on the truck in time to slam two rounds into the side of the engine, stopping the rig in place as the flaming gasoline crept down a wet line on the blacktop toward it. Four of the five rigs were burning or out of commission.

No more firing came from the broken, burning line of trucks.

"Let's move," Murdock said into his mike, and the SEALs came out of hiding unscathed and ran forward toward the trucks. They went through a twenty-foot-wide gap in the burning wreckage with their MP-5's and M-4A1's on full automatic. Once clear of the trucks, they saw no more opposition.

They formed their two inverted-V formations and moved up the street at a steady jog.

That was when they heard the Hornet high overhead. Murdock knew the Hornet would have to be at almost Mach 1 and at a two-to-three thousand-foot altitude to get off a launch of a Maverick-65 AGM missile. It was the best antitank weapon in the cupboard, and could be used for air-to-ground or air-to-ship.

The Maverick had several types of guidance systems to direct the missile on the target. The explosion ahead and to the right blasted well before the aircraft pulled out of the shallow dive.

Murdock changed directions to the right down another open area, and saw no opposition. Past two buildings, things opened up.

Across an open square block, he saw the two tanks. One burned, and a secondary explosion rocked it. The second one had one track off.

The SATCOM radio bleated, and Holt ran up beside Murdock. He held out the handset.

"SEALtime, how is our tank?"

"Cover Bird, scratch one tank. The other one is disabled. Any sign of their leader?"

"SEALtime. I'll make another pass. Thought I saw a convoy of two limos and two armored trucks heading for the west gate. I'll make another check."

Murdock stopped the platoon, and put the men on the ground. Holt kept close by with the radio. They heard the Hornet F-18 streak overhead. Then the radio talked.

"SEALtime, that's affirmative on that convoy. How about some twenties on them?"

"Cover Bird. I like it. We're still legal. Take them out."

They heard the fighter make two more passes, and the rattle of the 20mm Gatling-gun Vulcan cannon rounds exploding. The weapon could fire four thousand rounds a minute.

The radio spoke again. "SEALtime, convoy seriously disrupted. Three vehicles out of commission, the fourth abandoned." He paused. "I do see another pair of weapons carrier-type rigs heading for the west gate."

"Cover Bird, this is Rover."

"Yes, Rover."

"Your mission is finished. We have CNO orders to do no more air attacks on Kenyan soil. I'm sure this order comes directly from the Kenyan President to our President. Break it off and come home."

"That's a Roger, Rover. Sorry, SEALtime. The other two rigs are all yours."

Murdock looked at his troops. There was no way to know if the general was in the convoy that had been blasted, or if he was still on base or running out the west gate. Murdock called in DeWitt and Jaybird. Jaybird always surprised him with his sharp grasp of a situation and the strategy needed.

He told them about their loss of airpower.

"So the general might have been in that first convoy, or it could have been a diversion while the old man slipped out the side gate," Jaybird said.

"Yeah, I'm inclined to go with the general trying to make a move," DeWitt said. "I'd look at those weapons carriers heading out west."

Murdock grinned. "That makes it unanimous. Let's see what we can find for transport."

"Those trucks we trashed," Jaybird said. "One of them looked undamaged."

"Let's take a look," Murdock said.

Five minutes later, they were at the trucks that had blocked the street. Ross Lincoln, their top mechanic and driver, stepped into the driver's seat on the third truck in the line.

"Keys in it," he called. He turned over the engine, and it powered into life. Quickly he cramped the wheels, and got the 6 x 6 out of the line. Murdock and Jaybird joined him in the front seat, and the rest of the SEALs piled into the back. The canvas top covering the roof's wooden stays had been burned away, but the rest of the rig was intact.

"Gas gauge shows almost a full tank, L-T. The west gate?"

Murdock gave him a thumbs-up, and the truck powered down one street after another westward until they saw the gate ahead. There were no gate guards. The lift pole that usually swung down across the exit had been smashed and battered aside. Outside the gate, there was one paved road that headed west, but quickly turned north toward the mountains.

Jaybird found a map in the trash on the floor. He folded it twice, and tried to figure out where they were going.

"You sure the half-tracks came this way?" Murdock asked.

"I been watching the shoulders. Only road in this direction, and nobody has driven off it so far."

"How much head start?" Jaybird asked.

"Maybe twenty minutes. I can get forty miles per hour out of this mill, but I can't push her any faster than that."

Jaybird kept looking at the map. "Near as I can tell, we're heading somewhere toward Fort Hall, which is just south of Mt. Kenya. Tall sucker, over seventeen thousand feet."

"We got taller ones in the States," Lincoln said.

"Not a chance."

"What about Mt. McKinley, twenty thousand two hundred thirty feet up in Alaska."

"Alaska don't count."

Lincoln grinned, and Jaybird fumed.

They had been driving for twenty minutes when the road narrowed. They met little oncoming traffic, and no one passed them.

Lincoln pulled the truck off the road to a wide hard shoulder. He got out with the other two in the front seat. In back of where he turned off, he showed them tracks and a small puddle of oil.

"One of them rigs isn't running so well," Lincoln said. "Maybe we can catch them before they get lost up here."

They got back in and drove. Lincoln pushed the old truck up to forty-five mph, but had to back off to forty.

"Now that I think of it," Murdock said, "why didn't I ask to have the Hornet stay up there and be a spotter for us so we would know where those two half-tracks were going."

"Too damn late now," Jaybird said.

"Yeah, and when the CNO gives an order, best to get the aircraft back home before somebody gets busted bad."

Murdock scowled, and looked ahead. They were coming out of the plains and into some low hills. They could be the start of the foothills that led up to the peak of Mt. Kenya. He wasn't sure if the hills would have any more growth than down here. So far all they had were low-lying shrubs and some grasslands.

Ahead he could see higher hills. Murdock scowled. That couldn't be good. Whoever was in those trucks could get lost in those hills and brush and trees. The higher the hills the more rain, and more rain meant larger vegetation and trees.

Murdock set his jaw and tried to will the truck to go faster.

26

Friday, July 23

Murdock figured they had been on the road for about an hour. They had made one sighting of the two half-tracks ahead where the road lifted into more hills. So they were on the right trail. The hills became larger, and real trees began to show along the road. He wasn't sure what kind they were.

Jaybird had been reading the English map. He looked outside and pointed out some of the trees he recognized.

"There's a good old cedar tree, and up there some wild olives. I remember something about some podo trees, whatever they are. We're too low for the bamboo. It doesn't show up until we get to the eight-thousand-foot elevation."

"Hey, watch it," Lincoln shouted. Ahead in the narrow road no more than a quarter of a mile, one of the half-tracks had pulled to the side of the road. Before Lincoln could do more than ease off on the throttle, a round smashed through the windshield, missing them and sinking into the rear of the seat.

Almost at once they heard the machine gun chattering over their heads as someone in the back of their truck returned fire.

The three in the cab bolted out both doors, and dropped into shallow ditches on both sides of the road.

229

In the back of the truck both Les Quinley and Horse Ronson had their H&K machine guns up and firing. They alternated, and sent the half-dozen men from the half-track scattering into the brush on the side of the road.

Magic Brown lifted his big McMillan M-93 fifty and fired three incendiary rounds into the rig as fast as he could work the bolt. He hoped to hit the gas tank. They missed the tank, but he saw a hiss of steam coming from the front. The radiator. The engine must be dead.

The machine gunners moved their sights to the side of the road where the soldiers had vanished, and riddled the brush with the 7.62 NATO rounds. The return fire stopped.

Murdock talked to his lip mike. "First Squad except Ronson. Into the brush on the right-hand side of the road. We'll circle around them. Second Squad keep up fire for four minutes."

First Squad sprinted across the road and into the brush, which wasn't all that thick. They circled to the right, then when four minutes were up, they worked ahead slowly, soundlessly. Twice they stopped to listen. They heard whispers ahead.

Another twenty yards, and Murdock spotted a uniformed soldier prone and facing the road. Murdock's silenced MP-5 stitched four rounds up the man's back. His dead hand fell away from his rifle.

They moved in closer. Murdock heard the crack of the AK-47 to his left. They worked ahead another ten yards, and found three soldiers trying to get out of their uniforms.

"Hold fire," Murdock whispered. "Move in, but don't fire. None of them have weapons."

Seven cammie-clad SEALs stepped out from brush and trees and faced the three Kenyan men. Two had their uniform shirts off. The other was pulling his pants off. They all held up their hands.

"English?" Murdock asked.

"Yes, I speak English," one of the men said.

"Why did you stop your vehicle?"

"We knew you were behind. The general said we were to be the rear guard, stop you if we could. Die if we couldn't."

"How many men are with the general," Jaybird asked.

The Kenyan looked at Jaybird, who held his MP-5 trained on his belly.

"He has twelve, maybe fifteen men with him. All fanatics. Two machine guns, a flame thrower, grenades, rifles, a rocket-propelled grenade."

"Thank you. Why are you taking off your uniforms?" Murdock asked.

"We quit. The revolution is busted. We're going back to our old Army units, or just become civilians. Our war is over."

"Too much killing," another man shouted. "We've seen him kill too many good men. He's crazy."

"Where are your weapons?"

They pointed to a tree. Red Nicholson went over there and brought back three AK-47's and six magazines filled with thirty rounds each.

Murdock gestured to the Kenyans. "Go. Your truthfulness saved your lives. Get out of here."

The men looked uncertain. Murdock waved them away, and one ran south. Then the other two ran, taking off their army shirts and throwing them away.

Five minutes later, the SEALs had checked the half-track and taken out two more rifles, four loaded magazines, and six hand grenades. Then the big truck moved on up the hill again.

"How's our gas supply?" Murdock asked.

"Half full," Lincoln said. "A real gas-guzzler. We can't be getting more than seven miles to the gallon."

The road made a switchback, and climbed higher on the hill. Now there was a real forest. Tall trees, lots of cedar, and other trees they didn't know. Hardwoods with moss on them. It was more of a rain forest here in the higher elevations of what was mostly a desert country. All of that cover could be a death trap for the SEALs, Murdock knew.

"Look sharp now," he called to the men in back of the truck.

The road was narrower here. It looked bulldozed to Murdock. It twisted and turned, but they knew the quarry was ahead somewhere. There had been no place to turn off for the past five miles.

Twice they had seen men walking ahead of them. Murdock figured it was a rear guard. But when and where they would attack was the problem. Twice they fired rifles at the truck, but missed. Magic Brown had slammed two .50-caliber rounds at them and missed, but maintained that he'd scared the shit out of them.

Murdock looked at the turn ahead. Sharp and uphill. He hoped the big truck could make it. They might come to one soon where the truck couldn't get around, and they'd have to walk.

Lincoln ground the big rig into the turn, and stopped.

"Ambush dead ahead!" Lincoln shouted. They started to dive out of the cab, but the machine gun chattered at them even as Lincoln screamed the words. Half-a-dozen rounds hit the windshield, mashing it into jagged wedges. No safety glass in this one.

Murdock slid out of the passenger's side, and Jaybird fell on top of him. They dove and rolled into the scant cover of the ditch.

"Lincoln, you okay?" Murdock called. The machine gun chattered at them again and again.

In the back of the truck, Willy Bishop used the cab as his cover, and got his H&K machine gun over the roof and laid down a steady stream of answering fire. The Kenyans were two hundred yards off. Horse Ronson began pounding at them with his MG, and a minute later half the weapons with the range on board fired at the two men at the side of the big tree ahead.

Then the incoming stopped.

"Cease fire," Murdock told his Motorola. The weapons were silenced, but the machine gunners kept watch.

"Anybody hit?" Murdock asked.

He heard one growl from the cab of the truck, and jumped up the step and inside. Lincoln hadn't made it out of the truck. He lay against the back of the seat bent down under the dash. That must have saved his life. He had a bullet graze on one arm, and held his hand over his belly. Blood seeped between his fingers.

"Doc, get up here fast," Murdock bellowed.

Doc Ellsworth came up to the driver's-side door, and frowned when he saw Lincoln.

"Hey, buddy, you picked up a scratch. Move your hand, let me look at it."

He picked up Lincoln's bloody hand so he could see. "Yeah, Linc, caught you one in the side. Looks like it went right through. Missed most of your gut. We'll get you in the back."

He gave Lincoln a shot of morphine, put a pad over the front wound, and felt in back.

"Yeah, little zinger came out. That's good. Now I don't have to go lead mining."

"Anybody else hit?" Murdock asked into his lip mike.

"One nipped my arm a little, messed up my shirt sleeve," Holt said. Murdock knew his voice. "No sweat, LT. Band-Aid stuff. How's Linc?"

"We'll need a new driver. Who can handle this rig?"

"I can," Jaybird said. "Used to drive a furniture-delivery rig about this size back in Michigan."

They moved Lincoln carefully. Doc put bandages on both wounds, and had most of the bleeding stopped. Lincoln wouldn't be walking anywhere else on this mission. They laid him down in the back of the truck on some sacking. Doc stayed with him.

Jaybird rolled the truck. They cleared the curve and then the next one. Each time Jaybird slowed. They were getting into the higher country now, and the trees and underbrush covered the narrow road. They met nobody, and no rig tried to pass them. Murdock figured they were moving about ten or fifteen miles an hour, grinding along in second most of the time.

Murdock had Horse Ronson's H&K machine gun in the cab now, with the nose pushed out through the hole where the windshield used to be. He was ready for any more ambushes.

A short time later they drove around another corner, and

Murdock saw a flash of sunshine off something ahead. He let off a burst of six rounds, and a moment later they took return fire. Jaybird hit the brakes hard, stopped the rig, and killed the engine. He went to the floor of the cab. Murdock kept firing, driving three dark-green shirted troopers off the side of the road.

They had planned what to do if this happened again. Magic darted away from the back of the truck into the brush. Murdock was right behind him with Ching and Nicholson. They charged up hill through the brush fast as they could run.

Red stayed closer to the side of the roadway, and lip-miked what he saw.

"Three of them in the brush on the other side of the road," Red said as he ran. "Looks like they're waiting for something. Another fifty yards ahead."

The SEALs ran again.

The next time Red came on the Motorola, it was a whisper.

"Yeah, we're far enough now. There's a big cedar tree here with two tops. Bastards are right across the road."

Murdock got there first. They were screened by some brush. Three Kenyan soldiers lay across the road with their machine gun aimed down toward the next small curve the SEALs' truck would have to round.

Murdock settled in with the MG and waited. Magic came in next, silently saw the situation, and found a field of fire for his H&K PSG1 sniper rifle twenty feet up the road. Ching came in on silent feet, and he and Red stood behind the big cedar tree.

The SEALs traditionally started their firing on the first shot from Murdock. He got off half a burst of six before the other three weapons joined in. The three prone soldiers across the road didn't have time to swing their guns around. They all died instantly with six or eight rounds in each one.

The SEALs stopped firing and waited. There was no response from any other unit. After three minutes, Murdock motioned to Red, and he and Ching ran across the dirt road.

They picked up the two AK-47's the men had and four magazines, and ran down the road.

A few minutes later the big truck ground up the hill, and paused while Murdock and Magic climbed on board.

Red Nicholson rode on the front bumper. They came to a turnoff into a narrower track, and Nicholson jumped off and checked it.

"Turned in here, L-T," he called. Murdock waved them forward. This road was barely wide enough for the 6 x 6 truck. The vehicle swept branches on both sides of the road. The first turn involved twice backing up and going forward.

They worked along a road cut into the bank of a slope that went up fifty feet. They were halfway up. Murdock kept watching the slope, wondering. He saw something come out of some brush, and yelled for everyone to take cover.

The grenade bounced once to the side, then hit the road thirty feet in front of the truck. Red Nicholson had jolted off the bumper and dove behind the front wheel as Jaybird stopped the rig.

Murdock sprayed the brush with rounds from his MP-5. He'd taken the silencer off it. Two M-4A1's opened up as well, and DeWitt sprinted up the road with three of his men. He was next up on the ambush patrol kill schedule.

Horse got his MG warmed up, and chewed up the brush where the others had been shooting, then hosed down the area on each side.

"Hold it," Murdock called. DeWitt had vanished around the bend ahead where the road took a switchback heading up the sharp slope.

They heard firing from above. Then the Motorola spoke.

"Fernandez, over there by that tree. Yes." It was DeWitt. More rattling fire sounded from above, and DeWitt came on the radio again.

"Clear on top. See if that bucket of Kenyan bolts will get up this far."

It did.

Jaybird stopped on the rise and picked up the four men. They had three more AK-47's and two more thirty-round magazines of the 7.62 ammo.

Quinley moved over to Doc Ellsworth.

"Caught one," Quinley said. Doc looked at the arm wound.

"Not too bad. Missed the bone, went on through. Your lucky day." He put some healing salve on the two wounds, then some sterile compresses, and wrapped it tightly with roller bandages.

"Now flex your fist. Make a hard one. Relax. Do it again. Any burning along your arm?" Quinley shook his head. "Okay, *joto ichiban*. Have two blondes, and see me in the morning."

Quinley grinned. "Wished to hell I could. The blondes, I mean."

The road flattened out then as it wound through the highlands. There were more trees, and brush, and some strange plants that Murdock couldn't identify. They saw no more rear guards, and knew they had reduced the general's force by at least ten men. He might have ten still with him, or maybe fifteen. The men they'd questioned might not have known for sure.

Murdock looked at the AK-47's. Always a potent weapon. The thirty-round magazines were attractive right then.

"How we doing on ammo?" he asked. He got reports from half gone to two-thirds gone. Two men were down to two magazines left.

"We've got ten AK-47's here. We'll use them until they run dry. All the men with the MP-5 pick up a forty seven, and get used to it. We'll have more long-range work now anyway. One thing we don't want to do is run out of rounds, so be conservative. Use single-shot if that will do the job."

They came to another rise in the narrow road. It didn't look as if it had been traveled for some time. Weeds had begun to show between the tire tracks in the middle of the road. Soon they came to another hill. The road rose along the side of the slope, and Murdock watched upward wondering about another grenade attack.

None came.

They were halfway up the slope when Murdock yelled at

Jaybird. "Floor this fucker, Jaybird. We've got some rocks rolling down the hill."

They all looked up then. What had probably been started as two or three large rocks had gouged out dirt and more rocks, and those had hit more loose rocks, and now the SEALs had a full-sized landslide pounding down toward them.

Jaybird kicked the throttle to the floor, and the old truck wheezed, spurted ahead, then stalled. Jaybird ground the engine. The rocks and dirt came at them in a wall four feet high.

The motor turned over, caught, and Jaybird eased it forward, then gave it more fuel gradually, until they finally tore up the slope.

They almost made it. Murdock watched some of the larger rocks hit and jolt to the left and right instead of coming straight down. That gave the landslide a wider footprint. Jaybird coaxed more speed out of the truck, and Murdock saw that most of it would miss the truck.

Then it was on them. Half-a-dozen rocks the size of basketballs slammed into the side of the rig and the undercarriage. One bounced upward and shattered one of the bows across the top.

The road behind them was covered with six feet of rocks and dirt. The old truck kept moving. When they were out of the danger zone, Jaybird stopped the truck, and they got out and looked at the damage. One of the duals on the back had been slashed and had gone flat.

"One tire's enough with this light load," Jaybird said.

Just then several shots from above snarled, and angry lead slapped into the truck. The men scattered into the near ditch and any other cover they could find when they heard the rifle fire. The men all had their weapons with them. Four rose up and sent AK-47 messages up the slope. They used single-shot, and put twenty rounds into the brush they thought might be hiding the enemy. They had no reaction, and no return fire.

They waited five minutes.

"Let's mount up and get out of here," Murdock said.

The next turn also involved backing up and going ahead twice. Then they were on another fairly open stretch. They were a quarter of a mile from the last turn when the engine sputtered, coughed, and quit. Jaybird ground the starter, but it wouldn't catch.

Quinley came up from the side of the rig. "I'd say you're out of gas, Jaybird. One of those last rounds from the cliff caught the gas tank. We've been leaking fuel the last quarter mile."

"Everybody out," Murdock called. "We're foot soldiers from here on. That's what that L is for in SEALs."

Doc came up and shook his head at Murdock. "L-T, what in hell do we do about Lincoln? He isn't much on taking a hike right now."

27

Friday, July 23

1245 hours
Hill country
North of Nairobi, Kenya

Murdock knelt beside Lincoln where he lay in the rear of the 6 x 6 truck.

"Hey, Linc, how's it going?"

"Not the best, L-T. I heard about the gas tank. So why are you guys hanging around here? Hit the road. Hike a little. I can take care of myself. Just leave me my MP-five and I'll be fine."

Doc Ellsworth moved in and checked the bandages. He changed both front and back and eased Lincoln down. "At least the bleeding has stopped, Linc. You stay quiet and don't bust it open again, y'all hear?"

"Hear, Doc. Now get the troops out of here."

"Quinley, get up here," Murdock called.

He crawled into the truck. "Yeah, L-T?"

"You're staying here as a rear guard with Linc. Figure the two of you can stop anybody coming up this road."

"But L-T, Linc said—"

A stern look from Murdock cut Quinley off in midsentence. "Yeah, L-T. The two of us should be able to hold this spot for the rest of the day. I'll have my shotgun and one of them Kalashnikovs with the thirty-round magazines."

Linc started to say something, then shook his head and eased down on the bed of the truck.

Murdock put the rest of the platoon in motion. He had twelve men besides himself to face whatever was ahead. He hoped that would be enough.

They hiked up the road at a good pace, with Red Nicholson out ahead of the rest of them by fifty yards as lead scout. He watched the tracks on the dirt trail, and kept a lookout for any bushwhackers who might have been left to harass the troops.

They rounded two more curves in the road, and then it straightened out across a small meadow. Ahead, almost into the woods again, they saw the weapons carrier. It had stopped in the middle of the road.

Red dove into the ditch, and the rest of the platoon followed him.

"Can't see any troops around it, LT. Just sitting there," Red reported.

"No fire coming from it. Work up and check it out. But don't get yourself killed."

Red sprinted ahead ten yards and dove into the ditch.

Nothing happened around the rig.

Red did another spurt with the same results. He lifted up and used binoculars. He checked the whole area twice, then stood and ran for the rear of the Army vehicle.

No shots sounded. A moment later, he vanished around the side of the weapons carrier.

"L-T, nobody home," Red said to his lip mike.

The SEALs moved up quickly and looked at the vehicle, but didn't touch it or anything around it. They knew too well about booby traps in equipment and gear abandoned on purpose.

"Ran out of gas, my bet," Red said. He scanned the ground beyond it, and waved the platoon forward. "Now the big guy is hoofing it like the rest of us." Red soon saw that the Kenyans had kept to the road, where it was easier walking.

"How many men?" Murdock asked Red.

"Hey, I ain't no Chiricahua Apache who can track a pussycat across a lava field." He shrugged as they kept walking. "My guess is maybe ten or twelve. No more."

The platoon hiked for fifteen minutes, but had no way of knowing how far ahead the general and his men were. Most of the SEALs carried two weapons now, including one of the heavy AK-47's. But they didn't complain. The side that ran out of ammunition first was bound to lose this battle.

Red fell in step beside Murdock. "L-T, you know, if they split up and left twelve trails the way the Indians used to do, eleven of them would get away and be home free. This way we get a shot at all of them. If we catch them."

The flat crack of an AK-47 jolted into the mountain silence, and the round slanted past Murdock and dug into the road. The men darted into the ditches on each side or behind trees.

Murdock got off the first shot when he saw movement in the roadside brush two hundred yards ahead. "Use your AKs," Murdock said on the Motorola. The SEALs slammed ten rounds into the brush, then more on the other side of the road. Would they put just one man as a rear guard?

"Hold it," Murdock said to the lip mike. "No more fire. I think he's bugged out."

They went into the brush, and worked up to where they had seen the shots come from. No one was there. Red showed them where the man had trampled down some grass and weeds and broken off some branches to have a clear field of fire.

Back on the road, Murdock moved them out faster. They needed to catch the men ahead, not just chase them. He wondered if the Kenyans were heading for a specific spot or were just on a frantic run.

Murdock changed his usual formation, and spread the men out at ten-yard intervals to make a less-enticing target. He and Red took the point, and moved out fifty yards.

They came around another turn, and saw the road slanting upward again. The hills were getting higher, the ravines sharper, but still there were more trees and brush than Murdock liked.

Red held up his hand and went down on one knee. "Take cover, L-T," Red yelled, dove, and rolled to the side of the road.

Murdock sprinted five yards into the brush just as he heard a machine gun pounding out rounds from somewhere ahead. The rounds were aimed on the other side of the road toward Red. He rolled again, then lunged into the brush and behind a sturdy hardwood tree.

Murdock touched his mike. "Hold it, platoon. Take cover. We've got an MG up here somewhere. Red and I'll check it out. We move up on each side, Red. How in hell did you know he was there?"

"Saw something that didn't compute, L-T. Wasn't an animal, so had to be the rebs up there somewhere. Then there was the click of something metallic."

They worked slowly uphill in the brush, taking care not to break a dry branch or scuff dead leaves. The brush and trees were thick enough so they could see only twenty feet ahead. Murdock figured the MG had to be 250 yards up the hill. If the men working the weapon stayed there, the SEALs could even the odds more. Maybe he could encourage the Kenyans to stand pat.

"DeWitt. Move somebody up to see around the bend and put some rounds up the road. Ten or twelve. See if you get a reaction. Keep your fucking heads down."

Murdock and Red kept easing forward. He heard the slap of the AK-47 rounds, then an answering chatter of the machine gun. Good. Sounded a lot closer.

"About a hundred yards," Red said in his mike.

"Sounds right. Figure he's on my side." Murdock moved up again. The MG sputtered out more rounds down the roadway, where DeWitt must be baiting him. The sound helped cover Murdock's cautious movements. When he figured he was twenty yards from the machine gun, Murdock went on hands and knees and slipped under and through the brush, trailing his AK-47.

He stopped suddenly. There was a small opening in the brush, and he could see the MG in the ditch with some fallen logs dragged in front of it as a shield.

Fifteen yards. Three men worked the weapon. One feeding in a belt of ammo. One on the gun behind its bipod and resting the gun on the log. The third man looking around the barricade down the road.

Murdock stripped two fraggers off his harness, then changed his mind and used one HE and one WP. He pulled the pins on both, and threw the fragger first, then the white phosphorous grenade.

The fragmentation grenade hit six feet from the gunner, and bounced once on the soft forest floor, then rolled forward almost to the edge of the ditch four feet from the machine gun. Murdock threw the WP quickly. The HE went off with a deadly whump. The machine gunner slammed forward over his weapon. The ammo bearer was thrown sideways. Four seconds after the first explosion, the WP went off, showering all three with the sticky, unstoppable burning phosphorus. The third man took a dozen globs of the material on his uniform. He tried to brush them off, but they burned through the cloth into flesh and bone and kept on going. He screamed again and again, until Murdock had an open shot at him and put him dead in the ditch.

Murdock touched his lip mike. "Move up, we're clear here."

They had a brief conference in the woods beyond the three dead Kenyans. Red Nicholson came back from scouting up front. He said it was all clear for at least a mile ahead past another small hill and around the side of a little valley.

"How's the ammo?" Murdock asked. Three of the men had used up their AK-47 ammo and discarded the heavy rifles.

"That damned AK really chews up the rounds in a rush," Ron Holt said.

Most of the others had two or three magazines left.

"Ammo is going to be critical on this one," Murdock said. "Use it, but with some caution. When we're out, we're out."

"Anybody hit?" Doc asked. Nobody replied.

"We're going to go double time now. Magic, how many rounds left for the big one?"

"Last magazine, and it's getting heavy as hell. Find me a target, L-T."

They went ahead on the trail of a road. Red stayed a

quarter of a mile out front now, keeping in touch with the Motorola.

Murdock kept them at the slow trot for a half mile, then went to a walk but with a long ground-eating stride.

They met Red Nicholson at the next corner. He pointed upward. The road took a long turn and headed up a sharp slope.

"See those figures on the road?" Red asked. Magic pulled out his McMillan fifty and looked through the scope.

"Oh, damn, yes," he yelped. "I count eight of them." He lifted the big weapon and looked for something to lean it across. Horse Ronson went on his hands and knees, and Magic dropped to the ground beside him and slanted the heavy barrel across Ronson's back.

"Oh, my, yes, this is good," Magic said. He had a ten-round magazine in the big weapon. He sighted through the scope and fired. At once he jerked the bolt to the rear and slammed a new round into the chamber.

He watched through the sight, and screeched when he saw the round hit between two of the men. He sighted and fired again. Then he fired four more times as fast as he could pull the bolt. He saw the men on the road scatter and vanish from his sight. He aimed once more and pulled the trigger, but he knew he was out of rounds.

"Give the bastards something to think about," Magic said.

"You gonna dump the fifty now that you're out of rounds?" Fernandez asked him.

"Shit, no. They might not buy me another one."

They marched again. Nicholson had vanished around a bend ahead of them.

A half hour later, they climbed the long slope and came to the spot where the troops had been when Magic had fired on them. They found one man in the far ditch with half of his chest blown out. The .50-caliber round had almost cut him into two pieces.

Murdock checked his watch. Just after 1400. Should be five more hours of daylight. They had to get this wrapped up before dark, or they could lose the big man in the night and the wilderness.

They marched again. Red held his lead of three hundred yards. The road leveled out some, then rose again. They could see the footprints of the others ahead of them. Red figured there were no more than seven of them now.

It could be getting close to desperation time for the general plodding ahead. The big man must be out of shape. This hike would kill him. What would Murdock do in the general's place? What? He'd make a stand. Find a favorable setup, and try to cut down the odds against him or wipe out the chasers. Murdock considered it, and watched the country on both sides of the road.

The woods closed in again, and Murdock watched closer. Red pulled back so he was one hundred yards ahead of the main body, where the men were still stretched out ten yards apart. That separation was basic combat technique. At ten yards a chance mortar round, grenade or machine gun couldn't get more than one or maybe two men with a lucky hit or a sudden attack.

Murdock was tired of hiking. They had been going uphill now for what he figured was seven or eight miles, maybe more. Some kind of a bird called in the woods. Murdock frowned. He hadn't heard any birds before. He studied the growth on both sides, then took a breath and relaxed.

That was when small-arms fire broke out on both sides of the road. The SEALs were in a cross fire. They hit the dirt, and returned fire on full automatic. The attackers were twenty yards ahead on each side so they didn't shoot each other. Murdock felt a round tug at his shirt sleeve. Then he was down returning fire on full auto with the AK-47.

All of the SEALs, scattered as they were, had perfect fields of fire. The first incoming rounds did the damage. Then the eleven weapons all on full automatic cut a swath through the brush, and the SEALs heard two men scream.

Red came running down the road, but it was over before he got there. Ronson brought his machine gun into play, and riddled the left side of the roadway where he figured the rounds came from.

Ching used his M-4A1, and emptied a new thirty-round clip of 9mm parabellum rounds into the right-hand side. All of the SEALs fired their magazines dry, and slammed in new ones.

"Hold fire," Murdock said into his Motorola. The sound of the weapons trailed off. Murdock stared at the ambush. The general and his men had used their heads this time, waiting for the cross fire.

"Ed, check the left side. I'll take the right. Everybody else cover us. If anybody in there fires a shot, blast them." Murdock lifted up and charged into the brush. He worked ahead carefully, making as little noise as he could. Twenty yards forward he came on the death scene. Two green-uniformed Kenyan troopers lay sprawled in the grass and weeds. Both had been riddled by more than a dozen rounds. They'd had no protection to the front. He kicked the weapons away. Both AK-47's had run dry of ammo.

"Clear right," Murdock said.

"Clear left," Ed DeWitt answered.

Murdock ran back to the road. He saw what he feared he might. Doc Ellsworth was busy. Murdock came up beside him where he worked on Horse Ronson. The big man grinned through what Murdock knew was searing pain.

"He took two rounds in his right leg," Doc said. "Doubt if the bone is broken. He'd be screaming by now if it was. Guess that one round slanted off the bone and came out sideways. No more hiking for Horse."

"Anybody else?"

"Yeah, me. Got a scratch on my left arm," Doc said, and sat down suddenly. His face went white, and he struggled to stay sitting up. He shook his head.

"L-T, could you get me one of them morphine shots. Think I'm going to need one. Oh, one for Horse here too."

It was ten minutes before they got Ronson to the side of the road in a trampled-down patch of grass where he could stay until they came for him. Murdock gave him a WP grenade.

"Hey, Horse, if you hear a chopper coming, pop that Willy Peter out there in the road and we'll be sure to stop by."

"Can do. Go knock down that General Fuck up there.
Wanted him myself. Have to give him to you."

Ronson wouldn't let them leave anyone with him. They
were down to eleven men. Doc came around and joked
about almost passing out. Murdock wrapped up his left arm.
Doc could flex his hand. He said he could shoot, and that
was what mattered.

Murdock looked up the road. They were coming to the
top of this particular hill. It looked as if the road went
directly to the summit. Maybe that was the end of the road.
It had to lead somewhere. The general might be down to
three or four men. Which should make it easy, if they could
catch the guy. He shouldn't have much of a lead by this
time.

Murdock saw Red Nicholson jogging down the sloping
road toward him. He was out of breath.

"Might have something up front," Red said. "Road goes
right to some kind of a rock building, an old house or a fort.
I know the general and his men are inside. I heard him
yelling at them. It's not more than a quarter of a mile
ahead."

28

Friday, July 23

1532 hours
Mountain country
Near Nairobi, Kenya

Murdock and Red Nicholson slid into brush at the edge of the road. Murdock had moved the platoon up in the brush to the closest place to the structure, which was fifty yards away across a grassy area. He looked at the sturdy rock building. It wasn't a house or a storeroom. It had more the look of a fort. On the front he saw what could only be firing slots.

"Could have been a strong point early on when the British were here," Red said.

Murdock nodded. "Makes it just that much harder to capture." The platoon commander studied the structure again. Two stories, maybe thirty feet showing on the front side, slate or tile roof so it couldn't be burned out. Six firing slots out this side. One regular-sized door that looked to be covered with an iron facing had been built into the center of the front. Outside the door was a pile of furniture. Murdock got his glasses on it, and froze.

"They've got a barricade outside the front door. Could be some rifles in there."

Just as he spoke they heard two weapons fire, and rounds nipped through the brush around them.

Murdock got his MP-5 up. He'd taken the silencer off so it was good for a range of 150 yards. "Dig them out,"

Murdock said, and fired a six-round burst. The others began slamming lead at them as well, with the heavy snarl of the AK-47's and the sharper sound of the .223 rounds from the carbines.

Automatic bursts came from the barricade. Murdock squirmed farther behind the cedar tree. He heard somebody bleat in pain, then fired again at the pile of furniture.

There were three more bursts of rounds from the front of the house. Then they stopped. Murdock saw the door open a foot, then close a few moments later.

"Hold fire," Murdock said in his mike. "The gents have moved into their fortress. Who got hit?"

Ching spoke up. "Hey, just a scratch, not even a Baid-Aid needed. Not to worry. What's next?"

"Take a look, Doc. That's why we pay you the big bucks."

Ellsworth worked over to Ching, and found a graze that had plowed up a half inch of flesh across Ching's arm just below the shoulder. He put on some disinfectant salve, and then wrapped it with a roller.

"Ching is fit for duty, L-T. Just a graze," Doc reported.

"Good. Ching, glad you're still with us. Hey, no wonder the general wanted to get here," Murdock said. "This place looks like a fortress. Red, circle around the whole thing. See if there's any closer approach through the brush and trees. Check for any windows in back and look for more doors. See if they all have metal shielding. We've got three hours to darkness with any luck. Go."

Red Nicholson bent over and ran through the brush. This was the job he had asked for in the platoon, and one he loved. A little thing like a slug through his left arm wasn't going even to slow him down. He moved thirty yards in the heavy brush, then worked forward to where the growth thinned and then stopped around the top of this small hill. Evidently it had been cut down and dug out at one time. Now the new growth was starting to recapture the lost ground.

The side of the structure looked much like the front. Two stories, six firing slots, no doors or windows.

He crawled into the brush and circled around to the back.

The cover was sparser here, and he moved with caution. If they were any kind of soldiers at all, they would have lookouts at those firing slots.

Again he came up on the clearing. The rear was a little different. There were two doors, and two windows with close-set bars on them. He estimated the iron bars were only three inches apart. He saw one of the doors open. A man appeared briefly, threw out some water from a bucket, went inside quickly, and closed the door.

Red wondered if he should have shot the guy. No. He had no go on it from the L-T. He squirmed into heavy cover, and checked the last side. It resembled the other three.

The best place to attack would be the rear. It had the two doors, and grenades could be wedged between the window bars. The doors had the same metal facing, but a charge or two would send them flying off their hinges.

When Red returned to make his report, he found the ten men spread out in the brush facing the rock house. He gave his report to Murdock.

The platoon leader had his plan at once. He looked at Ed DeWitt. "Keep two men with an MG and AK-47. You'll be the diversion. I'll give you a signal on the Motorola. Gonna try those two doors in back. Keep up a good-paced fire, but don't run out of ammo. How much you have left?"

Willy Bishop reported he had a little over a hundred rounds. DeWitt gathered the AK-47 ammo from his squad, and had four full thirty-round magazines and two partials.

Murdock nodded. "Should be enough. We're hoping to blind them and get inside quickly. I'll call you off if we get a door open." He looked at the men spread out, then used the mike.

"How many flashbang grenades we have left?"

The reports showed they had only one.

"Bring it up," Murdock said.

"How many WP forty-millimeter or hand grenades we have?"

This time he found out the M-4A1 men had twelve of the smoke grenades. He still had one WP hand bomb.

"Okay. Ed's two men stay with him. Find yourself some

good cover with a good field of fire at those shooting slots. The rest of you on me."

They went deeper into the brushy cover, and circled the rock house, coming up at the back under Nicholson's direction. Murdock looked over the chances. The last good cover was thirty yards from the rock house, the closest brush was on any side.

"Red, any wind?" Murdock asked.

"Very light, L-T. Some, blowing left to right."

Murdock put Nicholson and Ching on one side, and Al Adams and Lampedusa on the other with their rocket-launching M-4A1 carbines.

"Ching, when I give the word, I want one WP round at the left side of the back of that rock house. We'll see how high the smoke blows and what effect it has. Then we'll do six rounds and if it works, we'll charge the place. Who brought the TNAZ that Lincoln usually carries?"

"I got the package, L-T," Ching said.

"When the smoke works, you and I charge up to that left-hand door and you put on two charges and blow the fucker. I'll be pushing some grenades into those windows."

Murdock had been on the mike. "Everyone have the game plan?"

"If the smoke doesn't cover?" Red asked.

"Then they have us outgunned and we wait for darkness. Pretty sure they don't have NVGs, so it'll be a walk in the park."

"Yeah, let's get this over with," Ching said.

Murdock adjusted his throat mike. "Ed, do it," Murdock said.

They heard the firing from the front, the chatter of the MG and the deeper crack of the Kalashnikov. Murdock waited twenty seconds, then pointed at Ching. He fired one WP round, letting it bounce before it hit the rock wall. It burst into a Fourth of July display with its hotly burning phosphorus. Then the trails began giving off smoke and it drifted slowly to the right rising, for a moment blanking out the whole wall.

Just as it did, rifles fired from two of the slots overhead.

The rounds came close to Murdock, who rolled to the side behind a six-inch-thick hardwood tree.

Ching had moved as well, and the rest of the men in deeper brush took cover.

"What the hell now, L-T?" Ching asked.

"We wait for the smoke to clear, then we use our long guns and blast those firing slots. Looks like they were made to fend off arrows and spears, not high-powered weapons. Everyone hear? Get a firing position along this front."

The troops moved up and spread out with fields of fire. The smoke drifted away lazily. When it was gone, Murdock reacted. "Open fire."

The rifles and carbines slammed thirty rounds into the slots. Murdock could see some rounds hitting the sides of the angled stone and ricocheting inside.

"Smoke now," Murdock said. "Fire for effect." The four SEALs fired six more rounds of WP at the same spot as the first one. Murdock watched the rounds burst and the smoke rise. Ching looked at Murdock. Murdock got up on one knee in a sprinter's stance. Ching did the same.

"Now," Murdock said, and the two men ran the thirty yards flat out for the rear of the building. Murdock knew there would be some firing from the rear window slots. They sprinted and zigzagged. A bullet splattered in front of Murdock, but only some dirt and gravel hit him. They covered the thirty yards quickly, and panted as they crouched against the wall.

"Hold fire, rear," Murdock said into the mike. He could hear DeWitt's team firing at the front, and knew there were also return rounds from inside the rock house. Murdock heard rounds fired from the wall above him, but the smoke had blinded the shooters, and he figured his men were safe.

Ching already had out the high explosive that succeeded C-5. It was TNAZ, twenty percent more powerful and lighter in weight than its cousin. Ching plastered a pliable one-eighth pound of the explosive on each door hinge, and attached timer-detonators. He had preset them for ten seconds. He motioned to the L-T that they would go around the corner to get away from the blast.

Murdock looked at the windows, held up his hand in a wait signal, then ran to the nearest window, broke the pane with the butt of his MP-5, and pushed two fragger grenades between the bars and through the window. He ran for the near rock wall corner, then nodded at Ching.

The SEAL pushed in the timer-activation switches, then hurried around the corner.

They heard the karumph of the two hand grenades inside the building after their 4.2 second fuse train burned down. Ten seconds is a year when you're waiting for a charge to go off, and Ching had started to go back to check it when Murdock caught his arm. Just then the twin explosions blasted half a second apart.

Murdock and Ching were around the wall in seconds. The rest of the squad raced across the thirty yards to join them at the rear wall. The two hinges had disintegrated, and the door had pivoted on the heavy lock and then broken off. A yawning black hole showed inside.

Ching hosed it down with ten rounds from his carbine. Murdock leaned toward the hole and threw in the flash grenade. The SEALs covered their ears and eyes. Murdock pulled up his night-vision goggles, and as soon as the six pulsing explosions and the six white-hot strobe lights faded, he rushed into the void.

In dull green light, he saw he was in a kitchen area. The grenades had trashed some kitchenware and furniture, but no bodies were present.

He charged to the connecting door, kicked it open, then knelt beside the protection of the wall. A burst of automatic-rifle fire buzzed through the opening. He rolled in a fragger grenade and waited the 4.2 seconds for the explosion.

When the shrapnel from the bomb stopped snarling through the open door, Murdock surged into the room. He took the right-hand side, and Ron Holt with his NVGs took the left. Through the faint green patina, Murdock saw two men trying to rise on the right-hand side. He drilled both with three-round bursts and they flopped to the floor. The sound of the firing in the rock room was like an echo chamber. Murdock wasn't sure he could hear much.

"Clear right," Murdock said into his mike.

He heard Holt on the left kick something, then send a six-round burst into the corner. The rounds echoing in the rock room sounded like doomsday itself. When the sound faded, Holt reported.

"Clear left, L-T."

The room had one door leading off it. Holt kicked it open. There was no reaction.

"Scrub it down," Murdock said.

Holt reached his MP-5 around the door frame and squirted twelve rounds into the room, covering most of the floor space. Again there was no reaction.

Holt leaned around from floor level and checked the room through his NVGs. He lifted up, and did the same thing again.

"Looks clear to me, L-T," Holt whispered. The two SEALs burst into the room, and found it empty.

Ching and Nicholson were right behind them. Ching saw the door leading from this room, and pushed it open gently, staying well to the side. The hinges squeaked. When the door came fully open, someone in the room spat six rounds through the void. Then there were footfalls, and a door slammed.

Ching checked the area from floor level by leaning out to look around the jamb. He jolted out, and came back. Just as he cleared the frame, it shattered with three rounds of angry bullets. Ching caught some splinters in one hand. He swore softly, pulled a fragger off his webbing, jerked the pin, and rolled the bomb inside after letting it soak for two seconds with the arming spoon popped off. The bomb went off two seconds after he threw it.

At once, he checked again, and pulled back. He did that twice, then stayed looking inside. "Look's clear, L-T," Ching said. As he did, he lifted his M-4A1 and emptied ten rounds from his magazine into the room. Then he charged in, and confirmed it was clear.

Murdock found a firing slot at the front wall. He looked at a door to his left.

"How do you get to the second floor in this place?" he

asked. Nobody knew. They cleared the next room. The rest of the eight men Murdock had brought with him were in the rooms behind. He could split up and send some men upstairs if he could figure out where the stairs were.

Murdock saw two doors out of the room. He opened one slowly. Light poured in through two firing slots in the thick rock wall. No one was inside.

"Over here," Magic Brown said.

Murdock went to the second door that Magic had opened. There were stone steps set against the wall that led upward. Murdock closed the door softly.

"Anybody up there isn't coming down, and they won't give up easily. Any suggestions?"

"Grenades," Magic said.

"Yeah, sure, and what if it bounces around and falls down the stairs?" Nicholson asked.

"Flashbang grenade," Jaybird said.

"Good, but we're out of them."

"One man go up them fucking stone steps quiet and cautious," Doc Ellsworth said.

"Who?" Murdock asked.

Nicholson shrugged. "Hell, gotta be me. You other guys would spook a herd of turtles."

Nicholson took off everything on his gear that would make any noise, hefted his M-4A1, and moved the rest of them to the other side of the room.

Then he opened the door soundlessly, slid through a foot-wide slot, and closed the door.

Red moved up one step at a time. The stone gave off no squeaks or rattles. He moved standing up, hoping that he could see over the floor level soon. He had on his NVGs, and they helped in the nearly dark upstairs. Red wondered if there was more than one big room upstairs.

He crept up higher, but still couldn't see over the floor. He paused, listening. Nothing. Not a chirp of a cricket, or a bird, or a man wheezing or breathing loudly. Another step. Still not high enough.

One more step and he lifted on tiptoe so he could see over the landing. There was no wall beside the stairwell, just a three-slat board railing. He checked under the lower rail, and saw in the green-tinted light two beds without linens or mattresses, a pair of chairs, and a large closet.

Slowly Red inventoried every square foot of the room.

There was no one there.

Except maybe in the closet. He lifted up another two steps, and angled the carbine's muzzle over the wooden floor. He had taken the silencer off the carbine. Red triggered a dozen rounds, drawing a line of bullet holes two feet off the floor across the wooden doors of the five-foot-wide closet.

When the sound stilled, there were four more SEALs just behind him on the steps. He put six more rounds into the closet, then surged up the last three steps and charged the doors. One had opened an inch. He threw open the door, training his weapon on the inside.

Nothing was there.

He jerked open the second door, and found the same situation.

"Nobody up here, L-T. If there was somebody here, he squeezed through that six-inch firing slot."

Murdock pushed past the others and checked every corner of the one big room.

Nobody.

"Where did they go?" Murdock asked. "We know there was at least one more live one in here."

"What about that other fucking door downstairs?" Ching asked.

They ran for it. When Murdock got there, Ching was ready to kick in the door in the next room. He did, staying clear at the side. No shots slammed through the opening. He bellied down, and took a look into the half-lit room.

"Sonofabitch!" Ching bellowed. "This is where that second door comes out of the place. Has that other window, and the fucking door is open."

Murdock ran to the door and looked out. "Oh, shit. We didn't leave anyone outside to cover this door. We must have chased them around in a circle, and they hauled ass through this door. Nicholson, on the double."

Red spent ten minutes outside looking at the grass, leaves, and weeds just beyond the second door. He took off in a line directly in back of the building, looking carefully at the ground as he went. A minute later returned.

"Okay, here's what we've got. I found tracks of four different kinds of boots. One set is deeper into the mulch than the others, which I'd figure is our fat general. They couldn't be ahead of us by more than twenty minutes. It's downhill from here. That fat guy is going to slow them down."

"Good, we'll go get them," Murdock said. He frowned. "Ammo report."

The three in front of the building were down to ten rounds each. The rest of the platoon members were on their last thirty-round magazines, except two, who had one more spare. The AK-47's were dry and discarded. They all had their belt pistols, the heavy H&K special Mark 23s with two twelve-round magazines. "If we get down to fighting with our forty-fives, we're in shit city," Murdock said. He scowled and walked around a minute.

"This all means we're damn short on ammo," Murdock said. "We use it only when we have to. We have four more guys out there to waste, but we have to do it carefully. Let's go, Red."

29

Friday, July 23

1602 hours
Rock fortress
North of Nairobi, Kenya

The platoon scout headed down the trail of footprints leading from the now-benign rock fortress on top of the Kenyan hill. The remaining men in the Third Platoon followed stretched out at ten-yard intervals.

Murdock was in his usual place just behind Nicholson, and Ron Holt shadowed the Platoon Leader with his SATCOM radio. The trail wound through the woods, not along the road they had come up. It angled down a slope through heavy trees and brush, but Nicholson had no trouble following it.

At one point on hard ground with little vegetation, he had to do a small circle to pick up the trail, but he found it again and they moved out.

Ten minutes later, Red called for Murdock to come up. He pointed at the ground.

"Fuckers are finally getting smart. They split up. Two of them went each way. I'd say the general is on the trail to the right, but I can't be sure."

Murdock looked at the evidence, and was glad his tracker was along. "Ed, come up," Murdock said in his mike.

Ed DeWitt hustled up, and went on one knee beside Murdock.

"So?"

"Split up, two each way. You take your squad and go left. I'll take the right hand. We want them down before dark."

"How am I going to follow them? I'm no Indian," DeWitt asked.

Red showed him the bent-over grass, the broken sticks and twigs on the ground, the scuffed mulch. "These guys are in a rush and not trying to hide their tracks, L-T. You shouldn't have any trouble."

"Easy for you to say, kemo sabe."

"Ed, you have four men?"

"Right."

"Take Doc with you. Nail these guys fast."

Ed called his men out, and they moved down the trail that slanted away at a ninety-degree angle to the other one.

Murdock nodded, and Red hiked out along the other trail. They had gone about two hundred yards through light trees when two weapons fired ahead of them on full automatic. Red Nicholson went down hard and rolled over.

The other four men hit the dirt, and returned fire at the location. The two weapons ahead chattered again on full auto, and bullets sang and ricocheted through the trees and brush. Murdock waved Magic Brown to swing to the left, and Ching to move right. The Platoon Leader and his men fired on the site for another minute. Then Murdock's command on the mike stopped the attack.

They waited. Two minutes went by with no fire from the front. Another minute, and Magic Brown came on the Motorola.

"Bastards are gone, L-T. Nothing up here but a pile of brass."

Murdock got his men moving. Red Nicholson hadn't been hit when he went down—just a precautionary move, as he called it.

He got back on his tracking mission. They moved ahead. Murdock evaluated his squad. They were beaten up. Ching, Doc, Nicholson, and Magic all had gunshot wounds. Ronson was out of it for now. Only he, Jaybird, and Ron Holt hadn't been shot up. He worried about it.

Ahead, Nicholson went flat on the ground, and the rest of them behind at ten-yard intervals dropped as well. Murdock bent over and hurried forward, sliding into the forest mulch beside his scout.

"So, what?"

"I saw somebody up there. Less than two hundred yards. We must be catching up with them."

"Let's go get them," Murdock said. Red moved out faster, charging down the slight slope. He didn't see the trip wire until he was on it. Then he screamed a warning, and tried to dive away from it. The trip wire snapped, releasing the arming spoon, and the grenade went off almost at once.

Red slammed into the ground too late. More than a dozen chunks of the shrapnel tore into his body. Two hit him in the chest, one in the throat, and four more large ones in his belly and legs. The ten-yard interval between men saved the rest of them. By the time Murdock dropped to the ground beside Nicholson, he was choking on his own blood. He looked up at Murdock and gave a small shrug.

"Been a good tour, L-T," he said. Then he gave one last long breath and died.

Murdock slammed his fist into the ground.

"Jaybird, stay with him. Keep some rounds so we can find you when we're ready to bug out of this firetrap. The rest of you, let's go get those bastards."

Magic Brown took over the point. He had left the big Fifty with Ronson when he ran out of rounds, and now moved along the plain trail. Fifty yards ahead he stopped and knelt.

Murdock went down beside him.

"No fucking expert, L-T, but looks like they split up again. One that way, one straight ahead."

"Brown and Holt, to the left," Murdock said. "Ching and I'll take the straight ahead. Let's get this thing wrapped up."

Murdock took the lead now, running when he was sure of the trail ahead, slowing to check the dirt and mulch of the woods floor. The brush thinned out, and he could see ahead thirty to fifty yards. He caught the glimpse of a green shirt vanishing into some trees, and put a dozen rounds into the area.

When they got there, Murdock found no body, only hurried tracks going along the side of the hill. They ran again. This time the brush petered out, and only a few trees remained. Ahead, Murdock saw a figure working along a rocky slope.

Ching lifted his M-4A1 Carbine and fired twice to get the range on single-shot, then flipped the lever and emptied his magazine at the target two hundred yards away.

The Kenyan soldier had turned to look behind him just as the rounds reached him. Murdock figured it was four or five hits. The man crumpled, then dropped his rifle, and flopped on his back.

Murdock nodded. "Yeah, splash one bogie. That one's not the general. Magic has him on the other trail. Let's get to where we left Red."

They turned and began working along their trail to where the dead SEAL lay on the ground.

Magic Brown had started out fast along the trail in the grass and leaf mold, but slowed as he watched for trip wires. He saw that the impressions in the mulch were deep, and hoped it was the general ahead.

Twice they took incoming fire. Both times they did not shoot back. Brown was down to his last magazine in his sniper rifle, and he wasn't sure how many rounds he had left. Then came an opening in the brush, and he saw a figure moving ahead. Three hundred yards. He lifted up and fired twice. The figure moved, and he had a good shot. But when he pulled the trigger, there was no round. He should have noticed when the magazine ran dry.

Ron Holt held fire. The target was out of range of his submachine gun. Both of them ran down the trail. Magic Brown worked ahead of Holt. The radioman tried to keep up, but he couldn't. He came around a small turn in the trail, and saw Brown twenty yards ahead. He put on a burst of speed, failed to see a root sticking out of the ground, and tripped and went down hard.

Holt threw out his arms to break his fall. His MP-5 fell to

the ground, and he hit hard. A jolting pain streaked up his arm, and he rolled over. He'd lost the radio, and he reached for it. The stabbing pain caused him to cry out. He looked at his left arm. It hurt like fire. Broken, he was sure.

He gritted his teeth to hold down the pain, and crawled over to the fifteen-pound SATCOM radio. Once it was safe, he touched his lip mike.

"L-T. Holt here. I'm down. Think I broke my fucking arm. Brown is still after the guy over here."

"Hang in there, Holt," Murdock answered. "Get back to where we left Red. We'll make that our assembly point."

Ahead, Magic Brown heard the cry behind him, and figured that Holt was down. It was up to him, with no rounds and a worthless rifle. Still, he carried it. He could bluff with it. Yeah, maybe whoever was up ahead was short or out of ammo too.

He rounded a bend in the small canyon they had worked down to, and ahead, just vanishing behind a rock, he saw the general. Had to be him. The man was huge, tall, and wide. He carried a rifle.

Magic slid behind a large hardwood tree and watched the spot. It was no more than thirty yards ahead. For a minute nothing happened. Then the general lifted the rifle and rested it over the rock that shielded him. So maybe he did have rounds left. One way to find out. Magic surged into sight of the general, then jolted back. The rifle ahead fired almost at once. Good reflexes. At the same time Magic felt a blow on his right hip. He dodged out of sight and stared down at his hip looking for blood.

The holster holding his .45 auto had been almost torn off his hip. He pulled out the big H&K Mark 23 and looked at it. The AK-47 round had slammed into it on the side of the slide, denting it inward a quarter of an inch. He tried to charge a round into the chamber. The slide wouldn't move. He tossed the useless weapon aside. What the hell now? He was really out of ammo. He couldn't go back and get Holt's weapon. He scowled. Then his hand brushed his K-Bar.

Magic left his rifle against a tree, drew his knife, and

moved into the denser brush to his right. He found what he wanted, a dead branch on the ground two inches thick, six feet long, and fairly straight. He used his knife to smooth the shank of it, then with some all-purpose tape from his vest, taped his K-Bar on the small end of the branch with the blade extending over the end.

He had a six-foot-long spear.

Magic moved silently through the trees and brush. At one point he saw the general through the brush. He was resting below the rock. Twice he lifted up to look toward where Magic had been on the trail.

Magic stepped gingerly along another twenty feet to the rear, then worked out to the fringe of the brush.

General Umar Maleceia sat on the rock thirty feet away and slightly ahead. The general was too far away for a charge even with Brown's spear. How?

Magic found a fist-sized rock, lifted up, and threw it as far as he could beyond where the general hid. The rock hit some brush and made a racket. The general jolted upright, and fired three rounds at the noise. Then he fired again, and the thirty-round magazine on the AK-47 ran dry. He threw it away. He drew a handgun and looked around.

One more fist-sized rock slanted out of Magic's hand, and crashed in much the same area. General Maleceia fired five rounds into the brush, and then the revolver ran out of bullets.

Magic moved out of the brush into the open to the edge of a dry streambed. He walked silently toward the coup leader. When he was ten feet away he called.

"The party's over, Colonel."

Maleceia turned, surprised. He saw the spear and laughed.

"You, a black man, fighting another black man? Don't be stupid. I can make you rich. We'll hike out of here. I have many friends in this area. We'll find transport, get into Tanzania where I can tap a bank account, and the two of us will live like kings. All the food, drink, and women we want."

"Not a chance," Magic Brown said.

The general snarled, and drew a knife. It was an inch shorter than the K-Bar, but just as deadly.

"Come on, nigger," Maleceia said. "Know you hate that name, but you're just a nigger used to taking commands from the white trash over you. I don't see you with any officer's bars on your shoulder. Just a poor little nigger boy working for the massa."

Magic walked forward, the spear in front of him. "You just killed one of my best friends, you bastard. You want to die slow or fast?"

Maleceia held the knife in front the way a fencer would, with the point aimed forward so he could stab or slice either up, down, or sideways.

"Come and get me."

Magic moved closer. He took a swing with the spear at the big man, who stepped back. Magic feinted one way, then drove ahead the other way, and the sharp K-Bar cut a groove a half inch deep along the general's left arm.

"Bastard! I told you I'd make you rich. What else do you want?"

"Everything you own, all the account numbers in Tanzania."

"Said I'd make you rich, not that I'm stupid. I give you the numbers and you kill me anyway."

"Probably. You're not in a good bargaining position." Magic darted forward again, stabbed, missed, sliced, and drew blood from a cut across the big man's chest. Blood soaked his shirt. He glared at Magic, turned the knife, and held it by the blade.

Magic drove in before the general could throw it. The K-Bar on the end of the lance jabbed again, dug into the general's right forearm, and came out leaving a smear of blood.

General Maleceia screamed in fury. He charged.

The move caught Magic by surprise. He backed up a step, sliced at the man's torso, missed, then spun the limb so he held it like a staff, and slammed the large end of it against Maleceia's left arm. He could hear a bone snap. The general growled in pain and came forward again, his right arm back to throw the knife.

Magic dove to the ground with the staff crossways in front of him, came to his feet, and swung the staff like a baseball bat. The wood on the knife end hit the general in the right leg, smashing the leg sideways, and the general went down.

Magic saw the hand go back. He darted to the side, then back, and the thrown knife sailed past him, missing by two feet.

The big black SEAL moved in slowly on the fallen general. The man held up both hands, but must have known they would be little defense.

Suddenly Magic was tired. Tired of the chase, tired of the man's insults, tired of seeing his buddies killed. He leaped forward, wielding the spear like a long knife. He slashed it at the general's chest. The Kenyan ducked, and the blade bit into his neck, severing one carotid artery and his jugular vein.

Magic continued the swing of the blade, reversed it, brought it back, and with both hands on the shank, drove the big blade deeply into Maleceia's heart.

Magic dropped to one knee. He panted. Blood spurted from the general's neck wound for a few seconds, then stopped. The general's uniform was starkly red. His eyes stared unseeing at the small clouds drifting past the sun.

The black SEAL touched his mike. "L-T, clear down here. The general is dead."

Murdock slumped down beside Red Nicholson's body. "Good, Magic. Reverse up the trail to where we left Red." The dead man would be going out with the rest of the SEALs. Almost never did a dead SEAL get left on the battlefield. The general was down, their main mission over. He wondered how DeWitt had fared.

"DeWitt, what's happening over there?"

"Yeah, Murdock. We nailed one of them. The other one is so damn sneaky we can't find him. Just melted into the brush somewhere."

"Don't sweat it, get back to the trail. We need to find a

space open enough for our chopper. Get back to the main trail, and we'll hook up. Watch for an LZ."

Holt came out of the brush a few minutes later. He carried his sub-gun in his right hand. His left arm hung at his side and pain etched his face.

"Damn sorry, L-T. Tripped over something running flat out."

"Happens. Can you work your magic box?"

"Oh, yeah. Heard the general is wasted. Good. Magic did it, knew he could."

"Kick up the antenna and let's try the tac band for the carrier. She still the Rover?"

"That's a Roger."

Holt opened the radio cover, and set up the antenna to align it with the Milstar satellite orbiting at 22,300 miles above the earth in a synchronous journey around the equator. It might not matter, but he aligned it anyway.

"Rover, this is Murdock, can you copy?"

There were some pops and whines out of the set; then the voice came over the small speaker.

"Murdock, this is Rover."

"We're ready for that pickup. We're ten to twelve miles, maybe more, northwest of Nairobi in some hills. We'll use flares when we hear the bird. Two hours? I have 1715."

"Yes, two hours. Be dark by then, Murdock. Spot an LZ with small fires if you can. Any enemy action expected?"

"No, Rover. Mission accomplished on the papa bear. We lost one Kenyan soldier, but he's probably still running. We'll find an LZ."

Magic came up the trail and dropped beside Nicholson. He shook his head. "Damn, never should have happened. Red stayed on point too fucking long."

"Wouldn't let anybody else walk it," Holt said.

"Yeah, we should have outmuscled him," Magic said. "Goddamn it to Hell. Damn lousy fucking way to die."

They moved up the trail they had used since leaving the rock house. Magic picked up Nicholson in a fireman's carry and marched up the trail without a word.

By the time they found DeWitt and his men, they were

less than a quarter of a mile from the rock house. DeWitt suggested they use the open spot in front of it for the LZ. Murdock agreed.

They hiked to the rock house and checked. The cleared spot in front was more than big enough for a safe landing.

DeWitt put two men to gathering up dry grass, twigs, and larger limbs they could use to light for signal fires when they heard the chopper. They laid four fires at the sides of the LZ, and waited for the signal to light them.

Doc looked at the men who had been injured or shot since he saw them last. He put a wooden splint on Holt's left arm and gave him a pain shot.

Murdock sent Ching and Bishop down the road to find Ronson. "See how close you can find a good LZ down there," Murdock said. He gave them two flares and one more WP grenade. "We'll get picked up here, then go down for you there. We shouldn't have any trouble finding the truck where Lincoln and Quinley are. Just be a matter of spotting an LZ down there." The two took off hiking down the road.

"Who has any ammo left?" Murdock asked the men who had flaked out on the ground. "I've got about half a magazine. Anybody else?"

Three more men had a few rounds. Murdock set them on the perimeter facing outward. "Let's have a little fucking security here," he said.

It was dark and 1922 when they heard the big chopper. DeWitt's men lit the four fires, and blew them into flames. Soon they burned brightly. The big bird made one pass, then dropped down and sent a tornado of dust and debris at the men as it settled on the ground. The big chopper blew out two of the fires. The men stomped out the last two, carried Red Nicholson to the bird, and laid him gently on the floor.

Murdock called on the Motorola, but couldn't raise Magic Brown. They all climbed on board, the bird took off, and traced the road with a searchlight.

Murdock tried again, and Brown came in scratchy but readable.

"Yeah, Bird. About a quarter of a mile more. Good LZ on

the left. I'll put up a flare." They landed, and brought in Horse and the two others.

Ten minutes later, they found Lincoln and Quinley by the Kenyan truck, picked them up, and headed home.

The pilot told Murdock they might not have enough juice to get all the way to the carrier. She was supposed to steam within four miles of the coast to cut down on flight time.

"We're pushing the limit in this baby even without all the hardware," the pilot told Murdock.

"If it's only four miles, we can swim that with no sweat," Murdock said.

"Yeah, maybe *you* can," the copilot yelped.

30

Friday, July 23

The Seahawk settled down on the deck of the nuclear-powered carrier at 2158. Medical corpsmen rushed on board and took off Lincoln on a stretcher. Corpsmen lifted Horse Ronson to another stretcher and carried him out the chopper door. Ed DeWitt went with them to the ship's sick bay, where both would be operated on. The rest of the SEALs got off and waited near the chopper.

Inside, Murdock sat cross-legged beside Red Nicholson's body. In all his years with the SEALs, he'd lost only two men. Now Red was the third. There must have been something he could have done differently. Something. Red loved being out in front, leading the pack, as he called them. Leading his pack of wolves.

If it hadn't been Red out there, another man would have sprung the trip wire.

This was one fucking dangerous game they all played. Somebody was bound to get hurt.

Murdock shook his head and blinked back tears. "Goodbye, good buddy. It was a great ride."

Two medics came on board and stood behind him waiting. Murdock stood and let them take the body. He knew the routine. He'd write a letter about how Red had

271

been killed on board a carrier in a freak accident that somehow could not be prevented. He had been a good and loyal warrior in the service of his country, and it was appreciated. He would be awarded the Purple Heart and the Navy Cross. His casket would remain closed during the funeral.

Murdock led his men into the carrier for the last time on this mission. Doc had medic tags on most of them:

Magic Brown for a wound in his left arm.

Les Quinley for a shot-up arm.

Kenneth Ching for a graze on the left shoulder.

Ron Holt for a broken left arm.

James "Doc" Ellsworth for a shot-up left arm.

Horse Ronson for a wounded left forearm and two rounds in his leg.

Ross Lincoln for a shot-up side.

Murdock went with them to the emergency room in the carrier's sick bay, and watched them all get their wounds checked over, treated, and bandaged.

Ronson had been rushed into surgery, and Lincoln would be watched for another few hours before they went to work on his side wound.

Murdock and DeWitt went to special chow with the men, and when the two officers came out they wanted only to find their quarters and the showers. Don Stroh stopped them and introduced them to three sailors.

"Sir, we were on the *Roy Turner* when you boarded her. We were the three nuts up on the superstructure firing at the Kenyan soldiers coming from the front."

"Yes, I remember," Murdock said. "You three did fine work that afternoon, saved us some casualties. We appreciate it."

"Thank you, sir," Gunner's Mate First Class Vuylsteke said. "There's a favor we need from you, and we're not sure how to go about it. We talked to Mr. Stroh here, and he set up this meeting."

Stroh shrugged. He led the way into a nearby room.

They all leaned against the walls inside, and Stroh got it started.

"These three guys were off ship when it was attacked and taken over by the coup. They hid out for three days with a lady in Mombasa. They kind of promised her they'd help her if she would keep them hidden."

The rest of the story rolled out with the three sailors adding bits and pieces.

"So that's it, sir," Vuylsteke said. "We figured if anybody could help Pita, it would be you and Mr. Stroh. I hear he can order our carrier's Captain around."

Don chuckled. "Only when I need to."

"You promised Pita you'd help her get to New York where she could try to be an entertainer?" DeWitt asked.

Murdock was suddenly more tired than he'd been in a long time. He looked at Don. "So, Stroh, do it. Get her a passport, a visa to the U.S., and a round-trip plane ticket to New York. She might decide to come home. Charge it to the Navy. Hey, she saved the lives of three U.S. servicemen here, and maybe a couple of SEALs. It's a damn cheap price for five or six Navy people's lives."

Stroh grinned. "Yeah, I figured you might ask for something like that. Talked to the new acting U.S. Ambassador on board. He said he'd set it up in a week or two, as soon as they get temporary quarters for the embassy."

Murdock looked at the three sailors. "Thanks, guys, you did a great job. Now I'm getting a shower and some sack time."

Ten minutes later his head hit the pillow, and he knew he'd kill anyone who woke him up before he had at least twelve hours of sleep.

Murdock got up at noon the next day, put on fresh cammies, and went to check on the men. Half of them were in the assembly room they had used before. Jaybird had them cleaning their weapons and making a list of lost or used-up equipment. Looking around at the men, Murdock saw more white bandages than he did fighting men.

He counted up. Eight of his platoon had been either killed or wounded. It was the toughest assignment he'd had yet. Stroh would have to get another platoon if anything popped in the next few weeks. He was going to authorize two weeks' leave for each man, and recuperation time for the worst hurt. Then he'd need at least two new men, and have to pick out a new scout. Ted Yates would be in Balboa Naval Hospital in San Diego for a couple of months or more. Chances were that he'd not be fit for duty as a SEAL when he did heal. Murdock would have to find out how bad that shot-up leg was that Ronson had. It was possible that he and Lincoln wouldn't be fit for duty for six months. Damn!

Murdock still battled a wave of fatigue.

He wanted a two-week leave starting right now. Yeah, sure.

He'd send Ed DeWitt on a fortnight's leave if he had to hogtie him and throw him on board an airplane himself.

An hour later, Murdock talked with Don Stroh in his quarters.

"The President says good job well done," Stroh said. "He'd give you a commendation of some kind, but you could never wear it."

"An early battlefield promotion to lieutenant commander would be nice," Murdock said.

"Sure, just what you want. Then you couldn't lead a platoon anymore."

"He could change that too. Talk to the CNO. You must have some clout."

"I do. How long do you want the carrier to babysit you here before you fly home?"

"Two days. I'm going to sleep straight through. Then too, I want my wounded guys healed up a little. Never had this many men shot up before. Are these assignments getting harder, or are we getting softer?"

"Maybe you're all just used up for the moment," Stroh said with a slight frown.

"Not by a fucking hindsight," Murdock bellowed. They both laughed.

"Third Platoon is off the action board for at least two months, Stroh. We need two new men, maybe four new bodies. We need to get men well and back into shape and train on some new weapons I'm considering. You ever heard of the Heckler & Koch G11?"

"Nope."

"It's a weird-looking sub-gun that can kick out two thousand rounds a minute, carries a fifty-round magazine, and shoots a special caseless cartridge which is simply a block of explosive with a bullet buried inside it. Shoots a 4.7 round, and looks like a winner. I want to test it out."

"So you want some time."

"We must have some time, two months at least. I'm getting each man who can walk a two-week leave, and then we'll think about getting back to work. Heal first, train second."

"You're getting conservative on me. What if the world blows up in a week?"

"Call on the duty SEAL platoon in that sector. That's the way it was supposed to work, remember?"

"Yeah, I remember. So in two days I'll get you and me out of here and flapping our wings back to the good old USA. Unless you want to settle down in Kenya. I hear the local Army has a lot of openings for field-grade officers."

Murdock threw a pillow at him, and went to check on his men in the sick bay.

Wednesday, August 13

2010 hours
Ardith Manchester's apartment
Washington, D.C.
Murdock had been in the Nation's Capital for three days. It had taken him more than two weeks after the platoon arrived in Coronado to get the paperwork done, have new and replacement weapons ordered, pick out two new men for the platoon, and then fight with DeWitt to take a leave. He'd finally sent him on a two-week trip to Maui, Hawaii, where he could fish and swim all he wanted.

Murdock stayed at his folks' place the first night in D.C. to take care of family responsibilities. He had lunch with his dad the next day in the House dining room, and then called Ardith.

She knew he was in town. He had been at her place ever

since. She'd said she had to work for her father for the next two days, but then she'd take the rest of the week off and they would explore the Virginia mountains.

He was looking forward to it. Some hills where no one would be shooting at him.

She came home early that day, and said she had cleared her calendar.

"Now, is it the mountains, or did you have enough of the outdoors for a while? We can stay here and gorge ourselves with great order-in food, wine, and cheeses you've never even heard of. I found this great little place. . . ." She stopped. "What?"

"It's just good to hear your voice again. Going to take me a while to figure out that foreign language that you're speaking, but I'll come around."

She leaned back against him and pulled his arms around her. "I'm sorry that Kenya was such a bad one."

She felt him flinch. "Hey, don't be so surprised," she said. "I told you I know what you do. I also have some connections so I know where you go, when, and why. The senator can find out just about anything he wants to know that's going on in this town, in the country, or in the armed forces. He says it's part of his job. If he knows it, I know it."

"Damn few people know what we do or when we do it," he said softly.

"That's the way it's supposed to be. You're the under-cover attack force of the CIA."

He turned her around to face him. "Don't you ever tell my mother. Dad knows, but don't ever let it slip to Mom."

"Promise. You like that lady, don't you?"

"A little."

She pinched him. He pretended he didn't feel it. She settled back with her head on his chest.

"Two-week leave, right?"

"True. Your spies do good work."

"Nope, just a guess." She turned and faced him. Her clear eyes stared into his. "Have you thought about what we talked about the last time? About maybe moving into some other area of Navy work?"

"Thought about it. You know we lost one man this tour. I've been with Red for over two years. A good man. Blown away by a damn trip wire on a hand grenade."

Ardith shivered. He held her tightly.

"Sorry," he said.

"No, that's why we need to talk, but we have time. We have most of two weeks left. I told Dad to expect me when he sees me come in the door."

She kept watching him. "I so desperately hope . . . I so hope . . ." He kissed her and she whimpered, and kissed him back .

He held her gently. "How about a week here in the lap of unmitigated luxury, making love all night and sleeping until noon. After a week of that, we'll decide on the mountains or the sandy beaches of Florida."

"Aye, aye, sir. Right now I want to be the only platoon you're concerned about."

Wednesday, August 20

1014 hours
Ardith Manchester's apartment
Washington, D.C.

Murdock woke from a dreamless, relaxing sleep to the chimes-type ring of Ardith's phone. Usually such a soft ringing wouldn't wake him. Ardith reached a bare arm across him and picked up the instrument.

"Yes?"

She paused and frowned. "Who?" She scowled. "Why would you think that?" Ardith listened a moment, then silently handed him the instrument.

"Yes?"

"Murdock. You're a hard man to find."

He recognized the sound of Don Stroh's voice. "How did you?"

"Hey, I have friends in high places too. Doesn't matter. Just wanted to alert you. There is something nasty building out there. No cause for action just yet. But we're keeping our eyes on it. Some of the satellite stuff is on the scary side.

Didn't mean to spoil your leave. It's only half over. So enjoy."

"Stroh."

"Yeah, Murdock?"

"Why don't you . . ."

"What, Blake?"

"Never mind. When we have more secure communications, I want you to keep me up to date with briefings. Right?"

"You got it, tiger. I'll call you in a week. We're worried about something that's brewing. Nothing immediate. Two, three months off. Probably. I'll stay in touch."

"Oh, I bet you will. You sound worried."

"Could get terribly nasty. But not for a while. Have fun."

"Yeah, Stroh. You have fun too."

They hung up.

"How in the world did he find you . . . here?" she asked.

Murdock grinned. "Hey, lady. He's with the CIA. You think you have contacts? He probably knows what kind of wine we had last night with that amazing Indonesian dinner we had sent in."

"Oh."

She pushed over her bare body against his and purred. "Just so he doesn't have a camera in my bedroom." She yelped and sat up suddenly and looked around.

Murdock laughed and pulled her down beside him.

So, something big was brewing. Two months off at least. That would give him just about enough time to get two or four new men integrated and working smoothly with the platoon, get the new weapons tested and see if he wanted to order half a dozen, and go through some rigorous field training again with the whole platoon. Yeah, sounded about right.

"Blake Murdock, where in the world are you right now?"

He grinned, slid under the covers, and attacked her gently with her complete approval.